Training the Cowboy Billionaire

A Chappell Brothers Novel: Bluegrass Ranch Romance Book 3

Emmy Eugene

Copyright © 2020 by Emmy Eugene

All rights reserved.

No part of this book may be reproduced in any form or by any electronic or mechanical means, including information storage and retrieval systems, without written permission from the author, except for the use of brief quotations in a book review.

ISBN-13: 979-8559712956

Chapter 1

Trey Chappell loved his mother's cooking, and while she'd lured him here with the promise of chicken and dumplings, he didn't entirely hate it. It was time anyway.

The conversation had been fine. Better than fine. Good. He'd talked about the upcoming yearlings sale, as well as Blaine's engagement, and he hadn't once had to answer a question he didn't want to.

Trey didn't actually mind answering questions if he knew the answers to them. The problem was that his mother liked to ask him things he didn't know how to answer. He wasn't sure why he couldn't let go of Sarah. He wasn't sure why he'd put all the blame on God and lost his faith.

Deep down, he still believed in the loving, benevolent God his parents had taught him about. At the same time, he couldn't believe that the Lord would allow his heart to be so completely trampled on, despite Sarah's ability to make her own choices.

He didn't know why he hadn't been able to make another relationship work, though he'd tried. He didn't know why he was so drawn to Bethany Dixon, and he had no idea why he hadn't been able to give a sure answer to her proposal. She'd asked him to marry her so they could enter the Sweetheart Classic together.

Really, so *she* could enter *her* horse into the Sweetheart Classic. She hadn't gone into details, but Trey could still hear her saying, "I need the money, Trey. Plain and simple."

He'd said he'd let her know when he came to clear her garden. That had been last week, and while they'd gotten the work done, when he'd gotten a moment alone with Beth, he'd told her he needed more time to come to a final decision.

Her time was running out, and Trey felt it ticking away second by second, the clicking actually loud in his ears.

They had to be married by Halloween, with his name on the horse's certificate before she could register it for the Sweetheart Classic. It wasn't October yet, but it would be in a few days, and he really needed to come to a decision.

"Are you seeing anyone new?" Mom asked, and Trey put the last bite of his chicken and dumplings in his mouth.

He took a few seconds to chew and swallow, trying to formulate the right answer. "Kind of," he said.

Mom's brow furrowed. "How can you *kind of* be seeing someone?"

"Jules," Daddy said, and his mom lifted one hand.

"Sorry," she said. "Sorry, Trey. I know how dating goes these days. You like her, and you're not sure if she likes you, and you want to be her boyfriend, but maybe you're not yet, so there's this middle ground where *kind of* exists."

Trey gaped at his mother. It was the third Sunday in a row he'd eaten with them alone, and he found all of his hard feelings softening and falling away. "Yeah," he said. "It's a little bit like that."

He looked back and forth between his mother and his father, and the interest in their eyes wasn't lost on him. He also wanted to tell someone about the things that had been tormenting him for the past two weeks, and maybe those two people were sitting right in front of him.

Part of his brain screamed at him to eat his mom's famous peach cobbler and homemade vanilla ice cream and keep his thoughts to himself. That had been working for him for the past forty-one years, and if he wanted to talk to someone, he could go back to therapy.

"If we can help," Mom said. "Let us know." She stood up. "Now, did you eat too much to have cobbler now? We can sit on the upper verandah if you'd like."

"I can take my cobbler up there, right?" he asked.

Mom smiled as she picked up his empty plate. "Of course, baby." She bent down and pressed a kiss to his head. "I'll get it all out."

Trey nodded and watched her go into the kitchen. She sang to herself as she got out bowls and spoons, the dishes clacking against each other.

"Thanks for coming," Daddy said in a low voice. "It means a lot to your mother."

"I know," Trey said. "She's been doing really great."

"She loves you boys," he said. "We both do."

"I know that." Trey reached up and tipped his hat forward. "Listen, I did want to talk to you about something."

Daddy leaned into the table. "Go ahead."

Trey swallowed. "All right now." He took a moment to find the right words, but they weren't there. It was the same reason he hadn't said anything to Cayden or Blaine. There wasn't an adequate way to explain the situation.

"Do you know Beth Dixon?" he asked right as his mother came back to the table.

"Are we staying in here?" She set a bowl of ice cream and cobbler on the table in front of him.

"No," Trey said, getting up. "Let's go outside." Maybe then he'd know how to explain what was in his head. He carried his bowl and steadied Daddy as he went up the steps to the second half of their back porch.

He took a bite of sweet ice cream and tart peaches. "Mm, Momma, you're a genius."

She laughed and continued to help Daddy get settled, tucking a blanket around his legs. Trey wore his jacket too, as autumn had definitely arrived in Kentucky.

"You said something about Beth Dixon," Daddy said, and Trey caught the sharpness in his mother's eyes.

"Yes," Trey said. "I've been helping her around her farm

the past little bit." He shifted a little bit, because that wasn't entirely true. It was true, but that wasn't entirely altruistic. "Her son's been hangin' around the ranch, and I take him home. Then Beth hurt her hand a few weeks ago, and we've been helping."

"We know about that," Mom said. "Blaine's told us."

"Yeah." Trey took another bite of his treat. "Well, I like her. I asked her to dinner, and she said her father could watch TJ." He cleared his throat. "We haven't done it yet or anything."

"Well, why not?" Mom asked.

"Things are busy, Mom," Trey said, a touch of darkness in his tone. "The yearlings sale is in two weeks." November first was barely beyond that, and Trey's throat closed.

"I know," Mom said. "Sorry. Go on."

Trey didn't know how to go on. "I don't want you to get upset."

"Why would I get upset?" Mom asked.

"Julie, let the man talk," Daddy said.

"Sorry, sorry."

Trey took another bite of cobbler. The breeze blew past the white fences and through the pastures beyond. "She's been in a...tough place since her husband died, and she wants to enter one of her horses into a race."

"Mm hm," Mom said.

"There's a catch," Trey said, watching his parents out of the corner of his eye. "It's the Sweetheart Classic."

Daddy didn't understand, if his perplexed look was any

indication. Mom got it though, because her eyes widened. She sucked in a breath, but to her everlasting credit, she didn't say anything.

"The deadline to enter is November first," Trey said, driving home the immediacy of the situation.

"Trey Travis Chappell," Mom said, not moving when Daddy put his hand on her leg. "Did you marry Beth Dixon?"

"Marry Beth Dixon?" Daddy asked at the same time Trey scoffed and said, "No, Mom. Come on now."

"The Sweetheart Classic requires the entrants to be *married* and own the horse together," Mom said, looking at Daddy. "By November first."

Daddy's eyes widened too.

"What should I do?" Trey asked.

Mom opened her mouth and promptly closed it. She looked at Daddy, but there was no help there. Trey had a feeling there wasn't help for this situation anywhere.

Unhappiness pulled through him, and he finished his dessert and set the bowl on the ground beside him.

"Well, honey," Mom finally said. "You have to do what you think is right."

"How do you know what that is?"

"Just be honest with yourself and with her. Pray and ask for help. You'll know what to do."

"Mom," Trey said with a sigh.

"I know, I know," she said. "You don't think praying will help."

"No, Mom, I don't."

"Have you tried it?"

"No, ma'am," he said quietly. He'd prayed plenty of times for the solution to his problems, and he'd never gotten an adequate answer. God didn't seem to hear him, and if he did, he just didn't care enough about Trey to answer.

"Just an idea," Mom said. "Trey, we love you no matter what. You're a good man, and I believe you'll make the right choice for you and for Beth."

Trey looked at his father. "Dad?"

"I like what your mother said," he said. "Be honest with yourself and with her. Pray about it. Do what you think is right."

"That can't be the answer," Trey said, beyond frustrated. Be honest? Pray about it?

No, he wanted a *solution*. He wanted *an answer*.

"Why not?" Daddy asked.

"It's too easy. Be honest. Pray. Do what's right?" He scoffed. "I'm not a six-year-old. I don't need the cookie cutter answers."

"Trey," his mother started, but she cut off when Daddy put his hand on her arm. They exchanged a look with one another, and she returned her attention to him. "You do what you think is right."

Trey wanted to roll his eyes. Instead, he got up and collected all the dishes. "Thanks for dinner and dessert, Mother." He gave her a kiss. "I'm gonna head out."

"Take some cobbler," Mom called after him, and Trey said he would.

He did dish himself some cobbler, and he took it back to

the homestead. "Cobbler," he called to whoever might be in the house, but it was likely just Cayden. No one answered him, so he put the container on the counter and went out onto the back deck.

Kentucky sure was a slice of heaven to Trey, and he looked up into the sky. It had rained a lot last week, but today the evening sky shone with gold and blue.

He wrestled with himself and whether he should say a prayer or not. Surely the Lord already knew what the issue was, and he'd been decidedly silent.

"Maybe you don't know how to hear," Trey muttered to himself. "What can it hurt? It'll take sixty seconds, and then you'll get nothing, and you can go find Cayden—or better, Lawrence—and ask them what to do."

Trey took a deep breath and exhaled. He did that over and over, trying to work up the courage to pray. He knew how; he'd done so as a child and teenager and even into his adulthood. It had just been quite a long time.

"Dear Lord," he finally said. "Bethany Dixon is a good woman, and I sure do like her. She needs help, and I can help her. Should I marry the woman so she can enter her horse into the Sweetheart Classic?"

The wind kicked up, and a dog barked somewhere in the distance. Trey closed his eyes and tried—really tried—to hear something. He never heard anything with his ears, but rather his heart.

The things he should and shouldn't do came as feelings, and in that moment, Trey felt like he should help Beth if he could.

"Should I?" he asked again.

There was no squirming in his stomach. The worry that had been needling his mind for weeks disappeared. The unrest in his very soul was simply not there anymore.

Part of him was disgusted, and the other part sagged in relief against the railing on the deck. The sun continued to go down, and the day died degree by degree.

"Why are you standing here?" he asked himself. "Get over to Beth's and talk to her. The clock is ticking."

He pushed away from the railing and hurried to his pickup truck. The drive to Beth's didn't take long. The longest part of the drive was getting down the dirt lane from the house to the road. Beth's was just a bit down the highway, and he pulled up to the charming, white farmhouse before he knew it.

While he still had a well of courage, he got out of the truck and marched toward the porch. He made it to the door and rang the doorbell.

"C'mon in," TJ yelled, and Trey took a deep breath.

He opened the door and stepped inside the farmhouse, already looking for the child. In the very next moment, a deluge of cold water hit him straight in the face.

Trey sputtered and reached up to cover his face with his hands. "What the devil?" he asked at the same time wild laughter met his ears. He cleared the water from his eyes and hair—his cowboy hat gone completely—and looked down at his soaking wet shirt. The front of his jeans looked like he'd wet himself, and water ran down his legs toward his cowboy boots.

"That's not your uncle Hugh," a man said, and Trey's eyes flew to an older gentleman whose smile faded right before Trey's eyes. Beth's father, Clyde.

"Trey," TJ said, his smile staying in place. He ran toward Trey, who scooped him up despite being a wet mess. "What are you doin' here?"

"I..." He looked at Clyde, who'd found a towel somehow and was hurrying toward him too.

"Sorry," he said. "I'm real sorry about the water. We're expecting Beth's brother, and I was just showin' TJ how to set up a prank." He smiled at the child and exchanged TJ for the towel.

They shook hands too, and Trey used the towel to mop up the water in his hair. This wasn't a good time to chat with Beth, clearly. Beth's family was here, and she obviously didn't know about this little prank lesson going on in her living room.

He didn't think she'd like the standing water on her hardwood floors, for example.

Trey turned around to find his cowboy hat. He located it sitting in a pool of water, stepped over to it, and had just picked it up when Beth said, "Trey?"

His heartbeat spiked, and he jammed the hat on his head as he straightened and turned in the same movement.

Beth wore a pale yellow tank top that flowed around her frame in a classy, sophisticated way. She made soft, loose pants look like a ballgown, and Trey promptly swept the cowboy hat off his head again.

Aware of water dripping from his ear and sliding down his face, he held his cowboy hat to his chest with one hand and wiped his forehead with the other. "I'll do it, Beth. I'll enter the Sweetheart Classic with you."

Chapter 2

"The Sweetheart Classic?" Daddy asked, and Bethany Dixon flew into action. She strode forward and put both hands against Trey's chest, as if she could really move a man muscular as him.

He did fall back though, and he turned and walked out onto the front porch, Beth right behind him. She brought the door closed behind her a little harder than she meant to, and she pressed her eyes closed as she leaned into the solidness of it.

She inhaled through her nose and realized her feet were wet. She opened her eyes and looked down. "Why is my porch wet?"

"Same reason I'm soaking wet, sweetheart," Trey said in a very dry voice.

She looked up from the puddle where she stood to find Trey standing at the top of the steps, facing her. He really was wet from head to toe, and she could only stare at the sexy way his hair spiked up with water in it.

Everything about the man called to her, and she forgot for a moment why her pulse was pounding and why she'd ushered him outside before he could say anything else.

The door behind her opened, and Daddy said, "Sorry about the water, sweetie. I'll get TJ to clean it up right now."

Beth reached up and brushed her hair out of her eyes. "Thanks, Daddy."

The door closed again, and Beth wished she could lock it from the outside. Hugh should be here soon too, and of course Trey would pick now to make his decision and come tell her about it.

She took a step forward as she tucked her hands in the pockets of her sweats. "You'll do it?"

"Yes," Trey said.

Beth nodded, her throat suddenly closed. She'd admitted so much to him already, and she really didn't want to lose more of her dignity. She moved over to the railing and leaned against it, pleased when he joined her.

She didn't look at him but gazed out over the graveled driveway and down the lane, which was bordered by pastures on both sides. "Why are you wet?"

"Your son and your father set up a prank for someone named Hugh."

"My brother," Beth said. "You'll probably need to get to know all of that, so we can..." She trailed off, finally looking up at him. "You look different without your cowboy hat on."

He automatically reached up and ran his hand through his hair. "My hat's ruined now."

Beth followed the trajectory of his hand with hers, and he froze the moment she touched him. He pulled in a slow breath while she brushed water off his forehead and curled her fingertips along the curve of his ear.

With heat racing through her body, she pulled away. "Sorry."

"It's fine," he said, his voice sounding with a hallowed quality. "Can I hold your hand?"

Beth slid her fingers down his arm and into his hand, the only answer she could currently give. In the silence that descended on them, Beth heard her own heartbeat in her ears and not much else.

Her thoughts raced and then slowed as she accepted that she was holding hands with another man besides Danny Dixon.

"I was engaged once," Trey said. "Did you know?"

Beth cleared her throat. "No, I didn't."

Trey nodded, his gaze out on the pasture like it was the most fascinating thing he'd ever seen. "Her name was Sarah Samuels."

"How'd you meet her?"

"She worked in the markcting department at the printer we use," he said. "They make all our signs, fliers, even those little name tags we give to our champion horses. The ones made of gold?" He chuckled. "It's pretty ridiculous what we do for those horses."

Beth liked the sound of his voice, and she didn't want to

taint the conversation with hers.

"Anyway." Trey leaned further into the railing. "She worked with Cayden a lot, because he does almost all of the PR for the ranch, and I met her once...and it was like...I don't know. Magic."

"Sounds wonderful," Beth said, her mind wandering down paths she didn't normally allow it to. "I was married once, but I think you knew that."

His fingers tightened on hers. "I did know that." He glanced at her and grinned. "How did you meet Danny?"

"Everyone in Dreamsville knows the Dixons," she said, a smile automatically curling her mouth. "Danny was my best friend's older brother. I'd seen him around their ranch from time to time, but he was gone to college before I really started hanging out with Myra."

"You must've caught his eye when he came home on a break."

"Not really," she said. "I grew up and went to college with Myra. I didn't finish and came back. I started dating other men." She lifted one shoulder. "None of them were Danny. I didn't realize it until I went to Myra's college graduation party, and there he was. I guess you could say that was when we met."

Beth lost herself in good memories of Danny before he'd become her husband. He'd graduated from college too, but his engineering degree only got used for a couple of years before he realized how much he hated it. They'd gotten married and bought this beat-up farm on the outskirts of town, next to the wildly successful Bluegrass Ranch.

How hard they'd worked. Sixteen hours, from sunup to sundown. They'd built a lot of the structures on the farm from the foundation up, and Danny had built this porch where she and Trey now stood.

"You must have loved him very much," Trey said.

"I did," Beth said, pulling herself from her sadness. She drew in a deep breath, held it, and watched her brother turn off the highway. "That's Hugh."

Trey released her hand and put another two feet of distance between them. Beth felt the loss of his touch keenly, and she looked him. "They're going to find out, like you said."

"We have five weeks to get married," he said. "I think we should probably go on at least one date before then." He kept his eyes on her brother's huge black truck as it came closer. "What do you think?"

"Yes," she said, her lungs quaking a little bit.

"That's my stipulation," he said. "I should at least be able to tell my family that we're dating before I start packing my bags to move out."

Beth swallowed. "You'll move in here?"

"You have enough bedrooms," he said. "Might as well make it look real on the outside, don't you think?"

"Yes," she said again. Hugh parked beside Trey, and Beth's window to have this conversation was running out.

"What's your stipulation?" he asked. "I suppose you can have more than one."

"I just have one," she said, her throat so very dry.

"What is it?"

Hugh got out of his truck and lifted his hand in a wave. Beth did the same, and Hugh called, "I'm okay to park here?"

"Yes," Beth called back to him.

"I'm not going to stay," Trey said. "You're busy with your family." He faced her, and while his shirt and jeans were wet, he was still so handsome.

"That's why you should stay," she said. "If we're to be married in only a few weeks." She stepped toward him and reached for the buttons on his shirt. She touched one and then the other, waiting for him to take her into his arms. If he'd been engaged before, he surely understood a woman's unspoken wants.

He finally put one hand on her hip and bent his head down. Beth ran her free hand up the side of his face, enjoying his clean-shaven face and the texture of his longer hair. "I only have one stipulation too," she whispered, the crunching of Hugh's footsteps over the gravel getting dangerously close.

"What is it now?" Trey asked.

"The first time you kiss me can't be on our wedding day."

Hugh started talking as he came up the steps, and Beth kept her eyes on Trey's shocked ones as she backed up. She finally turned away when her brother arrived and embraced him. She laughed as he picked her right up off her feet.

"Who's this?" he asked as he set her down. His bright eyes focused on Trey, and Beth decided they better go for the gold from the very beginning.

"Hugh, this is Trey Chappell. We've started seeing each other." That was one hundred percent true, and neither of them could deny it.

"Well, I'll be," Hugh said, his smile a little too wide. It went well with his wide-eyed, shocked look. He stared at Beth for a moment and then back to Trey.

"Good to meet you," Trey said, stepping forward as if Beth had introduced him to dozens of her friends and family members.

"Why you all wet?"

"I think this was meant for you," Trey said. "I just got here ahead of you."

Hugh's eyes traveled down Trey's body, and he started laughing. "I guess I owe you one then."

Trey smiled, and Beth nearly fell down with how beautiful it made him. "I'd be careful going inside."

"I'll use the back door." Hugh turned back to Beth, already mouthing words. She rolled her eyes instead of trying to read his lips, because she hated that. Even worse was when he started texting her while they were in a group. She hated that; if he had something to say, he should just say it.

"Uncle Hugh?"

The front door opened, and TJ came outside at a run, headed straight for his uncle.

Hugh laughed and picked TJ right up over his head. "Were you going to prank me? Were you? Grandpa's here, isn't he?"

"Yes," their father said. "I'm here." She watched as the three of them embraced, and Hugh followed them back inside, no buckets of water in sight. She looked at Trey, and he looked at her.

"Do you have an hour or two to spend with us here?" she asked. "It's okay if you don't. I'm really good at making up reasons why someone couldn't stay." She smiled, because that was totally true. "Or rather, reasons I can't come to this, that, or the other."

Trey approached and tucked her hair behind her ear. "I can stay for a while."

"Great," she said. "Because I need to introduce you to my father."

"We've met a couple of times now," Trey said, his eyebrows drawing down in confusion. "Once...before, and just now again. I shook his hand and everything."

Of course he had. Trey wasn't awkward the way she was. He might not know what to do in a situation, but he took it by the horns and wrestled it to the ground.

"I need to introduce you as my boyfriend," she said. "Did you tell him that?"

"Now that—no." He looked at her, slight awe in his expression. "Are you going to use that word?"

"What word? Boyfriend?"

"Yeah, that one," he said.

"You don't want me to?"

"I'm just trying to figure it all out is all," he said. "Seeing each other, I get. We are seeing each other. I've been seeing you over the past several weeks." He looked toward the open front door. "Boyfriend...I don't know if that's true."

"Then I'll just say we've recently started seeing each

other," Beth said, liking that a lot better. She took the first step toward the door, and Trey went with her. "What—when do you cross the line into boyfriend?"

"About the time I kiss you," he said, dipping his head closer to hers. "Does that work for you?"

She shivered, because everything about him worked for her. "Yes," she whispered, passing through the doorway. Laughter came from the back of the house, where the kitchen sat, and Beth continued that way, determined to get the word out that she had started seeing someone again.

Trey would be the very first man she'd dated since Danny's death, and she hoped no one would find it odd that she married him in only a few weeks. She'd just say she didn't want to wait. She'd been alone long enough, and when she met Trey, she'd just...known.

Like magic, she thought, wondering what had happened to dampen the magic on his and Sarah's relationship.

She couldn't help wondering if such magic really existed, and she glanced up at him, searching for something she wouldn't find on his face.

"Daddy," she said once they'd reached the kitchen. "I wanted to properly introduce you to Trey." She put a bright smile on her face. "We've started seeing each other." She beamed at Trey and then her father.

Her dad didn't miss a beat. "Yeah, I saw you holdin' his hand out there on the porch." He grinned at Beth and cocked his eyebrows at Trey.

"Come on now," Trey said, a grin on his face too. "I think *I* was holdin' *her* hand."

Chapter 3

Trey looked over the top of his cards at TJ, who wore nothing but delight in his eyes. Across the room, Beth huddled with her father, and while Trey really wanted to know what they were talking about, he didn't attempt to read her lips or study her dad's face too hard.

"Do you have any blowfish?" he asked TJ, who immediately dropped his gaze to the cards in his hand.

His uncle looked at the cards too, and just by the look on his face, Trey knew there was a blowfish in the little boy's hand. TJ frowned and tilted the cards toward Hugh. "What does that say?" he whispered, as if he couldn't speak the question out loud.

"What's that first letter?" Hugh asked.

"B," TJ said. "I think that's a blowfish." He looked up at his uncle with a question in those round eyes.

Hugh nodded, and TJ took the card and handed it to Trey. "I have two."

Trey hesitated with matching the yellow blowfish he'd gotten from TJ to the pink one in his hand. "Why didn't you put them down then?" He watched as TJ pulled another card out, sudden recognition lighting within him

"I had a pair," TJ said, looking from Trey to Hugh. "I messed it up." He slammed his cards on the table in front of him, and Trey jumped.

He'd never seen the child react this way before, but Hugh leaned over and said, "It's a card game, buddy. It's not a big deal."

"Now he has the pair." TJ looked like he might cry. "Should I give him this one? Or do I get to keep it?" He reached up and wiped his nose. "But now he knows I have a blowfish. So he'll just draw one and then ask for mine."

"I think," Trey said, separating his two blowfish. "That since we're both still learnin' how to play this game, that I should just give you back this yellow blowfish and you can play your pair."

TJ's eyes widened, hope filling his expression. "Really?"

"But I should get to swap out my blowfish, so you don't know I have it," Trey said. "And I get to ask for a new card." He looked at Hugh, who watched Trey with something in his gaze that Trey didn't understand. He switched his gaze back to TJ. "Sound fair?"

"Uncle Hugh?" TJ asked, climbing onto his uncle's lap. "Is it fair?'

"Pick up your cards, bud," Hugh said. "That sounds fair

to me." Hugh ended up picking up the cards and holding them for TJ. The exchange happened again, and Trey slipped his pink blowfish into the draw deck and chose another card.

Then he said, "Okay, do you have any...flying fish?"

"Go fish," TJ said.

Trey did, and he managed to get a blue flying fish. "Flying fish," he said, turning it so TJ and Hugh could see. "Got my wish." He put down his match and asked, "Do you have—?"

"No, you have to sing the song,' TJ said.

Trey had no idea what he was talking about. "What song?" He looked at Hugh, who shrugged slightly. They'd all visited for several minutes before TJ's restlessness had prompted Hugh to take him out on the farm for an hour while Beth finished up their Sunday afternoon meal.

Though Trey had eaten already, he'd stayed, and he'd eaten a little of the rabbit stew Beth had put together. She was an excellent cook, and Trey had marveled at her nervousness to serve him her food. By the end of the meal, though, she'd relaxed.

Her father had cleaned up the kitchen for her while she and Trey sat on the couch and she told him about Hugh and Sally, her brother and sister, both of whom lived right here in Dreamsville. Both married. Both with children.

Hugh's wife had taken their two kids to visit her parents for the weekend, so he'd come alone. Sally was a bit of a black sheep, and according to Beth, she hadn't known how to relate to Beth after Danny had died.

"That's not true," her dad had said, coming into the conversation near the end of it.

"It is true," Beth said. "She said it right to my face."

"She still comes around the house."

"That's because she's not living the life you want."

Confusion had riddled Trey's mind too, and it manifested itself right on Clyde's face. "What does that mean, hon?"

"It means Sally feels guilty coming here. She has the wonderful, doting husband, and the three kids, and she knows I want that too." She looked back and forth between Trey and her father. "She doesn't know what to say to me. She doesn't like coming, because she thinks I'll feel bad."

"Do you feel bad?" Trey had asked, and one look at Beth's face had answered that question.

"No," she said with her voice, but her eyes had said yes.

About that time, TJ and Hugh had returned, and TJ had gotten a new game he wanted to play. Beth had gotten up, still talking with her dad about Sally, and they'd gone into the kitchen to make coffee.

"There *is* a song, silly," TJ said, bringing Trey back to the game. "It goes, Got my wish, got my wish, now I get to guess another fish."

Trey laughed, because there was no way that was true. "Do I have to sing it just like that?" he asked. "Holding out that last word like that?"

"Yes," TJ said, and he was dead serious.

"All right," Trey said, "But I'll warn you, I'm not a great singer." He cleared his throat and hoped Beth's attention would stay way across the room. ""Got my wish, got my wish, now I get to guess another *fiiiish*." The last word turned into a chuckle that Trey could not contain.

TJ laughed too, and Hugh's laughter covered both of them.

"What's so funny over here?" Beth asked.

"Trey singed a funny song," TJ said, still giggling.

"It's sang, baby," Beth said. "Trey *sang* a funny song."

"Trey sang a funny song."

She smiled at him and pushed his hair off his forehead. "Your hair is getting long, Teej. We should go see Miss Anna."

"Okay," her son said, clearly disinterested in a haircut. "Who's turn is it?"

"Mine," Beth said. "I need to borrow Trey for a little bit." She flicked a nervous glance in his direction. "Hugh?"

"I'll take his hand," Hugh said, lifting TJ off his lap and putting him on the ground. "Me and you will play."

Trey set his cards down and got to his feet, his heartbeat doing a strange dance in his chest. All he could think about was Beth's stipulation, and his mouth and throat turned to sand. Could he kiss her?

Today?

He hadn't come over here with that in mind, though he supposed kissing Beth was always on his mind.

Clyde watched him as he watched Beth take a couple of bottles of water out of the fridge. She handed one to Trey and said, "I figured we could walk around the ranch a little."

Trey wanted to say, "Sure," or "Okay," but nothing came

out of his mouth. He let Beth lead the way out the back door, and he paused next to her at the top of the steps on the back porch, just inside the line of shade the roof provided.

"How many horses do you have over there at Bluegrass?" she asked.

"How many do we own? Or how many do we board?"

"Either. Both." Beth looked up at him, and Trey met her gaze.

"We own something like sixty horses," he said. "We board and allow on the track probably five times that many. Our track times are full for the next six months."

"That's because you only schedule out for six months," she said.

He grinned at her and slipped his fingers through hers. "True."

Beth started down the steps, and Trey went with her. The sun wasn't terribly hot, especially with the breeze and the evening coming earlier and earlier in the day. "Why did you decide to go through with it?"

"With what?"

"With the Sweetheart Classic."

Trey nearly stumbled, but he managed to stay on his feet without too big of a stutter in his step. "Uh, I don't know."

Her fingers tightened in his. "I think you do," she said, her voice real quiet now. "A man of reasonably sound mind such as yourself would have his reasons."

"Reasonably sound mind?" He shook his head, his focus on the ground at his feet though it was graveled and flat.

"What I asked you to do was insane. *Is* insane," she said.

"You took twice as long to answer me as you said you would. There has to be a reason."

"There is," he said. "I just... I got the feeling that I should help you, so that's what I'm doing. I'm going to help you." He'd already whispered how he felt about her in her ear, once, a while ago now. Might as well own up to that again. "Plus, remember how I said I liked you?"

"I do distinctly remember that," she said, plenty of teasing in her voice.

"Plus, we're neighbors. Neighbors help one another." Trey kept his voice light, seeing no reason to open himself up for complete ruin. "I've been trying to help you for months, so I figured this was a good way to do it. It was something you'd let me do, and hopefully, you won't argue with me about everything."

"I don't argue with you about everything."

He chuckled. "You literally just argued with me."

Several steps went by in silence, and Beth stopped at the fence separating the road from a pasture. A black and white horse came toward her, and she released his hand to stand up on the bottom rung of the fence, one hand outstretched toward the animal.

"This is Somebody's Lady," she said as the horse arrived at the fence. "I thought you might want to meet the horse that you're marrying me for." She stroked her hand down the side of the horse's face, her smile beautiful.

"She's a mighty fine horse," Trey said, holding out his hand too. Somebody's Lady eyed him for a moment, and all horses had at least a hint of unpredictability in their eyes, at least until they trusted a person.

Somebody's Lady could bolt or nicker, snap or smile, and Trey wouldn't know until she did it. She huffed at him, and Trey grinned at her. "Oh, you think you're so tough," he murmured.

He ran his hand down the side of Somebody's Lady's neck. "Do you know how to run?"

"She does okay," Beth said. "She's gonna need some training, I'm afraid."

"Who's going to ride her?" Trey asked.

Beth didn't answer as she got off the bottom rung. "Uh, I haven't worked out that part yet."

Trey's world spun for a moment. "What have you worked out?" he asked.

Beth walked away from him, and he let her go, because he had an inkling of what she'd worked out. Nothing. She'd worked out nothing.

"I have the money I need to enter," she said, and Trey got himself moving toward her.

"That *you* need to enter?" he asked, not sure why that word *I* had bothered him so much.

"That *we* need to enter," she amended, glancing at him "And I have you."

"My word," he said, the reality of this situation pressing down on him. "You don't have anything worked out."

"I need help," she said, her voice tight. "You're the one with all the connections in the horse racing world."

She was using him.

Of course she is, he thought. *You knew that.*

"I'm sorry," she said quickly. "That's not what I meant." She exhaled heavily and stepped in front of him. Trey stopped, so many things zipping through him. He wasn't sure if it was electricity from her nearness or disbelief at the situation in front of him.

Training a horse to run and win a race in less than five months? Not only was that insane—absolutely insane—but he had to first marry the woman, move in with her and her son, and somehow answer all the questions that would be thrown at him from every side.

"I like you too, Trey," she said, looking right into his eyes. "I think you're kind, handsome, and talented. I said before that I knew a few cowboys, but I knew you best, and that's true. What's also true is that you're the only cowboy I know that makes my heart do weird things, and I figured we'd have the best chance of doing this without it being too awkward."

He took a few moments to think through what she'd said. "What kind of weird things?"

Beth burst out laughing and put her good hand in his. "Weird things, Trey. Like it skips beats and stops sometimes when you walk in the room."

"I think you should have that looked at," he said, though a flush worked its way through his whole body. "Sounds like you might have a heart condition."

"Stop it," she said, giggling.

"Should we go to dinner tomorrow?" he asked.

"I can't tomorrow," she said. "I have four of your guys

coming to clear my fruit trees. I'm going to be canning and juicing and saucing for days."

Trey's frustration kicked up a notch. He wasn't sure why he needed a date before they got married. Perhaps because he wanted this relationship to be real.

Not fake, he thought. He'd wanted it to be real for months now. When he'd whispered that he liked Beth, that was real. His feelings hadn't changed just because he'd agreed to a fake marriage for the Sweetheart Classic.

He didn't want to ask her questions she didn't know the answers to, and he didn't want to hear her say that their relationship wasn't real to her. She felt very real at his side, her fingers as real as anything between his.

"Maybe I could come help you," he said.

"Have you ever made applesauce, cowboy?"

"No, ma'am." He squeezed her hand. "You could teach me. I'll do what you say."

"Sounds like a fun date," she said, slipping her hand up his arm and around his elbow. She hugged him there, and Trey felt strong and invincible in that moment. "You can tell me all about your family."

"Beth, I have seven brothers and the most complicated mother on the planet. I'd need a whole week just for her."

Beth laughed again, and Trey wanted to make her life easier. He wanted her to be happy. He wanted to be the *reason* her life was easier and happier. He remembered the way he'd felt on the deck only a couple of hours ago, and he couldn't deny the peaceful feeling that had come over him then.

If he could help Beth, he should.

"It's really dark now," she said. "We should go back."

Trey turned around, the winking lights on the farmhouse in the distance the picture-perfect postcard of small-town America. "I have another stipulation," he said, his throat dry. He uncapped his bottle of water and took a long drink.

"Go on then," she said.

"I want to know about you, Beth." He looked away from the lights in the distance, but it was dark now and hard to focus on her face. "Not just your family. Not just surface stuff so we can show people we 'know each other.'" He swallowed, about to fillet himself alive. "I like you, and I want to get to know you, like I said."

"I want that too," she said, one hand moving up his chest.

Trey froze and held very, very still as the beautiful Bethany Dixon crowded into his personal space. Everything on his face felt too dry, and as she curled her fingers into the ends of his hair, he sucked in a breath.

"You know what else I want?" she whispered.

"What?" The word was made of air and little else.

"I want my stipulation fulfilled." Her wounded hand found a spot on his shoulder as she pressed into him. "Right now."

Trey used one hand to swipe his cowboy hat from his head and the other to slide along Beth's waist. He pressed his hat to her back as he leaned down, his aim sure and steady.

He hadn't kissed a woman for a while, and he hoped he didn't crash and burn, right here on her ranch.

His eyes drifted closed a moment before his mouth touched hers, but he still saw the most spectacular light show with this kiss. Everything inside him urged him to go faster, but thankfully, he managed to keep the movement slow.

Beth kissed him back, and she was every bit the woman he'd thought she was. Smart, determined, and beautiful.

He hadn't come right out and said he wanted their relationship to be real. She hadn't either. But a kiss like this... This level of pulse-pounding passion could only come from something absolutely real.

Chapter 4

Beth's whole world had narrowed to the man in front of her. The man holding her right where he wanted her. The man kissing her with a level of adoration she hadn't felt in a long time. Even when Danny was still alive, he hadn't kissed her like this. Not in the last six months of his life.

She couldn't believe where she was or what she was doing.

At the same time, standing in Trey's arms as he kissed her was the only thing she should be doing.

He eventually broke the kiss and settled his hat back on his head while she tried to inhale an adequate amount of oxygen. She needed to get her brain working again.

Trey draped his arm around her shoulders, still saying nothing. He'd always been the silent, hard-working type, though he usually had plenty to say when he offered to do something for her, and she refused.

She guided them over to a couple of errant hay bales and sat down. He took the spot next to her, and she leaned into his chest as she partially reclined to look up at the sky. The stars had started to prick through the blackness above, and she smiled at them.

"There's something magical about stars, don't you think?" she asked.

"Mm." He traced his fingers up and down her forearm, and she wished she wasn't wearing a sweatshirt so their skin could touch.

Beth let her mind go down any path it wanted, something she rarely did. Tonight, though, it didn't seem to matter, because within the safety of Trey's embrace, nothing could hurt her, not even her own thoughts and memories.

After a few minutes of lovely, comfortable silence, she said, "My husband was cheating on me," in a voice barely above a whisper.

Behind her, Trey tensed, his muscles and chest turning to stone for a second. "How do you know?"

"He was distant for at least six months before he died," she said. "He was in an accident on a highway twenty-five miles from where he'd said he'd be. From the egg exchange he was supposed to be at." She breathed in, the story she hadn't told anyone but her father tight in her chest.

As she exhaled, it left too. "There were no eggs in the car. His wallet wasn't there. The only reason they were able to identify him and notify me was because of the registration and the license plates."

Trey's hand gripped her forearm, and she liked that it grounded her slightly.

"About a week later, I got his wallet in a package in the mail. The funeral was the next day, and at the time, I was so glad to have his wallet back. It was like this personal piece of him, you know?"

"I can see that," Trey murmured.

"After the funeral, and after I don't even know how long—a few weeks probably—I opened his wallet and tucked right behind his driver's license was a note. Handwritten, by a woman." She could see it as plainly now as the first time she'd looked at it.

Her heart started to pound the same way too. But she'd come this far, and she only had a little bit more to tell. "It said, 'If you want to talk, you can call me.' It had a phone number on it."

"Did you call?" he asked when she didn't go on.

"No," she said. "I gave the number to Hugh, who had one of his friends look it up. I said it was for something Danny had ordered for the ranch, but I couldn't find the invoice. All I had was this number."

Danny had left the ranch in such a mess that Hugh hadn't questioned her.

"Her name was Darcy Cornish. She lives a mile from where Danny went off the road. I just...knew."

"Like a feeling," Trey said. "And you just knew."

"Yeah, like that," she said.

"That's how I knew I should marry you so we can enter the Sweetheart Classic."

A soft smile touched Beth's face, and she leaned into Trey's touch as he ran his fingers along her neck and into her hair.

"I'm so sorry," Trey said.

Beth took another deep breath, expecting the cool night air to sting her lungs. It didn't. The kiss she'd shared with Trey should've stung too. At least pricked her conscience and told her that she shouldn't kiss another man. That hadn't happened either.

"There's so much more to tell," she said, sitting up and letting Trey's hands fall to his lap. "But I think that's enough for tonight." She looked at him, and with her eyes adjusted to the darkness, she could see the highlights of his face in the moonlight. "Thank you, Trey, for following your feeling."

She leaned toward him, and he seemed to understand exactly what she wanted just from reading her body language. He kissed her again, keeping the union much sweeter than last time.

"I'm not going to cheat on you," he whispered. "I'll just tell you straight-up what I'm thinking and doing. Deal?"

"Deal," she whispered.

"Can you do that for me?" he asked.

"Yes," she said without even thinking about it. She wanted everything between them to be open and honest and…real. Fear plucked against her pulse, but she pushed it away. She didn't need to be afraid of another relationship.

She was ready—finally ready—to let go of Danny, let go of everything he'd saddled her with, and start living her life again.

* * *

The next day, apple juice dripped from Beth's fingers when her doorbell rang. Thinking it to be Trey, she called, "Come in."

The front door opened and someone wearing boots came toward her. Sure enough, the handsome cowboy she'd spent too much time thinking about last night when she should've been sleeping appeared in front of her.

When the crew he'd hired to come help her with the apples and peaches had arrived at six-thirty, she'd barely been dressed.

"Hey," he said, taking in the scene in front of him.

"It looks bad," she said. "But this is normal."

"Normal?" He looked at the island behind where she stood at the sink. She knew what he found there, and the shock on his face made her smile.

"Yes," she said. "Now get over here and finish peeling these so I can check the jars I have on the stove." A bead of sweat ran down her back, but Beth ignored it.

Trey came and stood next to her, but he looked like he had no idea what she'd said.

"You can peel an apple, right?" she asked.

"Uh, no, ma'am," he said.

Beth found him utterly charming and adorable. "You use a paring knife," she said, grinning at the thought of such a little knife in such big hands. Her stomach flipped at the thought of holding those strong, large hands. They'd been so warm and so comforting.

"It's right there," she said, indicating the black-handled knife beside the sink.

He picked it up and settled it in his hand.

"You hold the apple in the other hand," she said. "These are already cored for you. You get off the skin and chop them into little chunks. Put them all in this pot." She indicated the big pot of water she'd already prepped for the next batch of apples. She'd put lemon juice, a cinnamon stick, and a dash of salt to the water, and as soon as he finished the last half-dozen apples, she'd set them to cook.

She had some apples waiting to be cored. Some cooking already. Others she'd already pureed and put in jars that were waiting to go into the water bath and be sealed.

"How long have you been doing this?" he asked.

"Since they brought in the first bushel," she said. "I've already put the unsweetened applesauce in the jars and freezer. This is the sweetened batch." She turned back to the counter, where she had a box of silver ring lids, jars, three bushels of peaches she hadn't even touched yet, and a stack of apple cores she hadn't quite put in the trashcan yet.

"I forgot about this stack of paper towels," she said, horrified now. They looked like they'd been soaked in blood, but it was really just a bundle of red apple skins that had seeped through the paper towels.

"I have no idea how to do this," he said behind her, and Beth abandoned her idea to take the full trash bag out and put in a new one so she could clean up the counter. She didn't have time to do that right now anyway. She needed to check the seal on the jars in the water bath, and then she needed to stir the cooking apples beside the giant black pot on the stove.

She returned to Trey's side to find him holding an apple in his left hand and the knife I his right. "Do you do any carving at all?" she asked.

"Carving?"

"Wood carving?"

"I mean, I can shave down a horse's hoof."

"This is like that," she said, though it wasn't at all. "Here." She took the knife from him and then the apple, taking a moment to make sure it wasn't pressing against her wound. She'd changed the plastic glove she wore over her injury three times that day already, and she'd finally gotten out some medical tape and taped the opening to her wrist so liquid would stop getting into the glove.

"Watch." She put the blade of the knife just under the skin of the apple and pulled down. "You can do it in strips like that. Just drop the peels in the sink." She pulled, pulled, and pulled, and a few seconds later, the apple was peeled.

"That was incredible," he said, his voice awed.

A timer went off, and Beth smiled at him as she passed the knife back. "Quick as you can, Trey." A glance at the clock told her she needed to leave in a few minutes to get TJ from school. She had an alarm set on her phone for that, so she pushed it from her mind.

She cracked the lid on the water bath and tilted it away from her face so she wouldn't get a steam treatment she didn't want. One tap on the top right lid told her this batch was done, and she used her jar tongs to remove the piping hot and utterly beautiful jars of applesauce.

She took a moment to cover the water to get it back to boiling and then she admired her long rows of applesauce.

"How often do you do this?" he asked.

She turned back to him. "Once every three years or so," she said. "Next year, I'll sell the apples to Mary Watson. She takes them for her own applesauce every third year."

"What about the year after that?"

"I'll probably ask Merilee Fenton," she said, her voice turning airy. Trey looked at her, pausing in his peeling to do so.

"You sound like you don't like her."

"Do I?" Beth turned away from Trey and took the lid off the cooking apples. They looked ready to drain and puree, so she quickly switched off the burner and slid the pot to the back of the stove.

"That goes right here when you're done," she said. "In fact." She lifted the pot and put it on the burner, re-lighting it. "Get those in as quickly as you can."

"I didn't know this was a race," Trey said. "I've done one apple."

"You only have four more," Beth said. "I like Merilee just fine, by the way."

"Whatever you say," he said.

"She brought me a rhubarb pie after Danny died," Beth said, unsure as to why she was telling this story. "When she knows full-well it makes me sick. It felt like a personal attack is all."

"Was it?"

"Does it matter if it was or not?" Beth asked, annoyed by the conversation. "I threw the whole thing away and never returned her pie plate. That's why she doesn't like me either."

Trey's knife made clunking noises against the cutting board, and then his chuckle started to rise above that. It was such a joyful sound that Beth found herself smiling as she put her jars in the water bath.

That done, with the timer set, she picked up the heavy pot of cooked apples and said, "Scootch over a little, Mister."

He was still grinning as he did what she'd requested. "I'm almost done. Just two left."

"You're flying," she said sarcastically. "This is going to be hot, hot."

"Hot, hot," he said. "Is that what you say to TJ so he knows it'll be really hot?"

"Yes, you big meanie." She poured the apples into the colander in the sink and set the pot on the large, gray towel next to the sink.

"Talk to me as you work," he said. "What are you doing?"

"I just drained the cooked apples," she said, inhaling the tart and sweet scent of them. With the cinnamon stick, her whole house would smell like Christmas for a week or so. "Now I'm putting them back into the pan, where I'm going to puree them with my immersion blender."

She measured out a cup of the cooking liquid she'd caught with a big bowl beneath the colander and poured it into the pot. "I add the cooking liquid, and this is a batch of sweetened applesauce, so I'm adding brown sugar and a touch of butter."

"Butter in applesauce," he said. "Fascinating. How did you learn to do this?"

"My grandmother," she said. "My mother died when I was only twelve, and my grandmother came to live with us for a while."

"I'm sorry," he said. "I didn't know your mother had passed away."

"Yes," Beth said, trying to search back twenty-five years for the right memories. "It was a long time ago, but I remember her as a fun, vibrant woman who loved to dye her hair." She smiled at the memory. "She was a brunette like me, but she was always trying to go blonde."

Trey grinned at her and chopped another apple. "Done." He dropped the chunks into the pot. "Lid on this?"

"Yes, please," she said, checking the timer on the stove. The apples would finish about the same time as the jars—again.

"Anyway, while my grandmother lived with us, she taught Sally and me all kinds of things. How to cook. How to do laundry. How to mow the lawn. Everything."

"Your dad's mom or your mother's?"

"Funnily enough, my mother's," Beth said. "She still lives just on the other side of the Harvest Bridge."

"Oh, so she's close," he said.

"Yes," she said. "She's quite old now, but I'll take her a few jars of the sweetened stuff and spend an hour with her.

She'll tell me stories of my mother and of us as kids, and I'll wish I could stay longer and hug her harder."

Beth stopped talking, because the conversation had suddenly sparked her emotions.

"How long did she live with you?" Trey asked. He turned toward the island and emptied the trash can, letting the full bag rest against the cabinets while he put another bag in and started cleaning up the mess.

"A year or so," Beth said, glad her voice was semi-normal again. "Daddy just needed help. Hugh was only nine, and he played football and lacrosse. Granny helped get us where we needed to go until Sally turned sixteen and could drive."

"What did you do as a kid?" he asked.

"I took ballet and did art lessons," she said. "For a year when I was a sophomore, I thought I'd dance on Broadway, so I took voice lessons too."

"No Broadway?"

"I didn't even try," she said, a hint of sadness tugging at her mouth. "I went to college to study forensics, of all things."

"I think you said you didn't finish that," Trey said.

"Right," she said, ready to talk about something else. Anything, really. "What about you? College? Or have you been working at the ranch since birth?"

"About that last thing," he said. "We went out on the ranch with our father very early. I'm the third of eight boys, and by then, my dad would say, 'Let's go, boys,' and if I could get my boots on fast enough, I got to go."

"You wanted to go out and work on the ranch?"

"Of course," Trey said. "Spur was going. Cayden too. They were my older brothers, and they got to wear a hat like my daddy's and hold ropes and pet the horses." He smiled at Beth. "It wasn't for a few more years that I realized how hard the work was on the ranch."

"That's why I don't let TJ come over there," she said.

"You could, though," he said. "Especially in the afternoons. I know what to do with a five-year-old on the ranch." Trey finished putting the brown cores and stained paper towels in the trash and turned to the sink to clean up the peels there. "Do you need this water?"

"No," she said, stirring the apples on the stove so they wouldn't burn and stick to the bottom of the pan. She just needed the sugar to incorporate and not be grainy. Then she'd add the butter and blend until smooth.

"What would you do with him on the ranch?" she asked. "He's a bit of a wanderer. I'm worried you'd think he was with you when he wasn't."

"He's been over there a lot when no one knew where he was," Trey pointed out. "I'd have him lead a horse where it needed to go. I'd have him hand me a clipboard, open a gate, make a checkmark. There's plenty he can do." He turned on the sink and wetted the washcloth. He wiped down the whole sink and then the counter, and Beth thought she'd died and gone to heaven.

"I didn't know men knew how to wipe out a sink," she commented.

"Okay," he said dryly. "All men?"

"I've never met one who even seems to know the sink

gets dirty." The applesauce had thickened, and the sugar had made everything a beautiful, toasty golden brown. "Can you line up nine bottles for me, please?" she asked. "Right here next to the stove."

"Sure," he said, tossing the washcloth into the sink. He did what she asked, and Beth plugged in her immersion blender and got to work on the apples.

"Wow," Trey said above the noise. "This is kinda cool."

Beth finished and said, "Okay, let's see those muscles in action." She wasn't sure she had the strength to lift the heavy pot another time. "Pour that into those jars, stopping about an inch from the top."

"Just pour it in?"

"Yep. Just pour it in."

He picked up the pot like it was made of foam and not metal and did what she asked. She followed behind him, wiping the tops of the jars absolutely clean and then putting a lid on them, followed by a silver ring she didn't tighten down too much yet.

"Okay," she said, blowing out her breath. "Since that's our last batch, we get a little break." She glanced at the clock. "TJ will be done in forty minutes. Do you think you could pick him up?"

"From school?" Trey's eyebrows flew up.

"Yes," she said. "It's fine if you can't. I'll go, and you can take these jars out when the timer goes off. Then you tighten the rings on these and put them in the water bath—but you have to make sure the water boils again. Then you can—"

"I'll pick him up," Trey said, eyeing the pots and jars and

tongs like they might spring to life and bite him. "We're just coming back here?"

"Yes," she said. "Then we're going to make peach pie filling and peach jam this afternoon."

Trey looked like she'd just told him he'd have to eat raw liver for the rest of his life. "I feel like you tricked me," he said, grinning at her. "You said it wouldn't be bad."

"It's not," she said. "Both of those things don't require any canning, and we can freeze them both." She nudged him with her hip as he encroached on her space. "It's just a lot of peeling."

"You have three bushels of peaches," he said. "How much jam do you need?"

"I'm only doing one of them," she said, turning to look at the boxes of peaches. "My sister is coming to get the rest of them."

"Your sister," he said. "She's younger? No, you just said she turned sixteen and helped drive you guys. She's older."

"She's older," Beth confirmed. "I'm the middle child." Her alarm went off, and she silenced it. "That's my cue to leave to get TJ."

Trey just kept looking at her, something bubbling in his expression. "You set an alarm for that?"

"It's really easy to get busy and not pay attention to the clock," she said. "So yes. Monday through Friday, I have an alarm that goes off at twelve-fifteen." Her stomach grumbled, and she considered asking Trey to bring home some lunch with her son.

She couldn't quite get herself to do it, and she turned

back to the stove to stir the cooking apples though they didn't need to be stirred.

"Beth," Trey said, and she turned to face him. "Thanks for letting me go get TJ."

She didn't know what to say, and then she didn't have to respond, because Trey cradled her face in one hand and gently tipped her head back so he could kiss her.

He hardly moved, the kiss sweet and tender. Beth's pulse was the complete opposite of that for the first couple of seconds, and then she relaxed into the comfort of his simple touch.

He pulled away after only short time and whispered, "How about I bring some of that fried chicken from Cut and Cluck?" proving that the Lord had sent Trey Chappell straight from heaven.

Chapter 5

Trey entered the homestead where he lived with Cayden and Blaine. Until he'd gotten married a few months ago, Spur had lived there too. The four of them got along really well, and the four younger brothers lived in a house down the lane.

All of them were at the homestead tonight, though, even Spur.

Trey took a deep breath and adjusted the six boxes of pizza he carried. "Food's here," he called, knowing a roar would fill the house a moment later. When it did, he grinned at the enthusiasm of his brothers for something as simple as pizza.

Spur got out the drinks he'd said he'd bring, plenty of curiosity in his gaze. Trey ignored his oldest brother, because he wasn't telling this story twice. He didn't even want to tell it once.

You have to, he told himself, because he didn't want to

pretend with the people who mattered most to him. He didn't want to lie to them, and every single one of his brothers would know something was up the moment he announced he and Beth Dixon were going to get married—in only seventeen more days.

He swallowed just thinking about it.

To tame the nerves, he flipped open the pizza boxes and named the kinds he'd picked up. He'd helped at Beth's on Monday until all the peaches were done. He'd met her sister, and Sally sure was nice. Her eyes had rounded like dinner plates when Beth told her she and Trey were dating. She'd stared for a full minute before saying a word, and then she'd sputtered something about how happy for Beth she was.

Trey hadn't seen Beth yesterday, but they'd texted a lot. This afternoon, he'd run by to take TJ home after finding him near the stables, fully dressed, with good shoes on his feet. He'd shown Trey and asked if he could have his hour at Bluegrass.

Trey's first inclination was to say no, because he knew Beth wouldn't approve and hadn't given her permission. In the end, though, he honestly didn't mind if TJ went around with him for an hour, and he'd just said yes.

Once she'd gotten him settled on the couch with a cartoon, they'd gotten out a calendar—he smiled just thinking of her with that paper calendar. He'd teased her that there were about a billion calendaring apps now—and chosen a date for their wedding.

His wedding.

"Quiet down, you animals," Blaine said. "I have to leave

in forty-five minutes, and I want to eat and hear Trey's story. Let's get started."

The brothers quieted, and everyone looked at Trey. "Should we say grace?" he asked.

Every eyebrow went up, and Trey wanted to run from the homestead and never come back. In a couple of weeks, he'd pack up most of what he owned and move down the street. He really didn't want to return to the ranch only six months later the way Ian had.

"You want to say grace?" Cayden asked.

"I don't, no," Trey said. "It's—we usually do before we eat. That's all." He looked at Spur, silently begging for help.

"Lawrence," Spur said, removing his cowboy hat. "Would you?"

"Sure," Lawrence said, and he gave everyone a moment to take off their hats. Some of them closed their eyes while Lawrence prayed, but Trey kept his open. He looked around at the others, wondering how they all got along as well as they did. The hard work helped, as did their dad's no-nonsense rule for no fighting among the brothers.

"Amen," everyone said, and Trey repeated it a half a beat too late.

"All right," Blaine said. "Let's hear it."

"Should we get pizza first?" Trey asked.

"Yeah, let's get pizza first." Cayden picked up a plate and then four pieces of pizza, one from four different pies. Trey went through the line last, and there was plenty of pizza left. He sat beside Spur at the huge family dining table and popped the top on his soda. He took a long drink, letting the carbonation burn his throat.

"Any day now," Spur murmured. "You're going to cause Blaine to pop that vein in his head."

Trey looked at Blaine, who sat just below him in the child order. He did look a little perturbed as he took the largest bite of pizza Trey had ever seen someone take.

"All right," he said. "Might as well get this over with." He put down his slice of pepperoni and olive pizza. "How do I put this as succinctly as possible?" He looked at Cayden and then Lawrence, wishing he'd run his speech by one of them so they could help him refine it.

"I'm going to marry Beth Dixon on October eighteenth so she can enter one of her horses into the Sweetheart Classic."

Surprise ran through him that he'd been able to boil it down so easily.

A moment of silence filled the house. Then another. When the third ended, Spur demanded, "Are you crazy?"

"For real?"

"Is this a joke?"

"The Sweetheart Classic? Isn't that an amateur event?"

"You're not serious."

They all spoke over one another, and Trey didn't bother replying. He picked up his pizza and took a bite while they continued to clamor. Finally, Cayden held up both hands and said, "Okay, stop. Stop it."

Trey swallowed. "I'll answer yes-no questions for five minutes. Then Blaine has to go."

"I'm not going until I know everything," he said.

"Five minutes," Trey said.

"Is this a joke?" Ian asked. He looked like he'd just swallowed a lemon.

"No."

"How long have you been seeing her?" Duke asked.

"That's not a yes-no question," Spur growled. He looked at Trey, his eyes wide and shifting from annoyed to compassionate. "Is this real?"

"No." Trey took another bite of pizza, expecting another uproar.

He only got stunned silence. "That's it?" he asked around his food. "Two questions?" He finished eating and added, "Wow, that was easier than I thought?"

"Are you insane?" Lawrence asked. "You can't just marry Beth Dixon."

"Sure I can," Trey said. "It's not hard. It takes about ten minutes to get married."

"Why would you do this?" Cayden asked, his voice quiet and yet so powerful.

"She asked me to," Trey said.

"Why did he get to ask a question that wasn't yes-no?" Duke grumbled.

"Look," Trey said, sighing. "She asked me to, because she has a horse she thinks can win, and the rules for the Sweetheart are that a married couple enter a horse they own together."

"You said yes, because you like her, though," Blaine said. "Don't even try to deny it."

"I won't," Trey said. "Yes, I like her. I told her that weeks ago when I asked her out. This is just...accelerating it a little bit."

"Accelerating what, exactly?" Spur asked.

"The relationship," Trey said.

"Are you going to move in with her?" Cayden asked.

"Yes."

Spur glowered at Trey, and he nodded at him. "Are you going to try to make this real?"

"Yes," Trey said without hesitation. "I know she likes me too. We've, uh, already done some kissing. She said yes to going out with me. Like I said, this is just accelerating things a little."

"A little?" Conrad said, his first contribution to the conversation. "I can't get Hilde to even talk about marriage, and we've been dating for almost a year. He asks a woman out, and the next thing you know they have a date set." He sounded equal parts disgusted and furious.

"You're going to marry Hilde?" Ian asked, the conversation and attention immediately switching to Conrad.

Trey let it too, because he'd said enough. They all knew now.

"Guys, guys," Lawrence said, waving them all into silence again. "This isn't about Conrad and Hilde."

Trey pinned him with a murderous glare. "Listen," he said. "Mom and Dad know too. You guys know. No one else can know." He looked around at the seven of them. Some he trusted more than others. "No one. When we enter that horse, the rumors are going to fly. She's telling her family too, but I'm serious when I say no one else can know. We want everyone else to think the marriage is real."

"Can I tell Tam?" Blaine asked. "She won't tell anyone, Trey."

"And Olli," Spur said. "I have to tell her."

"I worry about Olli," Trey said. "She's so quirky. She knows so many people."

"Not horse people, though," Spur said.

Trey nodded, his teeth tightening against each other. "You can tell your girlfriends if they can promise to keep it all to themselves. I wanted you guys to know, so I don't have to lie to you."

"I can't believe this," Ian said, standing up. "You're going to have her sign a prenup, right? I mean, she could say anything she wants later on, Trey, and then you're screwed." He wore absolute fury on his face.

"I'm handling it," Trey said. He hadn't even considered a prenuptial agreement, if he were being honest.

"That means no." Ian made a scoffing sound of disgust. "I can't believe this. After what I went through, you're just going to marry some woman you don't even know. Unbelievable." He left his pizza on the plate on the table and stormed away.

The slamming of the door leading into the garage made Trey flinch, and he couldn't stomach the thought of eating more pizza.

He kept his head down, his hat providing some privacy for himself. "I prayed about it," he said very quietly. "I felt like it was the right thing to do. Period. The end. I'm going to do it. I'd like your help and support, because I'm not stupid. I don't think it's going to be easy. But I'm going to do it, because I feel like it's the right thing to do."

He stood up too. "Now you know. Thanks for carving a few minutes out of your lives to come listen to me." He took his plate into the kitchen, sensing and hearing movement behind him.

When he put his uneaten pizza back in the appropriate box and turned around, all six of them stood there too.

"Ian will come around," Duke said. "He's just really sensitive about this."

"I know," Trey said.

"We'll be here for anything you need," Cayden said.

"One hundred percent," Blaine said, and as the most sensitive and most touchy-feely of all the brothers, he stepped out of the crowd and hugged Trey. "For anything."

"Thanks," Trey said, and that got everyone else to huddle up right there in the kitchen.

Several seconds of silence pressed on them, and then Spur asked, "What about you praying about it and getting an answer? That's pretty incredible."

That cracked the tension, and someone chuckled. Before he knew it, Trey was too, and as the group broke up and went back to their pizza and soda, he couldn't help thinking that yes, the answer to his prayer was pretty dang incredible.

* * *

"Are you sure?" His mother looked up from her computer, her reading glasses perched on the end of her nose.

Trey looked at Beth, who turned and looked at him. They held hands right out in the open for his mom and dad to see, and Trey wasn't even embarrassed.

He thought about that warm feeling, that easy feeling, he'd experienced on the deck almost a week ago now. "I'm sure," he said.

"Me too," Beth said. She turned back to his mother, who'd set up a little cockpit for herself. She said she'd text some of her friends while others would get an email.

As Trey and Beth were up against the clock, when he'd asked his mother to help them get the word out quickly, she'd risen to the occasion.

"You know what everyone is going to think," she said.

Trey's face flushed, but he said nothing.

"I don't care," Beth said. "Let people talk."

His mother just looked at her, almost like she couldn't quite believe someone didn't care what others thought about them. Trey didn't; not really. He didn't know anyone who'd care that he'd gotten married anyway.

He wasn't a woman, though, and he knew women talked. They talked and talked, and Trey was a little surprised Beth wasn't worried about having to answer their questions.

"They'll think you're pregnant," Mom said, never one to beat around the bush. "Or that you guys got married just to enter that race."

"They won't even know about that for another two

weeks after the wedding," Trey said. "My wager's on the first one."

"Well, in nine months, they'll all know they're wrong," Beth said. "Besides, why can't two people meet and fall in love quickly? Does no one believe in love at first sight anymore?"

"Not around here," Mom said, focusing on her computer again. She looked at her notebook, her concentration sharpening. "How detailed are we making this wedding?"

"Detailed enough," Beth said. "You don't need to worry about it, Mrs. Chappell. I have a sister and a sister-in-law, and they've both said they'll help me."

"Telling Momma not to worry about something is like trying to tell the sun not to rise in the morning," Trey said.

"Hey," his mom said, but Daddy just started to laugh.

"I'm not wrong," Trey said.

"You're not wrong," Daddy confirmed.

"You two," Mom said. "I just think that if these two think they're going to fool anyone with a quick trip to City Hall, they have another thing coming."

"Mom, I'm not twenty," Trey said. "We have a lot of the details worked out already." She didn't need to know that he and Beth had finally left TJ with Clyde and gone to dinner. Alone. At a real restaurant.

Just last night.

They'd discussed where to get married. What time. The whole she-bang.

"You're getting married on her farm," Mom said. "That suggests you want to keep it secret."

"Small," Beth said, and Trey admired her for standing up to his mother. "We'd like to keep it *small*. There's nothing wrong with that."

"Mm hm." His mom started typing, her fingers flying across the keyboard. "Four p.m. wedding. Dinner afterward, right?"

"Yes," Trey and Beth said together.

"Nothing fancy now," Trey said, and not only because he was paying for all of it. The money didn't matter to him. How much he spent very much mattered to Beth though, and he'd promised her he wouldn't let Mom go wild.

She peered at him over the top of her glasses. "Define fancy."

"Anything more than salad and then a main dish," Trey said.

Mom's mouth dropped open, and Beth's hand in his tightened. "You can't be serious."

"Mom," Trey said, a measure of warning in his voice. "We talked about this."

"What about a soup?" Mom suggested. "Salad and soup. Main dish. And dessert. I mean, it's a wedding. You're going to have a cake, right?" She looked at Beth and then Trey.

"Yes," he said. Maybe if he stuck to one-word answers, this conversation would end faster.

"It's such a lovely fall," Mom said. "Soup would be wonderful at a wedding."

She'd obviously forgotten this affair was fake, and Trey didn't have the heart to bring it up again.

"Julie," Daddy said tactfully.

"Soup *or* salad," Mom said in a desperate attempt to fancy-up the wedding. "Guests could choose."

Beth drew in a deep breath and said, "Okay, ma'am. We can offer a soup or a salad."

Trey leaned over and pressed his lips to her forehead, because he appreciated her willingness to compromise with his mother.

"I've been married before," Beth said. "I've had the big, fancy to-do. I simply don't want it this time."

"That's actually really good," Mom said, her fingers tapping again. "I'm putting that in the email. It's her second time...doesn't want a big affair...send gifts to..."

"Gifts?" Trey asked, his voice pitching up. "Mom, they don't need to send gifts anywhere."

How mortifying. Gifts for a fake wedding?

"He's right," Beth said. "I have everything already. We don't need gifts."

"I could put something like, in lieu of gifts, please donate to your favorite charity."

Trey almost rolled his eyes but stopped himself just in time.

"Sure," Beth said, her voice as normal as ever. An alarm went off on her phone, and Trey had never been happier to hear the chirping chime. "I'm sorry, but that means I have to go get TJ." She started to stand, and Trey went with her. "Are we in a good place to stop?" she asked.

"Yes, I'll just go over the rest with Trey."

"I'm not staying," he said.

"Yes, you are," Mom said.

"I don't need you to come," Beth said, and Trey got whipped from woman to woman.

"I'm not making wedding decisions without you," he said, staring into Beth's eyes and trying to communicate with her so she'd know she couldn't leave him here alone with his mother. Especially a mother in full organizational mode. Mom could ask questions that went on forever, and did it really matter if the centerpieces were orange or gold? Weren't they really close to the same color?

"I do need to go with you," Trey said. "Remember how I drove us, and you don't even have your truck?"

"The party ends in fifteen minutes," Beth said.

"Let's go then," Trey said, guiding her toward the door with his hand on the small of her back. "Thanks, Mom. I'll text you later." He looked further over his shoulder. "Bye, Daddy. Love you."

His mother and father repeated the sentiment back to him, and Trey got out of the house as quickly as possible.

"You were seriously going to leave me there?" he asked, tossing Beth a dirty look.

"You seemed like you were having fun," she said.

"You have got to be joking." Trey opened the passenger door for her, and when he met her gaze, her eyes were full of laughter. "You are."

"She's great," Beth said through her giggles. "Really. She's a great lady. She's just so…"

"Intense," Trey said. "Crazy? Stubborn? Headstrong? Her-way-or-the-highway?"

Beth shook her head, her smile cemented in place. "Be nice. She's fine. I would probably pick intense out of all of those."

Trey nodded and went around to the driver's side. "I'd pick all of them," he whispered to himself. If he and Beth actually got married in her back yard, with just a few dozen people, while serving a dinner with only three courses, it would be a miracle.

Chapter 6

Beth put her SUV in park and said, "There's Lucas, Teej." Her son was already unbuckling his seatbelt, and if Beth didn't tell him to wait, he'd be out of the car and running across the parking lot before she could collect her purse. "Wait for me, TJ. You can't go alone."

"Okay." He still opened his door and got out while Beth turned off the SUV and made sure she had everything she needed for the next few hours. Hand sanitizer, Chapstick, wallet, sunglasses, tissues. She carried everything in pocket sizes in her purse, because she liked using the smallest bag possible.

She got out too, pleased with TJ as he waited by the front tire. "Good boy," she said, taking his hand with her good one. "Oh, wait. Will you help Mommy and lock the car?" She nudged her purse closer to him with her hip. "The keys are right in that front pocket, baby."

TJ pulled them out and looked at the fob. "The one with the lock, right, Momma?"

"Yep. Just push it once."

He did, and the SUV honked at them. "Ooh, that was loud," he said, sticking the keys back in the pocket. He put his hand back in hers, and a rush of love filled Beth. She hoped he'd want to hold her hand while they crossed the parking lot for many years to come.

Kait, Hugh's wife, stood from the bench where she'd been sitting with her four-year-old. Lucas got to his feet too, but she put her hand on his chest to keep him up on the sidewalk as Beth and TJ approached.

"Where's Hugh?" Beth asked, leaning in and giving Kait a quick hug. "Look at Tawny." She wanted to pick up the baby and breathe in the soft, powdery, pink smell of her. "She's adorable. Where did you get that hat?"

The six-month-old wore a soft-looking hat that had the perfect shade of Winnie-the-Pooh yellow on the top, with a pale pink band. Tawny was still bald, and Beth didn't mind that one bit. She loved stroking the baby's petal-soft skin and holding her close to her heart.

"My mother sent it with us," Kait said, smiling down at her daughter. "Hugh went to get ice cream bars."

"I want an ice cream bar," Lucas complained, and Kait gave him a sharp look.

"Daddy's bringing you one." She looked at TJ too and crouched down in front of him. "And one for you too, little man. Give me a hug."

TJ grinned at his aunt Kait and threw himself into her

arms. She giggled with him and listened with wide, interested eyes as he started telling her about the kittens under the woodpile, the dogs Kait knew all about, and then something about a horse named Thunder.

Kait said all the right things at all the right times, and Beth marveled at her. She'd taught preschool before marrying Hugh, though, so she did possess a special love for small children and the ability to relate to them.

"I heard your mommy is dating a man," Kait said. "Do you know what that means?"

"No," TJ said, looking up at Beth with wide eyes.

Kait tugged on his shirt, straightening it for him while she reached for Lucas to keep him close to her. There were quite a few people at the mall today, and she was especially concerned about her son wandering off. Lucas did tend to do that, and Beth wondered if that wandering gene came from her and Hugh.

"It means she's going on dates with him," Kait said. "And she likes him like I like Uncle Hugh. She might even kiss him, and he might be able to marry her and be her husband. Then he'll live with you and your mom and be kind of like your dad."

Way too much information, Beth thought, her heart pounding hard at the thought of all of that happening any time soon. All of it was happening soon, though. Absolutely all of it, and Trey would be in her farmhouse, "kind of" like TJ's dad in less than two weeks.

She swallowed and looked around, needing an escape.

"Who will do that?" TJ said. "I have a friend who could do it."

"Yeah?" Kait asked just as Beth spotted Sally coming toward them. "Who is it?"

"His name's Trey," TJ said. "He lives next door, and he lets me help him on the ranch. Thunder is his horse."

Beth whipped her attention from her sister and her youngest child walking down the sidewalk back to her son. "You've been over working with Trey?"

TJ looked up at her with wide, baleful eyes. "He said I could."

"But *I* didn't say you could." Beth's blood started to boil.

"Yes, you did," TJ said. "The other day when he brought me home. Then you gave me all those fruit rings and you and Trey sat at the table. When he left, he asked if it was okay if he let me work with him when I go to the ranch, and you said yes."

Beth blinked at him. "What day was that?"

"I don't know," TJ said. "I had art at school, and then Trey let me feed the chickens and water the goats, and I led Thunder to his stall."

Kait straightened, her eyes laughing. "Sounds like you said yes."

"Art is on Wednesdays," Beth said. "Trey did bring him home that evening and said he'd let him go around with him. I guess I don't remember him asking if he could do it again."

"I went yesterday," TJ said. "Trey had cookies in the barn."

"TJ," Beth said, bending down and taking her son's chin lightly in her fingers. "You have to tell me when you're going from now on, okay? Then I can text Trey so he can watch out for you."

"Okay," her son said.

Beth smiled at him. "Good boy," she said just as Sally said, "Hello, everyone."

"Hey." Beth turned toward her sister and swooped her into a hug. "How are you? I feel like I haven't seen you in ages." It wasn't true; her sister had come over just last week for peaches. It just felt like a lot of distance existed between them.

"Good." Sally held her tight, and Beth heard everything her sister wanted to say. *I'm sorry. I miss you too. I will try to do better.*

After several seconds, Sally released her and hugged Kait too. Her youngest, Myra, had climbed onto the bench with Lucas, and TJ stood in front of both of them while Lucas showed them something on a portable game device.

Kait looked at the kids. "You guys really think Hugh can handle these three kids?"

"It's two hours," Beth said. "He'll be fine."

"That's right, he'll be fine." Her brother sidled up beside Beth and gave her a quick side-hug. "Thanks for the vote of confidence, sis." He grinned at Sally and stepped over to hug her too. "How's Mick?"

"Still in Philadelphia," Sally said, an icy note to her voice.

Awkwardness descended on them, and Hugh nodded as if he understood. Beth wasn't sure she did, but she didn't feel like it was the right time to ask either.

Sally was always so buttoned-up. She'd always been that way. Reserved, her father said. She came off as conceited, in Beth's opinion, though she wasn't. Once she opened up, she was kind and thoughtful, and she'd never want to hurt someone.

"All right, kids," Hugh said. "I have ice cream. Who wants to go over to the park and then go to a movie?"

TJ raised his hand and bounced on the balls of his feet. Hugh laughed as he swept her son into his arms, and he took Lucas's game machine and handed it to his wife. "We don't need that, bud. All right, there's only one rule today, okay?"

He set TJ on the bench, the three kids lined up. "Two rules. Number one: no crying for your mommas. They're going to be busy and then they're going to be back. It's not a big deal." He held up another finger. "Two: you have to stay where I can see you at all times. All the time." He reached out and tapped his son's knee. "Did you hear me, Lucas?"

"Yes, sir," his son said.

"If you don't, I *will* put the leash on you." Hugh sounded like he meant it too, and Beth believed him.

"Let's go," Kait said, releasing the brake on the stroller. "We have a lot to do today and not much time." She turned back to her husband and kissed him quickly. "Thanks, baby. See you at four."

"Yes, thank you, Hugh," Beth murmured.

"Find the perfect dress," Hugh said, straightening and

smiling at her. "I just can't believe you're going to marry him so fast."

A river of unease ran through Beth, but she pasted a smile over it. "I just figured—what am I waiting for? He's great, and there's no reason to wait."

She nearly buckled under the weight of both Sally's and Kait's gazes, but Hugh just chuckled and shook his head. "He's a lucky guy, then."

Beth nodded and stepped away. Kait quickly fell into step beside her, as did Sally. "The best bridal shop is just down here," Kait said. Now that she wasn't teaching, she did a few private wedding consultations from time to time. Usually for the most high-profile weddings in Kentucky—those who had millions to spend to rent out the nicest facilities, feed eight hundred people at a distillery or winery, and buy designer dresses in New York City.

She came from a family of wedding planners that were heavily entrenched in the business, and when Beth had called her and said she was getting married in less than three weeks, Kait had just sat on the phone for several long seconds, stunned.

Then she'd flown into action, securing this appointment for a last-minute wedding dress and organizing babysitting for Beth and Sally so they could come too. Hugh worked as a private consultant for a tourism company, and his schedule was fairly flexible, thankfully.

"What are you thinking for food?" Kait asked. She and Beth had been texting almost non-stop about the dresses and the venue, the décor and the cake. Nothing about food yet.

"Trey is going to cater it," Beth said quietly. "Actually, his mother is taking care of it, so it should be nice."

"Julie Chappell? I would think so," Sally said. "She's organized some of the biggest fundraising dinners in the state."

Beth pressed her lips together and nodded. "Yes, we met with her on Saturday."

"You don't know the menu?" Kait asked.

"She said she'd text it today," Beth said. "We're trying to go simple, and I'm not sure Julie knows how to do that." She smiled at her sister and then her sister-in-law, finally relaxing a little bit. "I want a simple dress too, Kait."

"You've told me fifty times," Kait said, slowing down so she wouldn't get to the door of the bridal shop first. "Our appointment is with Caroline."

Sally opened the door and held it for Beth and then Kait to push her stroller through.

"You must be Beth," a woman said. She wore a sharp skirt suit and had every strand of hair in the perfect place. "I'm Caroline."

"Nice to meet you," Beth said, shaking the woman's hand. She shook Sally's too, and then hugged Kait, as they were old friends.

"I have three dresses ready for you back here," Caroline said, leading the way past a long counter where another woman in another equally pressed skirt suit stood. "Kait said simple but elegant. I know this isn't your first wedding, and we don't have a lot of time for alterations. She sent your measurements, and I chose dresses that typically don't require much tailoring because of the cut or style."

Beth felt like turning around and running to the nearest fried chicken shop. Maybe if she consumed enough fried food what she was doing would make sense.

Her phone chimed, and she plucked it from the pocket of her purse, hoping there was some problem with TJ she'd have to immediately attend to. The text wasn't from Hugh, but Trey.

Try to have fun today, he'd said. *I can't wait to see you tonight.*

A smile touched her lips and slid through her soul. How had he known she was about to flee? As Caroline continued to talk, Beth sent him a heart emoji, a brand-new feeling of calmness flowing over her.

She'd asked him to marry her so she could enter the Sweetheart Classic. Deep down, though, Beth wondered, then hoped, that a relationship with him could be...real.

He hadn't said as much, but he'd said he liked her before her crazy idea. He kissed her like he liked her and wanted their relationship to be real.

Maybe, she thought. Just maybe...

"Here we are," Caroline said, drawing back a curtain to reveal a room easily as big as Beth's oversized kitchen. "Everyone can come in. I'm assuming Beth brought you to hear your opinions."

The women all filed into the dressing room, and Beth hung her purse on Kait's stroller before facing the wall where three wedding dresses had been hung.

Caroline stood next to them, her hands clasped in front of her, that gloriously perfect smile on her face. "I'll go over them all," she said. "You tell me which one you want to try on first."

Beth swallowed and nodded. Sally slipped her hand into Beth's and squeezed, and that helped ground Beth a little bit more.

* * *

"No, you can't see it," Beth said later that night. She set a bowl of green salad in the middle of the table. "TJ, time to eat."

Her son had curled into the couch when they'd returned from the mall, and Beth had left him there while she went out to the ranch and did the few chores to sustain the animals until morning.

"I want to see it," Trey said. "It's not like the wedding is going to be canceled if I see the dress."

"It's bad luck," Beth said with a small smile in Trey's direction. TJ hadn't moved, and frustration filled her. She went back into the kitchen to grab the spaghetti and meatballs she'd thrown together. "TJ, now. It's time to eat."

She went around the island the other way so she could walk behind where he sat on the couch. He still ran his colored pencil over the pad of paper Hugh had bought for him. "Put it away, bud," she said. "You can finish it after dinner."

Beth took the pot to the table, a sigh leaking from her

mouth when she didn't hear any movement behind her. She looked back at TJ, still on the couch. Still coloring.

Trey looked up at her and then over his shoulder. "TJ. Dinner. Now."

Her son looked up as if he hadn't heard a word anyone had said until Trey had spoken. "Comin'," he said.

Beth glared at Trey. "I hate that he listens to you and not me."

Trey blinked at her, obviously surprised. "I...just tryin' to help."

She took her spot at the table as TJ skipped toward them, happy as a clam. "Spaghetti," he said, though she'd told him what she was making for dinner half an hour ago when she'd started it. "I love spaghetti."

He climbed into his chair across from Trey. "Do you like spaghetti, Trey?"

"Sure," he said easily, glancing at Beth with plenty of nerves in his gaze. "Do y'all say grace?"

"Yes," Beth said. "Get ready, TJ. You want to say it?"

"Okay." TJ knelt up to the table and rested his elbows beside his plate. He leaned his head against his hands and said, "Dear Lord, thank you for the food. Thank you for the ice cream at the mall. Thank you for the dogs. Thank you for the farm. Thank you for Mommy. Thank you for Uncle Hugh. Thank you for Grandpa."

Beth smiled at his gratitude, but a hint of embarrassment started to creep through her as he continued to name Aunt Sally, Aunt Kait, his teacher, and then Thunder.

She looked at Trey, who was staring at TJ with his eyes

wide open, clear surprise there. She wasn't sure which was funnier—TJ's lengthy prayer or Trey's reaction to it.

"TJ," she whispered. "Wrap it up, bud."

"I'm almost done," he said right out loud, looking up at her quickly. She nodded, and he pressed his head against his hands again. "Thank you for Trey. Bless Grandpa. Bless me at school. Bless Thunder."

Oh, dear, Beth thought. How had she forgotten that TJ could go on and on during a prayer?

"Bless Trey to be my dad and mommy's husband. Amen."

Beth's heart rammed into her throat, and she couldn't even repeat the *amen*. Trey certainly didn't, and she didn't dare look at him to see what he was thinking.

TJ had no idea what he'd said, and he stood on his chair, reaching for the tongs in the pot. Beth blinked and got her senses back to a certain degree. At least enough to know she couldn't allow her son to try to dish his own spaghetti.

"Sit down," she said, trying to make her voice as commanding as Trey's. "Let me get it for you. It's too messy." She knocked his hand away from the tongs and took them into her good one. She put the spaghetti and meatballs on his plate that he wanted and then she served herself.

Only then did she look at Trey. He wore a mask, everything he was thinking and feeling carefully concealed behind it. When their eyes met, Beth knew he could see all of her nerves, all of her worries, and all of her humiliation.

She didn't know how to hide it the way he did.

He took the tongs from her and looked back at TJ again.

"That was a good prayer, bud," he said, and as he put spaghetti on his plate, he added, "We got a new horse you should come see at Bluegrass."

"Can I?" TJ asked, his enthusiasm off the charts.

Trey chuckled, which caused Beth to relax. She supposed he better be ready for anything if he was going to marry her. The farm wasn't up to snuff. TJ could be a challenge. She knew she wasn't perfect either.

Danny had been gone for a while now, but Beth hadn't forgotten how hard marriage could be. There were highs and lows, and she hoped Trey was ready for it. He seemed like the kind of man who could handle anything, but if Beth wanted this marriage to last longer than five months, she should probably talk to him about a few things she hadn't mentioned yet.

Buoyed by the flirty glance he threw in her direction, she determined to do just that before he left tonight.

Chapter 7

Trey could hold Beth in his arms forever and never tire of it. Coming in off the ranch to dinner, a beautiful woman, and a movie night with her son had Trey thinking things he hadn't in a while. He was thinking long-term—longer than five months. He was thinking family—not just TJ as his and Beth's child. He was thinking about where he'd really work for the rest of his life.

Bluegrass Ranch? Or Dixon Dreams?

Beth had just put TJ to bed, and Trey should probably head back to the homestead real soon. He had to get up early to receive a pair of horses Spur had purchased as leads.

"I want to talk to you," Beth said, her voice almost a whisper.

"Okay." Trey wasn't worried, because Beth had curled right into his side and currently had one arm draped across his stomach. He'd put his arm around her, and his fingers lingered near her waist. Eight days had passed since his prayer and his declaration that he'd marry her, and Trey could honestly say he'd enjoyed every one of them.

"You should know...marriage is hard, Trey."

He nodded, because he didn't know how to respond to that. He'd never been married, and while a couple of his brothers had and had said that sometimes things just fell apart, he couldn't comprehend what being married to someone would really be like.

"Parenting is hard."

"I know that," he said quietly.

"You really don't," she said. "TJ listens to you. He worships the ground you walk on. He doesn't even hear me." She sat up, and Trey looked into her anxious eyes. "There will be times when he won't listen to you either. You'll be frustrated and angry. He's a child, but you'll have to discipline him. He's not perfect. He could grow up and become a real jerk to you, and to me, and to everyone. It's what teenagers do."

Trey's surprise darted through him for at least the fifth time that night. "Beth," he said. "Listen to what you're saying."

She searched his face, but Trey looked down at his hands in his lap. "Teenagers, Beth?" TJ was almost a decade from being a teenager. She'd asked him for five months. Did she want more?

She sucked in a breath, and that brought Trey's gaze back to her face. A beautiful flush colored her cheeks, and those pretty eyes were wide with fear. "I—"

"Tell me what you want," he said, hoping it sounded like a request and not a demand.

Beth took a deep breath and sat up even straighter, tucking her legs under her body. "I'll start at the very beginning," she said.

"Sounds like a good place to start." Trey stifled a yawn, because he wanted to be here. He wanted to hear what Beth Dixon wanted from beginning to end. He already knew if he could give her what she wanted—even part of it—he would.

"I want to keep my farm," she said. "It's all I've been focused on since Danny died. Things are getting better, but it's very slow, and every time I feel like I've taken a step ahead, something happens to set me back two or three paces."

"Like cutting your hand," he said.

"I've used all of the meager savings I'd managed to build to pay people to come do what I can't," she said, her misery heavy in her voice. "My dad has been supporting me and TJ for years. Clothes. Food."

Trey reached over and took her hand, hoping to lend support.

"That's why I wanted to enter the Sweetheart Classic," she said. "It's a lot of money, and I could pay off the debts, stop using my dad, and take some real leaps forward."

Trey thought about the money in his bank account. He could fund the Sweetheart Classic for a century and not even miss the prize money. He said nothing, though, because Beth already knew about the size of his bank account. Not the exact number, but enough.

"I want to be a good mom," she said. "I want to raise TJ right. I want a partner as I do it. There's a reason men and women have children together. It's so when he won't listen to me, he'll listen to his dad. And when his dad can't get through to him, I can."

Trey had never thought about his parents that way, but as Beth spoke, he could see the way they'd tag-teamed their kids as they raised them. Daddy was the softer parent. The one Trey felt comfortable going to when he had a problem.

He'd taught Trey to be honest, no matter what. He'd taught Trey to work hard. He'd taught Trey to say what needed to be said.

His mother had been the harder parent. The one always nagging the boys to do their chores, finish their homework, and get ready for church. She handled every little detail around the house and with the family, as well as all the charitable organizations the ranch was involved in. She didn't have time for back-talk, or disrespect, and she'd never tolerated either.

As a result, Trey had never done anything but agree with her. There were no discussions. It was Mom's way or no way.

"I want a loving marriage," Beth said, and Trey turned to look at her. She gazed right back at him. "I want to have more children. I want to eat fried chicken on Friday nights, and spend time with my family on the Sabbath." She smiled, but it wobbled a little. Her voice pitched up and shook when she said, "I kind of want it all, Trey."

"You should have it then," he said, his throat tight and his pulse pounding through his body.

"What do you want?" she asked.

He swallowed, his mind whirring. In the end, he simply said, "Everything you just said."

She turned her whole body toward him and rested her elbow along the top of the couch. "Everything?" She pushed her hand through her hair and rested her head in her palm, watching him with eagerness in her eyes.

"Sure." He cleared his throat. "I want a wife, a family, a good piece of land to work." He swallowed, trying to find the precise things he wanted.

TJ.

Beth.

This farmhouse.

This land?

The first three were absolutes.

"I want to be happy," he said. "With all of those things." He wasn't sure how much he could say. If he said he wanted to be TJ's father, that blew the fake part of their upcoming marriage right out of the water. It exposed everything he'd been harboring for Beth for the past few months.

He felt like he was standing on the tallest mountain in the world, looking down into a valley thousands of feet below. If he jumped, and spilled everything, would she catch him? Or had he misread her signals for the past couple of months?

"I want to tell you the truth," he said, unable to look away from her. "But I'm scared."

"You?" she teased. "I didn't know Trey Chappell could experience fear."

"Trey Chappell can," he said with a steady smile. "Especially when Trey Chappell is faced with Beth Dixon and telling *her* what he really wants." He cleared his throat, the smile slipping away too. "That *she's* what he really wants. Not just for five months either. I want to see if we can make this fake marriage into a real thing."

He couldn't hold her gaze for another moment, and he did catch her shock as he dropped his eyes back to his hands. "I want to be that boy's father," he said. "I love him in a way I can't quite describe, because I don't have the words. I know I don't know everything about him yet, and I know he'll drive me to the brink of madness sometimes. But I love him. I want the best for him. I don't know if that's me or not, but I guess I'm hoping it is."

He'd come this far, and Trey still had words to say.

"I don't love you yet, Beth," he whispered. "I've wanted to help you since I brought TJ home the first time, months ago. You make me crazy when you won't let me help you, and you irritate me when you argue with me. But I also like your stubborn personality and I admire the heck out of your desire to take care of yourself, your son, and your farm."

She said nothing, and Trey figured he'd confessed enough for one night. Probably for a lifetime. He waited and kept breathing in and out, praying she'd say she wanted him to be TJ's father, and that she wanted more than five months with him too.

"I guess I have one more thing now," he said into the

silence. "I don't love you right now, but I think I could. Quickly, too. Every day I spend with you, and the more I talk with you, the more I like you. The more I feel myself bonding to you in a way that I know develops into love. I've loved a woman before; I know what it feels like. I know what it takes to get there. I guess if you feel any of the same things I do, maybe we could take the fake label off our relationship and give it a real try. That's what I wanted before you mentioned the Sweetheart Classic, and it's still what I want."

He nodded, finally done. "That's it. I'm done. That's what I want."

She said nothing, but her hand slid up the side of his neck and gently turned his head to look at her. Tears welled in those beautiful eyes, and Trey smiled at her. When the water spilled down her face, he wiped it away with his clumsy fingers. "What do you want?" he whispered.

"Everything you just said." She leaned into his touch. "Is that even possible, Trey? Can we really try to do what you just said?"

"Why can't we?" he asked, reaching for her. He gathered her onto his lap, wrapping both arms around her as she curled into his chest. "Really, Beth. Why can't we work toward a real, loving marriage? With TJ as a family for now." He swallowed. "And this farm."

"It sounds too good to be true, that's why," she said. "Dreams don't always come true."

"Sometimes they do, though," he said, thinking of Spur and Olli, then Blaine and Tam.

"I want to try," she said.

Trey grinned at the darkness beyond the back windows. "Me too."

She lifted her head, and Trey kissed her. She seemed hungry for him, but he kept the kiss slow and gentle, only deepening it when she'd succumbed to him. He pulled away sooner than he would've liked too, because he needed to keep his hormones out of tonight's conversations and happenings.

"I think you want to tell me more about TJ," he said. "I didn't mean to upset you at dinner. You tell me what you want me to do and not do with TJ, and I'll do it. He's your son, and I'll respect whatever you say."

Beth opened her eyes and stroked her hand over Trey's beard. "It's not your fault he listens to you and not me. I think...let me try with him first, and if he doesn't respond, then you can step in." She leaned forward and kissed him again. "Okay?"

"Sure," he said.

"Or when I ask you to do something with him. Then you can."

"What if I need to get after him when you're not around?"

She cuddled into his chest again. "Like when he's at the ranch with you?"

"Yeah, like that."

"Then you do what you think is right. I'd like to be told what that is when you get back with him."

"Of course."

She lifted her head again. "And one more thing, Trey."

A blip of fear moved through him. "Yep."

"I told him he has to ask me or tell me he's going to Bluegrass before he goes. He can't just wander off and then get rewarded by playing with the horses."

Trey tried not to smile or laugh, because Beth was being serious. He tried nodding, but he couldn't quite hold it all in. He chuckled. "We don't play with horses over there, sweetheart."

She grinned at him too. "I know. You know what I mean." She laid her head against his shoulder, her breath washing across the skin right above his shirt collar. A shiver ran down his back at the nearness of her, at how close he felt to her emotionally and physically.

"I told him I'd text you when he was coming over. If you don't get a text from me, Trey, he didn't do what I asked him to. You should send him home to follow through with what I've asked him to do."

"I can do that," Trey promised. "Now, are you sure I can't see your wedding dress?"

* * *

"Don't tie it so tight," Cayden said. "His neck is bulging."

"It's not bulging," Duke argued. He stood in front of Trey, both hands at his neck, trying to get the bow tie right.

The other brothers continued to argue, but Trey stood still and silent. The days until this Saturday afternoon wedding had passed in a blur of work and sleep, more work, and then more work. He'd also had to interact with his mother a lot more than he usually did, and he couldn't wait for this day to end.

Then the wedding would be over. The meal finished. The stress of all the prep and the fittings gone.

"Ten minutes," someone called just as an alarm on Cayden's phone went off. Of course he had an alarm on his phone. He was a lot like Beth in that regard. He claimed it was because he had a plethora of tasks he had to complete each day, and over half of them were things he didn't want to do.

He'd learned that he could do anything for fifteen minutes. If there was something he didn't want to do, but had to be done, he set a fifteen-minute alarm and worked until it went off.

Beth used her alarms so she wouldn't forget to pick up TJ from school or when to get dinner out of the oven. Either way, the alarms worked.

"Good luck," Spur said, hugging Trey.

"You've got this," Blaine said. "You're lucky you don't have to endure a long engagement." He embraced Trey too.

Cayden took his turn, grinning at Trey before stepping into his personal space and clapping him on the back. "Happy wedding day."

Trey should've reminded him it wasn't real, but he didn't. He and Beth had professed real feelings for each other, and they'd both admitted they wanted to see if they could build something real out of this wedding.

Conrad hugged Trey. "You're a good example of doing what you think is right."

Surprise lanced through Trey, and he was so tired of the feeling.

Duke fiddled with his tie again and then hugged him. "Love you, brother."

"Love you too," Trey murmured, glad his voice was still working.

Lawrence grinned and hugged him. "I'm happy for you."

One by one, they left, and it was just Trey and Ian. He hadn't spoken to his brother much over the past couple of weeks, though he'd wanted to. TJ came to the ranch every afternoon, and Trey had been spending evenings on Beth's property.

There was a to-do list for Dixon Dreams ten miles long, and Trey didn't think he'd ever get through it all. He still had work to do at Bluegrass, and he didn't want to give that up. In addition to all of that, he'd started training Somebody's Lady.

He loved training the horse, and he felt more awake in the middle of the night while he worked with her than when he woke after sleeping. He'd put out a couple of calls for a jockey, but he hadn't heard back yet.

Somebody's Lady could come out of the gate easily. She loved to run—really loved it. But she still tried to lift her head, and Trey needed a lead horse to work with her, and that required two riders. Beth's hand wasn't in good enough shape for horseback riding, and she'd admitted she didn't do a lot of it anyway.

"Good luck," Ian said, and Trey reached for him. He hugged his brother, plenty to say but no time to say it. The pain radiating from Ian was enough for Trey to know his words wouldn't matter anyway.

Ian cleared his throat, stepped back, and nodded at Trey. He left the room right as their parents entered.

"It's almost time," Daddy said, a wide smile on his face. "Are you ready?"

"I don't know," Trey said, looking from him to Mom. "I know this isn't the wedding you wanted for me."

"It's lovely," Mom said, smiling. She reached Trey first and hugged him. "I will always support you when you're following your convictions." She stepped back but kept her hands on his shoulders. "My, you look handsome." She scanned him down to his shiny, black shoes, and then reached up to touch his hair.

"Mom, I'm wearing a hat." He brushed her hand away and turned to get his cowboy hat.

"You should've at least cut it a little bit. It's your wedding day."

"I like my hair how it is," Trey said. It grew incredibly slowly, and if he cut it for his wedding day, it would take a year to get back to this length that curled over his ears and that he could push his fingers through as he swooped it to the side.

He did that now and seated his hat on his head before he faced his parents again.

"We were hoping to have a quick prayer with you," Daddy said.

Trey's immediate reaction was to say no, but then he thought of TJ's prayer. Since dinner that night, Trey had been more focused on thanking the Lord for what he had before he asked for a single thing. "Okay," he said.

"I'll say it," Daddy said. He took off his cowboy hat too and tucked it under his arm. He took Mom's hand and then Trey's. With the three of them holding hands, Daddy closed his eyes and said, "Dear Lord, we're grateful for Thy bounty. Thou has always taken care of us, and we appreciate it. Please bless Trey and Beth as they start this life together. Bless them both with clear minds and the ability to communicate clearly with one another. Amen."

"Amen," Trey whispered, stepping into both of his parents and hugging them. "Thank you." He didn't know any more adequate words, but these still weren't enough.

"Let's go," Mom said after a few seconds. "We don't want to be late."

Trey followed them out of the bedroom where he'd be sleeping in the farmhouse and through Beth's kitchen and living room. The back deck had been decorated with flowers and twinkling lights, and three dozen chairs had been set up under the awning.

The altar stood to his left, right against the railing, and Trey went that way, wishing he could hide behind his mother and father. They both walked with their heads up, smiling and murmuring hello to those they passed.

Besides his brothers and parents, Trey's uncle had come

with his wife. Olli was there with her friend, Ginny Winters. And Tam had brought her parents. Sixteen chairs with Trey's family.

Beth had her sister and her family, as well as her brother and his. Her father, and her grandparents. TJ, of course, though he was walking out with Beth, so Trey didn't see him. Strangely enough, she'd invited Danny's parents, and they'd come.

Fourteen people for her, plus her son. Thirty-one people made a very small wedding indeed, and Trey glanced out to the grassy area that was the back yard. It wasn't very large, and then gravel and dirt took over as the ranch began.

Six tables had been set up underneath a wide, white tent. Tall, curved and tangled rods sat in the middle of each table, with orange, brown, and red flowers and berries hiding in the curls and bends in the wood.

Place settings were already there. Bows tied on the back of chairs.

He reached the altar and nodded to the pastor Beth had asked to come perform the ceremony. He looked out at the crowd, most of whom were looking at him. They were all dressed in their finest, as was he.

Everything was ready.

He just needed a bride.

His feet shifted, and he couldn't keep his eyes away from the back door, where Beth should have appeared already.

Two empty seats waited in the front row—one for Beth's father and one for her son. They were both walking her down the aisle…hopefully.

He met her sister's eyes, a woman he'd met a couple of times when she'd been at Beth's when Trey had come in the evenings. Sally got to her feet, her eyes wide. She held up one palm in a universal sign for Trey to stay.

He didn't want to stay. He wanted to run, especially if Beth was going to back out now.

Chapter 8

Beth ran her hands down her sides, the wedding dress smooth beneath her fingers. The dress fit like a glove, and it hadn't required many alternations. The fabric was shiny and bright, almost glowing in the sunlight. She'd loved it in the dressing room too.

The dress cinched everything tight above the waist, and Beth hadn't realized how much she had in the way of her chest until this wedding gown pushed everything into the right place. The neckline scooped, but not too low. Beads that functioned as buttons ran down the back, which also scooped. It was lower than the front, and Beth had allowed Kait to curl her hair and pin it all to her head in some immaculate bridal display.

She'd felt like a cake that was getting decorated as Sally had done her makeup while Kait did her hair. To their credit, neither of them had ever asked if Beth was pregnant.

Neither of them had asked her to explain more than she had, and they'd been there whenever she'd called or texted.

They'd both left her bedroom a while ago, and Beth knew she should've been on the deck several minutes ago.

"I've got it," Daddy said, rushing back into the room. He held her shoe in his hand and lifted it up. "I don't think you'll even notice. There's not a crack or anything." He presented the shoe to her, and Beth took it.

"Get up, bud. Let's see if this works." She slipped her shoe on and looked up at her father. He extended his hand to her, and she put hers in it. She leaned her weight on him as she stood from the bed, testing out the heel that had snapped with the first step she'd taken into the hall.

It had taken a lot of her courage to even take that step, and now she had to do it all over again.

"I think—" She grunted as the heel bent again. Her ankle twisted with it, and she went back down to the bed. "Shoot."

Daddy started to bend to retrieve the shoe, but Beth said, "Leave it, Daddy. We're not going to fix it."

Someone knocked on the door, a light rap that belonged to a woman. "Beth?" Sally poked her head into the room. "Is everything okay?"

"Her shoe is broken."

"It's okay," Beth said, slipping her left foot out of the shoe that wasn't broken. "I'm just not going to wear shoes."

"Maybe I can—"

"It's fine," Beth said, interrupting Sally as she came toward her. "I'm late, and it's just a shoe." She hoped it wasn't a sign of what her marriage with Trey would be like. Brittle. Fragile. Breakable.

She smiled brightly at Sally. "Go sit, Sally. We'll be right behind you."

Her sister nodded and left the room again. Beth turned toward her son, who wore a pair of black slacks, a white shirt, and a tie the color of the deepest, reddest roses. Beth loved that dark, dark red that was almost black, and she'd chosen it for this wedding.

She and Danny had been married in the winter, and everything had been silver, blue, and white. She didn't like any of those colors all that much, and this autumn wedding was more her style.

She'd even put pumpkins on the deck as part of the décor. Julie Chappell had probably gasped and removed them all by now.

Daddy stepped to her side and linked his arm through hers. "Ready, sugarbaby?"

"Ready." She reached for TJ's hand. "Right here, bud. Right by me."

He did what she said, and the three of them left the bedroom and journeyed down the hall and through the living room. The back door loomed, and Beth's pulse pounded against the neckline of her dress.

"Are we going out?" Daddy asked, and Beth realized she'd slowed to a stop.

She took a deep breath and thought about all she and Trey had already been through. "Yes," she said, taking another step. Then another.

With enough of them strung together, she exited the house, turned toward the aisle, and started down it.

Trey stood only ten paces away, his eyes bright beneath the brim of his hat. He stole her breath and calmed her heartbeat at the same time, and Beth smiled at him, her gaze refusing to go anywhere else.

His return smile made him doubly delicious, and before Beth knew it, she'd reached the altar. "Love you, baby doll," her father said, and she kissed both of his cheeks before she bent down and touched the tip of her nose to her son's.

"I love you, TJ," she said. "You want to give Trey a hug?"

"Can I?"

"He'd probably like it." Beth straightened and watched her son turn to Trey. He didn't just hug her son; he scooped the child into his arms, his smile as wide as the Mississippi River now. TJ took his face in both of his hands, and the brim of Trey's hat nearly covered both of their heads.

He set him down and TJ went to sit with Kait and Hugh.

Trey focused on her, his eyes sliding down to her feet. "Shoe trouble?" His voice could barely be heard, and Beth lifted one of her bare feet.

"I think they're pretty cute."

He grinned at her and offered his arm to her. "You look amazing," he said. "I love this dress." His eyes sparkled with desire, and Beth felt it popping through her whole body too.

"You look pretty great too."

"I'll take pretty great," he said. "This bowtie is cutting off my circulation."

"Are we ready?" the pastor asked, and Beth remembered they weren't meeting just to chat.

Trey faced him and nodded; Beth did too. Pastor Adams began speaking, and not two seconds later, Trey reached into his far pocket and took out his phone, bending his head to look at it.

Beth's horror mingled with her shock, but when he put the phone where she could see it, she read the name *Robert Merchant*.

Her eyes flew to his, and he cocked his eyebrows. An entire conversation was had in only a moment, and Beth loved that they had that foundation between them.

Robert Merchant was one of the jockeys Trey had reached out to. His top choice, actually.

She nodded, and he quickly put the phone back in front of his body. He didn't answer the call, but he hurried to thumb out a message before he slid his phone back into his pocket just as Pastor Adams said, "I've been told not to make this too long, so we're ready to move into the vows."

Beth looked at him, and he didn't look very happy. Probably because the groom had been texting during his speech. Beth could admit she hadn't heard any of it either, and regret made her offer him a small smile.

The pastor smiled back at her. "Beth, are you going first?"

"Yes," she said, turning fully to Trey. "Trey, I know I drive you crazy when I try to do everything myself, and I know you get irritated when I argue with you." She grinned at him as he chuckled and shook his head, his eyes dropping to the altar.

He looked back up when she said, "I appreciate everything you've done for me, and I love how you love my son. I can't wait to build a life and a home with you." She hadn't said she loved him, because she didn't.

She knew there was a difference between loving the service someone rendered and loving that person. She also knew that serving someone built a bridge that could easily lead to loving them.

"Beth," Trey said. "The moment I met you, I wanted to know more about you." He smiled at her and then over to TJ. "Every time your son came over to Bluegrass, I'd smile as wide as the sky, because then I'd get to take him home and see you. I love talking to you. I love learning about you. I love your son, and I think I'm going to love living at your farm. I'll do my best every day to be the man you deserve."

He nodded, and they turned back to the pastor. If anyone noticed that neither of them had professed their deep love for one another, Beth hoped they just wouldn't say so.

Pastor Adams performed the ceremony, and Beth said, "I do," when it was her turn. Trey said it too. Then the pastor said, "I now pronounce you man and wife. You may kiss your bride."

Trey turned toward her and took her face in his big, rough, wonderful hands. He kissed her like a gentleman while the crowd only paces away cheered. His brothers were loud, as was hers.

She giggled, breaking the kiss. She and Trey got separated

as his mom surged forward to hug him. He embraced her and then his father and Beth let her siblings and their spouses engulf her. After all the congratulations had been said, Beth migrated back to Trey's side.

"Momma," he said. "You're up."

Julie Chappell's face lit up, and she walked down the aisle, weaving through the crowd to the top of the steps. She put her fingers in her mouth and whistled, and Beth gaped at her. "She just whistled at our wedding."

Trey stared at his mother too. "We did put her in charge of the dinner, and she's a born and bred Kentuckian."

The crowd quieted, and Julie said, "Dinner will be served in five minutes. If you'll all come with me to the yard to find your seat, please."

She was a Southern socialite, that was for sure, and she did charm everyone who came her way. Beth watched Trish and Taylor Dixon smile and introduce themselves. Julie's eyes widened, and then she grabbed onto them in a tight hug. She personally led them to their table, and Beth couldn't think of a better person to be in charge of the dinner.

"We're being paged," Trey said, nudging her forward. Her bare feet ate up the distance across the deck and down the steps. She and Trey had been assigned seats at a table with her father, TJ, and Trey's parents.

Beth experienced true happiness as she took her seat, and that surprised her slightly. She'd thought having a real shindig for a fake marriage would be more taxing than this.

That's because this is not fake, she told herself.

The food arrived, and Julie eventually came to the table too. Beth went through everything required of her. She laughed. She talked. She danced with Trey and then her father.

Finally, the cake had been cut, the bouquet thrown, and another round of congratulations said. She hugged TJ tightly and said, "Be good for Grandpa."

"I will, Momma." He moved to Trey next, who stooped and said something to her son before the little boy skipped off to go home with her father.

When the last guest left, Beth waved at them and then looked at Trey. It was just the two of them now, and she couldn't help thinking about what usually happened once a newly married couple was alone.

"Ready?" Trey asked, offering her his hand. "My bag is in the bedroom."

"Mine too," she said, slipping her fingers through his. She only moved because he did. He collected both bags and set them in the hallway before going into his room to change. She slipped out of her wedding dress alone, admiring the fabric and the beautiful baubles.

She put on a pair of loose, flowing black pants and a dark gray sweatshirt covered with autumn-colored flowers. With shoes and socks on, she left the bedroom and found Trey in the living room, both bags at his feet while he texted.

"Robert is in," he said, glancing up. "I'm going to send him the contract when we get to the hotel, and he'll be at your place in the morning to meet Somebody's Lady."

"But we're not going to be there tomorrow."

"I'm asking Conrad to meet him for me." Trey looked up when he finished messaging, his expression changing in a split second. "Look at you."

"Look at you," she said, drinking in his jeans, that belt buckle, and a plaid shirt in green, white, and black. "Do you own anything but jeans and plaid shirts?"

He looked down at himself. "I don't think so," he said.

She laughed lightly and stepped over to him. He took her into his arms easily, and Beth's throat narrowed. He'd said so many wonderful things to her, and all she'd had to say was she agreed.

"Who does your shopping?" she asked. "Be honest."

"I'm going to plead the fifth," he said, staying as serious as ever. "Did you like your wedding?"

"It wasn't just my wedding," she said. "I've had one before. Did you like it?"

"I did," he murmured, his eyes dropping to her mouth. "As much as I thought I wouldn't."

"It was beautiful," she whispered. "Thank you, Trey."

"Mm." He kissed her, and Beth let him dictate the speed and depth of the kiss, simply going along with him as she enjoyed the taste and feel of him. He accelerated things quickly, and Beth matched him stroke for stroke.

He broke away from her and pulled in a noisy breath. "We should go," he said, stepping away from her almost violently and reaching for their bags. "Do you need anything else?"

"No," she said, feeling a bit abandoned. She wasn't even sure why. They weren't going to sleep together tonight. He'd paid for a suite in a five-star hotel in Louisville, an hour away, but it had two bedrooms. One for each of them.

Her feelings stung when Trey grunted and headed for the front door without another word. She almost didn't want to follow him. The wedding had been beautiful. *He* was beautiful, and she didn't want the night to end like this.

She followed him and watched him put their bags in the back seat of his truck. "Hey," she said gently. "What's going on in your head?"

He barely looked at her. "Nothing."

"You just ran away from me."

Trey paused with his hand on his door handle.

"You aren't going to open my door for me?" she asked. "Your wife?"

"I'm struggling with a couple of things," he said. He still didn't look at her. "I can open your door." He went past her without looking at her and walked around the back of the truck.

Beth once again followed him and paused right in front of him. "Talk to me."

Trey looked into the truck, not at her. "I'm not sure what I'm supposed to do," he said. "Open the door for my wife, but I can't kiss her the way I want. Carry my wife's bag, but only to a bedroom where she's going to sleep alone." He shook his head. "It's confusing. I get it. I know you're not…I mean, you are. I don't know."

He pulled the door open further. "Can you get in, please? We still have a long drive in front of us."

Beth got in the truck, and Trey closed the door. He

walked away, but he didn't come get in the truck. "Where did he go?" Beth asked. Should she get out? Go find him?

The seconds ticked by, and Beth did get out of the truck. Trey came down the front steps, saying, "Sorry. I left my phone charger inside."

"I thought maybe you'd left." She walked toward him. "I don't want things to be awkward between us."

He met her on the sidewalk. "I'm just going to need some time reconciling what I'm allowed to do with what I'm not."

"Fair enough," she said.

He reached her and cradled her face in one hand. "You light me on fire," he said. "In case you didn't know."

Beth hadn't felt attractive in a long, long time. Yet there was Trey, always telling her how beautiful she was and how much he liked her, her clothes, or her hair.

She swallowed, not sure what she was feeling or thinking. "Maybe we don't need the second bedroom tonight," she said, her voice a little froggy.

"I can't ask you to do that," he said. "Even if I want it."

"You didn't ask."

He shook his head. "Sweetheart, when we do that, I want it to be because I'm in love with you, and you're in love with me. Not because we had a beautiful wedding and we're finally alone." He laced his fingers through hers and led her back to the truck. "I'm fine. I just need to not kiss you like that again."

"I liked it, Trey," she said as she climbed into the truck.

"Men and women are different," he said simply. "I can't

kiss you like that and not want more. And I don't want to make love to you until I'm *in love* with you." He leaned into the truck, his face getting close to hers. "Okay? I'm not mad at you; I'm frustrated with myself that I first, kissed you like that, and second, that I didn't anticipate this. It's harder than I thought it would be, that's all. Doesn't mean I can't do it."

Beth's emotions quivered, but she managed to nod. "You're an amazing man, Trey."

"I'm still just a man." He closed her door, and this time, he came around and got behind the wheel. He took a deep breath. "All right. Let's have a good time for a couple of days, okay? I've been working like a dog, and I can't wait to sleep as late as I want."

Beth smiled into the darkness as he eased out of her driveway and onto the highway. "It's funny, but I was looking forward to sleeping as late as I want too."

They laughed together, and Beth reached over and took Trey's hand in hers, her gratitude for him off the charts. She didn't know how to adequately express it, but she hoped she'd find a way in the next few days as they spent time together away from the busyness of the farms and ranches they worked, away from the stress of parenting, and away from any other distractions.

Chapter 9

Cayden Chappell walked down the lane with Spur and Olli, the two of them hand-in-hand as they all chatted about the wedding. Cayden hadn't said a whole lot, though he'd certainly seen the way Trey and Beth had exchanged something personal and intimate at the altar when he'd shown her something on his phone.

Trey said the wedding was fake, but Cayden—and anyone with eyes that could see—could tell the feelings between Trey and Beth weren't.

Blaine had said that Tam had asked him to be her fake boyfriend, and they'd ended up engaged. All around him, not-real seemed to become real, and he hadn't given Trey's wedding much more thought since the night he'd asked all the brothers to come so he could talk to them.

Olli's phone rang, and she answered in a chirpy voice with, "Ginny, hey."

Cayden couldn't help the way he looked over to Olli. He'd sat right behind Virginia Winters during the wedding, and afterward, he'd sat at the same table with her, Spur, Olli, Conrad, and Lawrence.

He'd tried not to focus only on her, but she'd been right next to him for the second wedding in a row, and he'd already asked her out. She knew he was interested in her, and she sure seemed interested in him too.

They'd talked about her distillery, her family, and the ongoing festival that took all of her time and attention. She'd said that once the holidays were over, she'd have more time, and Cayden had taken Tam's advice and faded into the background. He did want all of Ginny's attention, and he didn't want to cause more stress for her.

He texted every once a while, and she did the same when they saw something online they thought the other one would like. The latest conversation he'd had with her was about a meme he'd seen for her favorite comedy television show.

She'd sent him a few laughing emojis and then claimed to be watching that show at that very moment. They'd had a couple of back-and-forth texts about eating in bed—okay or not okay?—and the appropriateness of wearing pants inside your own home.

He smiled just thinking about those texts. Ginny had been stunning tonight—absolutely stunning—in a sparkly, rose-gold-colored gown with shiny, sparkly heels that made her look like a princess straight out of a children's movie.

They'd danced together just once before her mother had

called and Ginny had retreated to the back deck to take the call. Cayden had sipped champagne and lingered at the table, watching her, until Spur and Olli were ready to go.

Holding Ginny in his arms, even with a foot of space between them, had reminded Cayden of all the things he'd liked about her months ago. He'd sort of thought his crush on the woman would fade while he waited, but it hadn't. Perhaps it lay dormant when he wasn't talking to her and with every day that passed where he didn't see her.

Then, when she walked back into his life, everything roared back through his bloodstream, making him vibrate in a whole new way.

"I'm sure we can," Olli said. "I'll send Spur over to see what's going on." She pulled the phone from her mouth and said, "Her car broke down, baby. Can you go look at it?"

"I'll go," Cayden said, his voice far too loud in the still, dark night. Spur looked at him, but there wasn't enough light to read his brother's expression. "I mean, you guys have that phone call with Frank really early in the morning."

"You're better with cars than I am," Spur said, his voice even and quiet. "Tell 'er Cayden will come."

"Great," Olli said, relaying the information to Ginny. "He's on his way." She ended the call and said, "She's only about a mile down the road, Cayden. You can't miss her."

"Okay," he said, reaching into his pocket for his keys. "I'm sure she'll update you."

"Oh, I'm sure she will," Olli said with plenty of knowing in her voice, and Cayden had forgotten that he'd told Spur about his crush on Ginny the moment it had sparked to life.

"Leave him be," Spur murmured, and Cayden appreciated his brother in that moment.

"The festival is almost over," Olli said. "He should ask her out again. Get something on her calendar before her mother fills it up again."

"*He* is standing right here," Cayden said, his heartbeat rippling through his chest. He fiddled with his keys, his truck to his right. "Do you really think I should ask her out again?"

"Absolutely," Olli said. "Ginny works in spurts, Cayden. She's busy and then not. Busy and then not. It's a lot like you guys on the ranch, some weeks heavier in workload than others."

"Okay," he said. "She said after the holidays. I thought that meant all the way to Christmas."

"No." Olli shook her head. "Cayden, the harvest festival ends on Halloween. She'll have a bit of time after that before she's into the holidays and all the schmoozing her family does." Her face brightened, and she looked up at Spur. He didn't even twitch a muscle. "Hey, you know what? Ginny hates going to all those holiday events alone…you should find a way to offer to take her."

"If they're dating, he can just go as her boyfriend," Spur said.

"Oh, Ginny doesn't use the word boyfriend," Olli said. "Don't use that word, Cayden, okay?"

"Okay," he said. His mind was stuck on Spur saying "dating," and he couldn't even comprehend "boyfriend." There was too much information coming at him while Olli continued to talk, and finally Spur said, "Baby, she's on the side of the road. Cayden's not an invalid. Let's let him get on his way."

He met Cayden's eye, and they both nodded. Cayden got behind the wheel of his truck and started down the gravel lane toward the highway. Beth's farmhouse still had lights on inside, and he wondered where they were going for the next few days. Trey hadn't been as forthcoming with those details, and Cayden hadn't asked.

If he really wanted to know, he could ask Lawrence or Blaine, but Cayden tried really hard to stay out of family drama.

He turned right instead of left once he reached the highway, and sure enough, he came upon Ginny only a couple of minutes later. Her luxury SUV sat on the shoulder, absolutely no lights to indicate the car was occupied or worth anyone's attention.

He pulled past her SUV and flipped around so his headlights shone on the hood of her vehicle. Taking a deep breath, he got out of the truck and walked toward her car. "It's just me, Ginny."

Her door opened, and the gorgeous, curvy, brunette stepped into the spotlight of his high beams. "Thank you for coming, Cayden." She spoke in a voice made for queens, everything round and smooth and so proper. No wonder her mother wanted her as the public face of their whiskey distillery.

"Of course," he said. "What happened?"

"I've been having some trouble with it for a couple of

weeks," she said, sighing as she leaned into the hood and looked at it. "It's never just died, though."

"Will you pop the hood?"

"Sure." She ducked back into the car and a moment later, a loud clunk meant the latch had released.

Cayden told his fingers to steady and his pulse to calm down as he lifted the hood. A rush of heat hit him in the face, and he said, "You're overheated." He got down on the ground, pulling his phone from his pocket.

"Cayden, you're in a suit," she said.

"Yep," he said with a grunt as he slid under the car. There wasn't anything leaking out of her engine, and he suspected her radiator was bone dry. He got up with another groan and grunt, because he wasn't in his twenties anymore. "I think it's your radiator, Ginny. I don't suppose you have antifreeze in your trunk or anything?"

"No," she said.

"We can put water in it," he said. "But I'm not sure you'd even make it home." He checked his phone. "It's too late for the automotive stores to be open." His mind raced. "I wonder if we have any antifreeze on the ranch."

She stepped to his side as he gazed at the engine. "Maybe you could just give me a ride home."

"Yeah?" he asked. "You have something else you can drive until you get this fixed?"

"Yes," she said simply, and Cayden didn't detect any frustration beyond being stranded on the side of the road. He also found it odd that she'd called Olli for help, not a family member.

"Are your brothers out of town?" he asked.

"No," she said.

Cayden finally dared to look at her. He knew better than to touch a radiator cap that had overheated. "Do you need anything from your car?"

"Just my purse." She left his side and went to retrieve her purse while Cayden closed the hood. He met her next to her door and offered her his arm.

"I like your shoes," he said. "I don't think I told you earlier." He was already looking at them, but Ginny looked down too.

"Thank you," she said, a smile greeting him when their eyes met. "I'm sorry my mother called earlier. I would've liked to have danced another song with you."

Cayden bit back on the urge to ask her if she was serious. Most things about Ginny were very serious, as she ran a business every bit as profitable as Bluegrass Ranch. "I would've liked that too," he said, finding himself speaking and acting more properly than he normally did. He tried to get rid of that, because he didn't want to be someone different with Ginny.

Either she'd like him for who he was, or she wouldn't.

He cleared his throat. "I know you said you were busy, but I'd still—uh, I was thinking we could get dinner sometime soon." He opened her door and waited while she stepped up on the running board of his truck.

Cayden let his hand drop to her lower back, his nerves rejoicing at the touch. She smelled like something flowery and spicy and full of vanilla all at the same time, and he was sure it was one of Olli's concoctions. He needed to find out which one. Perhaps he could sniff them all and tell Olli which one he liked best. Then, she'd tell Ginny, and surely Ginny would wear that perfume every time they went out.

You're way ahead of yourself, he thought, pulling back on his thoughts. He re-entered reality and closed her door. "Stupid," he muttered to himself as he rounded the hood, walking directly through the high beams. He'd asked her out, and she hadn't even answered.

She had answered, months ago. She was busy.

He shouldn't have asked again. "Stupid Olli," he said just before yanking open the door. He got behind the wheel and closed his door as quickly as he could so the interior lights wouldn't shine on him, giving away how he felt about the woman in his truck.

After easing onto the road and turning around again, he said, "I don't know where you live."

"Right." Ginny picked up his phone from the console and started tapping. Several seconds later, a cool, female voice directed him where to go. "There."

"Thanks," he said, glancing down. Twenty-four minutes to her house. His exhaustion suddenly caught him right behind the lungs, and he yawned.

"Sorry to make you drive me home," she said. "I should've told you how far away I live."

"I don't mind," he said. "I just have to ask, though... You can tell me to mind my own business. Why did you call Olli? You have three brothers who live nearby."

"I always call Olli when I need help," Ginny said quietly. "She calls me. I call her."

"Okay," Cayden said.

"Besides, I'm not really talking to my brothers at the moment. Well, Drake I am. The other two, I'm not."

Cayden worked very hard to keep his eyes on the road. "And your parents?"

"We're a bit at odds," she said coolly. "We discuss business and not much else. Mother has been pestering me to get a new car, and I suppose that's exactly why I haven't." She gave a light laugh that wasn't truly filled with humor. "It's also why I didn't call Daddy to come get me."

"I'd love to know more about all of this," he said. "I thought you got along with your parents, and I've never heard you say a bad word about your brothers."

"Maybe I'll tell you sometime," she said slowly, letting the last word hang there. "Cayden, I know you'd like to go out with me. I'd very much like to go to dinner with you too. I am wondering, though...perhaps you'd be willing to stay in?"

He came to a stop at an intersection and turned to look at her. Without other traffic on the road, he could take his sweet time. "Stay in?"

"I have several social obligations over the course of the next few weeks and months," she said. "They're mostly at the distillery, and the reason I'm not currently speaking to my Mother about anything but business. She's been badgering me to have a date for the parties, the dinners, the terribly *important* fundraiser soirées." She rolled her eyes.

"You'll be horribly bored, but the food is usually very good, and we'd get to see one another..."

She left the sentence there, her eyes filled with what Cayden could only describe as hope.

He gaped at her, his pulse crashing against his ribcage.

"It would require a fair bit of pretending," she said. "To be clear."

"What do you mean?" he asked, his voice sounding rusted.

"You have to wear a smile all the time," she said, her voice pitching up as she put an obviously fake smile on her face. "It never slips, even when someone says something unfunny or inappropriate. You just smile and let them kiss your hand, all while they're simply trying to get your money."

The gesture slipped from her face and she looked out her window. She took a deep breath. "I apologize," she said quietly to the glass. "I'm simply overwhelmed at the moment. Please don't think I dislike my family."

Cayden got the truck moving again, though he'd rather sit in it with Ginny for a good long while. "I understand the complications of family relationships," he said into the void between them. "I have seven brothers to deal with, and...let's just say all of us are in various stages of working out how to make things right with our mother."

Ginny crossed her legs, drawing Cayden's attention there. "Even you?" she asked.

"Yes," he admitted. "Spur's managed it. Blaine's always

been a momma's boy. Even Trey's been over there to have hard conversations."

"He certainly looked very happy tonight," she said.

"That he did," Cayden said, flashing a smile in her direction. His thoughts lingered on his mother, as he really did need to reach out and find a way to move past the barriers between them. "When you're...annoyed with your parents, what brings you back together again?"

Ginny took her time answering, and Cayden didn't hate the silence in his truck. The radio played softly in the background, and he just liked being with her. Very much.

"Time," she said. "I suppose. Forgiveness. Realizing that they're my parents, and I do love them. Getting outside of my head and remembering that they want what is best for me." She leaned her head back against the headrest and looked at him. Her eyes were soft and vulnerable. "Will you think on accompanying me to my parties?"

"I don't need to think on it," Cayden said, feeling so proper. "I'll come to whatever you want me to."

"You'll have to practice your plastic smile," she said. "I know you Chappells. You say what's on your mind and it shows on your faces."

"Does it?" he asked. "What am I thinking right now?"

"Why don't you just tell me?"

"Because then you wouldn't have read it on my face." He grinned at her, liking this game.

"You're thinking you wished you would've let Spur come rescue me from the side of the road." She grinned at him, and Cayden's whole being lit up with the flirtatious tone of her voice.

"Wrong," he said just before he laughed. She joined in, and Cayden would never feel tired when he was with her.

He approached the address she'd put in his phone, but she said, "You turn right here."

"This says it's straight ahead."

"It's a huge piece of property," she said. "We all live on it. My place is to the right."

He peered through the windshield at the street sign, which certainly didn't look like a public sign. "Virginia Avenue," he said, reading the white letters on the blue sign. "Fascinating."

She cleared her throat. "You do know I'm quite wealthy, don't you?"

"I've heard," he said.

"I've heard the same about you."

"Then you know I'm not interested in you because of your money."

"Why are you interested in me?" she asked. "I'm the house right there on the left." She pointed as if he couldn't see the enormous building that had lights glowing over every window and beneath every eave.

It looked made of the finest wood, brick, and glass, and Cayden knew she had a great deal more money than he did. Cayden pulled into the driveway and eased to a stop right next to the sidewalk that led to the front porch.

He put the truck in park and looked at her. "I'm interested in you, because the first time we met, your very presence sparked something hot inside me. You're gorgeous, and you're smart, and I would be honored to be at your side for whatever *soirées* you need a date for."

Ginny gave a light laugh that sounded like she'd practiced it many times, and Cayden didn't like this fake version of Ginny Winters.

"I can't be very sophisticated," he said. "Spur says I'm over the public relations, because I'm the most charming and I can hold my temper the best. But Ginny, I'm not like you."

"That's okay," she said. "All the more reason to bring you along." She grinned at him, uncrossed her legs, and slid from the truck before Cayden could remember his Southern manners and go around to help her out.

By the time he did, she was halfway down the sidewalk toward her front door, and he called, "Good-night, Ginny."

"Good-night, Cayden," she called over her shoulder without breaking her stride.

He watched until she went all the way inside, whispering, "I'll call you."

Then he got behind the wheel and pulled out of her driveway, the last thing she'd said to him filling the cab in her absence. *All the more reason to bring you along.*

"What does that mean?" he asked himself over and over as he started the thirty-minute drive back to Bluegrass Ranch.

Chapter 10

Virginia Winters always knew exactly what to say. She knew how to hold a glass of champagne without ever taking a sip. She knew when to smile and how wide to make it. She knew exactly what to wear for any event, and precisely the shade of lip gloss to go with whatever blouse or blazer she'd pulled from her expansive closet.

Tonight, though, her house was too big. Too big, with too many rooms and too much darkness.

She tossed her keys on the table just inside the front door, though she rarely used that entrance to her house. "I'm home," she called. "Where are you guys?"

The clicking of claws sounded against her hardwood cherry floors, and all three of her dogs made an appearance, one right after the other. Sarge led the way of course, and she giggled and scooped the pug into her arms.

"Hey, my boy," she said as she tried half-heartedly to

deflect his doggy kisses. Uncle Joe jumped up on her legs, and Ginny stooped to pick up the miniature poodle too. She couldn't really juggle Sarge and Uncle Joe, so she put the pug down.

Minnie brought up the rear, as she often did, and Ginny could handle the poodle and the yorkie, and she held them both as she kicked off her heels and left them next to whatever doorway she stood next to.

Cayden Chappell consumed her thoughts, as he often had over the past few months, and Ginny didn't even realize she'd gone upstairs and removed her makeup, her dress, and her slim-shaper.

All of her dogs waited for her on the bed as she put on her pajamas, and she sighed as she lay down next to them. "I asked him to come to the parties," she said. "Mother is going to be furious." She giggled again. "I hope he wears his cowboy hat. In fact, I'm going to text him right now and tell him to make sure he does."

She reached over and snapped off the light and then picked up her phone to text the handsome cowboy who had made her heart jolt the first time she'd met him too.

How many cowboy hats do you own?

Plenty, he sent back almost instantly, and Ginny grinned at the letters. She'd felt plenty of sparks the moment Cayden's eyes had met hers at Olli's rehearsal dinner. He'd taken a pot from her with, "Let me have that, ma'am."

She was definitely old enough to be a ma'am, even if she didn't like that fact. They'd had a great time that night, and Ginny had known Cayden was interested in her when he'd made up a reason why he'd needed to have her number in his phone.

Just in case we have to coordinate something for Olli and Spur, he'd said. They'd never once discussed Olli and Spur, and Ginny hadn't mentioned her budding and expanding crush on the cowboy from Bluegrass Ranch.

No boyfriend Ginny had ever had was good enough for her mother, as Ginny had carried the burden of marrying well since she was nine years old—the first time her mother had started talking about the type of man Ginny *should* marry, where they *should* live, and what Ginny *should* do from there.

She wasn't going to have biological children of her own, she knew that, and her smile slipped. She still hadn't told her mother about the hysterectomy she'd endured last winter; she'd managed to play off the recovery time as pneumonia, and since her mother suffered from an autoimmune disease and was scared to death of getting the flu or something like pneumonia, she'd stayed out of Ginny's hair for a full three weeks.

Ginny hadn't even told Olli about her surgery. Only one person knew, and Drake's wife, Joan, was the only family member Ginny was currently talking to about personal things in her life.

Do you need an exact count? Cayden asked, and Ginny giggled, those sparks moving through her body again.

Might be a good idea, she said. *I'd like to know how many ways we can annoy my mother.*

She doesn't like cowboys?

Ginny's fingers flew across the screen. *Not particularly.*

She quickly tapped over to her calendar, suddenly eager to see Cayden again. Tomorrow was Sunday, and she'd be expected at the mansion in the middle of this property for brunch at ten-thirty in the morning, and she'd go with one of her fake-smile masks securely in place. She'd wear the new dress she'd found that week, and Mother would comment on the length of it.

Ginny had bought it simply to see if she would.

"When are you going to stop caring what she says or does?" she asked herself, flipping to Monday. "You're almost forty-seven-years-old." She knew she'd never be truly free of her mother's comments and opinion, though, because Ginny lived, breathed, and benefitted from the distillery.

She was the oldest child, and she'd inherited the title of CEO the moment she'd been born. The whiskey operation came through her mother, through her grandmother, and through her great-grandmother, who'd been the only child of Alan Ellington.

He'd started Sweet Rose Whiskey, and sometimes Ginny felt like she'd die at the hand of the family company that she'd often loved more than anything. She'd chosen Sweet Rose over many things throughout her life, despite watching it ruin her father and harden her mother into the shell of a real person.

It was only recently that Ginny had made new resolutions for her life. When she'd accompanied her mother to Chestnut Springs to witness the marriage of her half-brother, Ginny had realized how lonely she really was.

She'd made a list on her phone on the plane ride back to Kentucky, and at the very top of her new to-do list was *husband* and *family*.

She wanted to give all of her attention to Cayden, and her heartbeat pulsed through her body when a few more texts from him came in. She couldn't read them all until she had a date they could get together, and she swiped them away so she could see her calendar for the upcoming week.

She'd taken the fall festival at Sweet Rose to a new level this year, and their attendance had doubled. The board was happy about that, as Ginny had single-handedly increased the cost of their advertising during the festival, and for the distillery in general.

More companies were keen to buy those ad spots with that many people coming out to Sweet Rose, and Ginny had been working for this event for seven months. She was extremely proud of how it had turned out, but she was also ready for it to be over.

Only two more weeks, and Ginny would have a few days completely to herself. She didn't want to wait that long, and she told herself that she ate lunch and dinner every single day. Why couldn't Cayden bring something to her house, where they could talk and eat for an hour?

Guilt tugged against her fingers, because she did live quite a distance from Bluegrass Ranch, and asking him to come for an hour would actually take at least two from his day. He was just as busy as she was, and she didn't want everything in the relationship to be about her.

Her phone rang, startling her enough for her to drop the

device onto her stomach. "Oh," she said. The ringer quieted among the blankets, and she hurried to pick it up. This late at night, it had to be someone important, and she prayed intensely for two seconds that it wouldn't be her mother.

Cayden's name sat on the screen—well, really, the name she'd put in for him. *Handsome Cowboy*—and she quickly swiped on the call. "Hey," she said.

"Sorry to call," he drawled. "I texted, but you didn't answer, and I...well, to be honest, Ginny, I need an answer so I can sleep tonight."

She frowned, as his voice didn't carry that fun, flirty tone she'd heard previously. "I was looking at my schedule for this week to see if there was a time we could get together," she said "I swiped your texts away for a moment."

"So you haven't seen them?"

"No." She pulled her phone from her ear. "Let me put you on speaker and see what they say."

"I can, uh, tell you," he said, but Ginny was already tapping. The call got put on speaker, and she tapped over to her texts. "I just need some clarification on something, particularly the point where you asked me specifically to be your date at all your fancy parties."

Her eyes scanned and her ears heard. She said, "Oh."

Why did you ask me to be your date when you know I'm going to annoy your mother? he'd asked. A minute later, he'd sent, *Is that the only reason why?*

A few minutes after that, he'd sent another message. *I really need to know tonight, Ginny. I hope you're not in bed already.*

Then: *I'm going to call you.*

She took him off speaker and put the phone back to her ear. Ginny Winters always knew what to say. She knew how to steer a conversation away from something awkward or political and turn it onto the other person so everyone would be comfortable. At the same time, she could sit at the head of the conference table and run a meeting with the board of investors without blinking an eye. She could quiet someone trying to take over, and she could present facts without getting emotional.

Now, faced with Cayden's texts and verbal question, Ginny had no idea what to say.

"I'm not very comforted by your silence," he said, his voice carrying a deadly edge. "Let's try a yes or no thing. Did you ask me to come to your parties just to annoy your mother?"

"Not just," she said.

"So that's a yes," he said.

"No," she argued. "That's only one reason."

"You said there would be a lot of pretending. Did you mean the smiling and nodding, or did you mean there would be pretending between me and you?"

"That's not a yes or no question," she said, hoping he'd laugh.

He didn't. "Do you intend to pretend that we're more serious than we are?" he asked.

"No," she said, though she couldn't truly answer that. If she had to hang on his arm so another man would leave her alone, she would. If she had to lean in close and whisper something in his ear to irritate her mother, she would.

"Parties are unpredictable," she said.

"I've been to plenty of parties," Cayden said. "I run the public relations and fundraising operations for the ranch singlehandedly. I've been to dozens of dinners and events, and I know what a fake smile looks like and feels like. I know what a false laugh sounds like and how it feels coming out of my throat."

"You'll be perfect then," she said.

"I know you gave me both a fake smile and a false laugh tonight," he said.

She had no idea what he wanted her to say. While her mind whirred, Cayden sighed.

"Ginny," he said very seriously. "Are you interested in me for me, or are you interested in me because I'm a cowboy with the exact type of hat and unsophisticated demeanor that will drive your mother mad?"

She sucked in a breath. "Cayden," she said. "Of course not."

"I'm not sure I believe you," he said.

"I was just looking at my calendar, because I don't want to wait until the fall festival is over to see you."

"Yet, that was exactly the reason you gave me a few weeks ago," he said.

"I said earlier that I'd like to go to dinner with you."

"You said that in conjunction to staying in," he pointed out. "Staying in to go to your commitments." He exhaled. "I'm just going to be honest. I think you might have been interested in me a few weeks ago, but you were overwhelmed with work and family. I don't think you lied to me. Meanwhile, I think something changed with your mother, and now you want to use me to irritate her."

"No," Ginny said, though she could've easily have said yes. Would Cayden annoy Mother? Yes, he would. "Why can't it be both?" she asked. "I *am* interested in you, and I think you won't be my mother's first choice for me." In her mind, that was a win-win.

"I'm a Chappell," he said. "We're respected all over the South. We produce the best racehorses from any farm across six states. I don't see why she wouldn't approve of me."

"It's complicated," Ginny said. Before she could explain further, her home security alarm blared, filling the air with high-pitched squeals and screams.

Ginny's heartbeat ricocheted around inside her body, and she jumped to her feet.

"Ginny?"

"My alarm is going off," she said, stepping over to her bedroom door and locking it. All three dogs started barking. "I have to go." She hung up before Cayden could say another word, and she swiped to get to the camera feed on the security app.

She had cameras everywhere around her house, and sometimes a slow-moving car would set it off. The public entrance to Sweet Rose was on the opposite side of the property from her house, across the highway. Any time anyone drove by her house too slowly or too often, her security system registered it and would sometimes go off.

It sent her anxiety through the roof every time, and Ginny would often pack her weekend bag and her dogs and go to Drake's for a few nights after the alarm got triggered.

Everyone in her family got notified whenever her alarms went off, just like she got notified if theirs did. Texts started rolling in despite the late hour, but Ginny ignored them all in favor of answering the call from the security company.

She grabbed Minnie and said, "Come on, guys," as she fled toward her closet. It was the quietest place in the house while the alarm rang, and it provided another locked door she could hide behind.

"Virginia Winters?" a man asked.

"Yes, sir," she said.

"I need your verification code, ma'am."

"7VHEDW4," she said. "I'm in my bedroom closet with my dogs." Sarge dashed in as fast as his puggy legs would carry him, and she closed the door. "The door is locked. I didn't have time to check the cameras."

"My name is Ronald Featherston. We have a broken seal on the north side of the property," he said. "I'm pulling your floorplan right now, and I can see it's a set of French doors that lead into a music room...or a library."

"It's the library," she said, and her room sat on the other side of the house from that room. The library was at the back of the house, and those French doors led out onto a beautiful patio that wrapped around to the back yard.

"Cameras on that side of the house don't show anyone there," Ronald said.

"How did the door get open then?" she asked.

"I'm checking the weather now, ma'am."

Ginny couldn't remember the last time she'd used the French doors in the library—or even been in the library itself. Those doors had been locked for a while, and no amount of wind was going to knock a deadbolt loose.

She put the call on speaker and pulled down her weekend bag. Clothes went inside, and Ginny thanked heaven above that she'd just looked at her calendar, so she knew what she needed for the next few days.

"We're sending officers," Ronald said. "I still see nothing on any of the camera feeds to suggest there's a person there, but that door was opened, and is in fact, still open."

"I'll wait for the police," Ginny said. "I'm packing a bag now, and I have family I can stay with."

"I'll stay right here on the line with you," he said.

Ginny thanked him, and they didn't speak again. She started answering her texts, and fifteen minutes later, Ronald said, "The police are searching the house now, ma'am. I've fed them your floor plan, and they'll come get you from the closet."

"Thank you," she said again, her exhaustion nearing a breaking point. The call ended, and she picked up her weekend bag.

In the next moment, she got a text from the security company, saying an alarm was going off at property number three.

"Drake," she said.

Another text came in. *Alarm sounding at property*

number one. Please check the status of your alarm and text the contact at property number one.

"Elliot," she said, and she knew none of them would be staying in their homes that night.

Her first thought was Olli, and then her phone rang again, and Handsome Cowboy sat there.

Perhaps she could stay at Bluegrass Ranch until they got things sorted at Sweet Rose. "Hey," she said.

"What's going on?" Cayden asked. "I came back to check on you, and there are cops everywhere."

"I have a huge favor to ask you," she said. "It's okay to say no, but I need a safe place to stay and lay low for a few days…"

Chapter 11

Trey woke the morning after his wedding, his internal alarm getting him up just after six o'clock, as normal. He picked up his phone to find a dozen messages, and his frustration grew.

Thankfully, the first few were from Robert, saying he was on his way to the ranch, and that he'd gotten the contract Trey had sent him last night.

He sent him a quick, *Thanks, Rob. I'll be back on Friday, and we'll meet Saturday morning. I'd love to hear your initial assessment on the horse then.*

Sounds good, Rob said, and Trey navigated to the several texts from Cayden. They were part of a group message, which included Trey, Spur, and Blaine.

Ginny's had some trouble at her house. She needs a place to stay, and I offered Spur's old room at the homestead. If you object to that, I'd love to hear it now.

Trey frowned but kept reading. Blaine had answered

instantly with, *What kind of trouble? Either way, it's fine with me.*

Fine with me, Spur said. *I think that bed is made and ready.*

It was, because Mom had made sure to lecture the three cowboys who still lived in the house to keep it that way. She wanted the bedroom ready for any guests that might need it. Blaine had argued back with her, laughing afterward, asking what guests would possibly come to the ranch and use that bedroom.

Turned out, Ginny Winters was that guest.

The other brothers had kept talking for a few minutes, and Cayden explained that they weren't sure what was going on at the property where Ginny lived with all of her siblings, but four out of the five houses had had their alarms triggered.

Blaine had asked if he and Ginny were dating, to which Cayden had answered with a very firm *No.*

They'd probably taken the conversation off the group, because there wasn't anything after that. Spur hated group texts with a passion, and Trey had to admit he wasn't that fond of them, either.

He sent a quick, *I hope she's okay. Keep me updated.*

Trey closed his eyes, the burning sensation behind his eyelids reminding him exactly how long it had taken him to fall asleep in this wretched hotel room. Alone.

His wife slept on the other side of the wall, and Trey put his palm against it. The rough texture of the plaster and the coolness of the paint infused into him, and he took a long, deep breath.

He could do this. Beth had asked him to marry her so they could enter a horse into a race. They'd taken things a step further only very recently, and Trey had to be patient if he wanted a real relationship with her.

He hooked another breath to his first, and then another to that one. Eventually, he drifted back to sleep, and that was the best gift the Lord could give him.

* * *

"Stay back here," Trey murmured to TJ, reaching down to take the boy's hand. "They're bringin' in the last one right now." He'd been working day and night for the past week, the lazy, relaxing days of his honeymoon a distant memory of seven days ago.

Once he'd returned to Dreamsville and Bluegrass Ranch, his workload had doubled. Not only did he still have all the scheduling of the tracks to deal with, as well as all the trainers who wanted special treatment and the perfect time slots, but Beth's farm needed a ton of work.

She'd hired a crew to keep it functioning while they'd been gone, and Trey thought they'd done a fine job. So fine, he'd called Marc Towers that morning to ask him to come back and work at Dixon Dreams until they were caught all the way up—and then some.

He hadn't told Beth yet, because he didn't want to argue

with her when they were already in the midst of stressful things.

Their application to enter Somebody's Lady into the Sweetheart Classic had to be submitted in less than two days, and they'd been holding off to avoid questions and speculation.

It really was insane how many people kept up with what the Chappells did, and Trey had taken the idea of waiting until the last moment to enter to Beth after speaking with his father.

Don't believe for a moment that they're not watching you, he'd said. *I made that mistake once and wasn't careful enough with the stud list I was using. Suddenly, everyone was hiring the same sires as me, and that took the better part of five years to overcome.*

"There he is, Trey," TJ drawled, and Trey pulled himself out of his head and back to the task at hand. He glanced right, and sure enough, the beautiful, dark bay he'd been most excited about during the yearling sale pranced toward them.

Conrad led the horse, and Trey wished he could wipe the smugness off his younger brother's face. He definitely needed a better mask, and the pride slipped as Spur stepped next to Trey. "He's a mighty fine horse," Spur said.

"Yep." Trey watched the horse go by, wishing they didn't have to sell all of their animals. They sometimes didn't, but Bluegrass made a lot of money from their yearling sales, and they couldn't afford to house and keep horses just because they were pretty and knew how to run.

They bred them for both of those things, and Trey reminded himself that he owned three horses personally. He hadn't had time to ride them much lately, and he vowed he'd do better.

Out in the arena, Cayden started to talk about the bay, and the auction for him began.

"That's it," Trey said to TJ. "We sell him, and we're done." Not really, but TJ didn't understand all the behind-the-scenes things that went on. The boy loved horses, though, and that was the first step to becoming a cowboy that worked with animals for the rest of his life.

Cayden would stay out front and answer questions. Lawrence, Ian, and Conrad worked back here, where the sales office was and the veterinary booths. Everyone had to pay for their horse before they could leave, and they all got a free check with the vet, so they could take their clean bill of health too.

Spur would oversee all of that, schmoozing and shaking hands while money got paid and exams gone done. Blaine, Trey, and Duke would clean the arena, then take their manpower to the sheds and rowhouses where the horses had been kept for the past few hours.

By six-thirty tonight, the trailers would be loaded and gone. The money counted. Everything sprayed down and scrubbed clean. The ranch would be quiet again, and the Chappell brothers would eat at the homestead together, just like they did after every yearlings sale.

His stomach growled, because Trey barely had time to think let alone eat. He stifled a yawn, because he didn't want to answer his brother's questions, and he wished he'd had the foresight to grab a granola bar and stick it in his pocket.

"How's it going?" a woman asked, and he turned toward Beth, recognizing her voice as he did.

"Hey," he said, smiling. "What are you doin' here?"

She tipped over TJ's head and kissed his cheek. He pressed right into the touch, a jolt of attraction moving through him. "I just came to see how it was going," she said. "Plus, TJ left most of his lunch on his plate in his excitement to get here, and I thought you might be hungry as well."

She's an angel, Trey thought, his smile growing.

"I brought ham and cheese sandwiches," she said. "If you can spare a few minutes."

"I can once the sale ends," he said. It would be madness for a few minutes while the crowds dispersed. "Thank you, sweetheart." His heart swelled and expanded at her kindness and intuition. She had to be thinking about him in order to bring him food, and he reached for her hand.

She held up her wounded palm, a look in her eyes that said he'd get to kiss her later, and he simply chuckled. "How is the hand?" he asked. "I haven't heard you say much about it lately."

She kept it wrapped all the time, and she hadn't complained or been taking nearly as much painkiller as she had weeks ago when the accident had first happened. He blinked, and he could see her standing in her bathroom, sobbing while blood dripped into the sink.

"It's doing great," she said. "Remember I have an appointment on Tuesday?"

"Right," he said, though he had forgotten. Trey found it easier to live for the next chunk of time. An hour to complete that chore. A few minutes to make a phone call. Once he finished a task, he simply moved on to the next one.

"I'll know more then," she said.

He nodded and looked back into the arena as the auction concluded with a rousing round of applause. "Let's go," he said, gripping TJ's hand harder. "It's going to be a surge of people, and if we don't need to be here, we shouldn't be."

"Have fun," Spur said. "See you back here in fifteen?"

"Yes," Trey said, forgetting his brother was even there.

The back of the arena started to fill with people, and Trey nodded Beth and the plastic bag of food she'd brought out the nearest door. They found a patch of shade and settled on the ground.

Beth handed TJ an apple and said, "Four bites, please."

He took the fruit and the first bite while Trey marveled at the calm, caring demeanor of the woman next to him. She looked at him, her dark eyes bright. "Did you want an apple, babe? I brought plenty."

"Yes," he said, the word grinding through his throat. She'd never called him anything but Trey before, and he sure did like the endearment in her voice. He took the bright red apple from her and took a bite too.

TJ took exactly four and put the apple on the ground. "Can I have a sandwich now?"

"Half or whole?" she asked.

"Whole."

"Let's start with half."

Trey wasn't sure why she'd asked if she was just going to do what she wanted anyway, but he said nothing.

"Daddy invited us to his house for Thanksgiving dinner," Beth said, her eyes trained on something in the bag. "I said I'd talk to you."

Trey took another bite of his apple, trying to come up with a response. His mother would work in the kitchen for a week to prepare for Thanksgiving, and Trey knew telling her he and Beth and TJ wouldn't be there would be hard for all of them.

"Okay," he said after he'd finally chewed and swallowed. "That sounds fine."

"You don't think your mother will have a problem with it?"

"She might," Trey admitted. "But she'll deal with it."

Beth nodded, finally raising her eyes to his. They held worry and doubt.

"What's goin' on in your head?" he asked.

"Just thinking about family dinners with you," she said. "I know you have a loud family, but they at least seem to understand boundaries. Mine doesn't. Not really."

"They were great for the wedding," he said, frowning at her.

"Yes," she conceded, her voice growing soft. "They were."

"They'll probably be fine," he said, not worried about something that was still almost a month away. "I talked to Rob again last night while we were training. He and Lady have really formed a bond. She listens to him, and he seems to know exactly how long to hold her back. He said he can feel it in her stride and her energy."

"That's great," Beth said. "I have the application ready to go."

"We're still taking TJ to your brother's, then dropping off the application, and then going to dinner, right? On Saturday?"

"Yes, sir," she said, flashing him that playful, flirty smile he loved. She handed him a full sandwich, and he started to open the zipper bag containing it.

"Great," he said. "Then I'm going to tell Rob we don't need him Sunday or Monday. He can't work Lady that much anyway, and I'm sure he could use a break." In all honesty, it was Trey who could use a break, because he'd been sneaking into the indoor track here at Bluegrass Ranch with Somebody's Lady for a week now. They didn't even leave Beth's farm until midnight, and Trey had been crawling back into bed about three-thirty after watching Rob run the horse, talk to the horse, and get the horse to trust him.

He'd scheduled regular time on their outdoor track for teaching her how to run straight, and how to pick up her step. He did that, working with her carefully each day, making sure not to run her too hard more than once or twice a week.

Part of him really wanted to win the Sweetheart Classic just to show Conrad and Ian that they weren't the only Chappells who understood racehorses. They trained horses exclusively on the ranch, sometimes getting their names in programs for their accomplishments with a horse.

Conrad especially was known around the Lexington area as the horse whisperer, as he hadn't met a horse yet that he couldn't tame, break, and love. They all loved him too, almost like they sensed a horse spirit inside his very human body.

"Listen," he said to Beth. "I hired Marc and his crew to come back next week."

"You did? Why?"

"Because, Beth," he said, trying to keep his voice even and frustration-free. "The farm is still hanging on by a thread. They can help us get it fully cleaned up in a couple of months I bet."

"A couple of months," she repeated. "I can't pay for that, Trey."

"I can," he said simply. Their eyes met, and hers stormed. He wasn't sure if it was because she didn't like taking his money, or because he'd made a decision about her farm without her. Probably both.

"There you are," Cayden said, and Trey looked away from Beth, about a quarter of his sandwich left. "I need you in here." He took in the scene on the lawn. "Can you spare a few minutes?"

Trey knew from the anxious yet determined look on his brother's face that it would be more than a few minutes. He stuffed the rest of his sandwich in the bag, got to his feet, and said, "Yep," He leaned down and kissed Beth quickly, adding, "TJ, time to go home, bud. I have a ton of work to do."

"Aw, Trey," TJ whined, but Beth shushed him and told him not to be ungrateful for the time he'd had here. She was patient and kind with him, but firm, and Trey admired her parenting skills. They could talk more about the crew later.

He followed Cayden inside, the man moving fast and sure. "We've got the mayor of Lexington here," he said. "Along with her press secretary, and three City Councilmen."

"Wow," Trey said. "Why?"

"They want to do a billboard about us," Cayden said, his grin popping onto his face. "They grabbed me, and we've been talking, and I need you since you do our schedule."

"A billboard?" Trey asked. "What in the world?"

"Mayor Densfield," Cayden said smoothly, that smile still on his face. "My brother, Trey."

"Nice to meet you, ma'am," Trey said, shaking her hand. He cut a glance at Cayden, who introduced everyone else. The names went in one ear and out the other, especially since plenty of people still loitered about, chatting and filling the silence with a din that made concentrating difficult for Trey.

"We're doing some campaigns for the city," the mayor said. "Our theme is champions, and we want Lexington to be on the map for where champions come from." She looked from Trey to Cayden, her eyes animated and bright. "Bluegrass Ranch has produced more championship horses than any other ranch in the surrounding area," she said.

"Not Derby winners, but across the board, even races in Australia and Saudi Arabia have winning horses from right here in Lexington."

Technically, Bluegrass Ranch existed within the city limits of Dreamsville, but Trey buried that information beneath his tongue. Dreamsville could be considered an outlying appendage to Lexington, and they had long been considered part of the region.

"We're thinking a huge billboard on the highway coming in from Louisville," the mayor's assistant said. "We want you Chappell men on it."

"All of us?" Trey asked.

"Yes," she said. "We have some preliminary ideas, but we'd love to work with the two of you to see what else we can come up with." She glanced at the City Councilmen, and Trey did too. "We want you all in the full regalia of your jobs. The very jeans you wear to work with the horses. The belt buckles. All of it."

She continued to talk, and Trey listened, his mind coming up with ideas that would morph and change and sometimes die by the time she finished a sentence.

"Athena," the mayor finally said. "Let's schedule something with them so we can provide all the nitty gritty. Then they can decide."

"Right," her assistant said. She met Trey's eyes and smiled. "That's you, I believe."

It sure was, and Trey pulled out his phone to see when he could meet with the mayor again.

***

Weeks later, Trey pulled up to a house in the middle of the Kentucky wilderness and said, "Don't forget that pie now, TJ. Your grandpa said it's his favorite."

He was tired already, but noon hadn't even gone by yet.

"We can leave as soon as lunch is over," Beth promised. "You look tired."

"I am tired," he said, looking up to the house. "You promise I won't have to eat any yams?"

She giggled, and that sound rejuvenated Trey slightly. They'd been married for six weeks now. He'd been sleeping in the bedroom across the hall from hers, and most nights, he was okay. He'd sleep for a couple of hours, get up, sneak onto the ranch, watch Rob with Somebody's Lady, and go back to the white farmhouse which he was quickly becoming attached to.

"No yams," she confirmed. "Come on. Let's go in." She got out of the truck and stepped to the back to help TJ down with the pecan pie the two of them had made last night while he'd been doing the invoices for the housing rentals on the ranch.

The farmhouse had a great big office off the front door, and Trey had set up everything he needed in there. The room had a comfortable couch, and sometimes he slept there after stumbling back into the house from the indoor training arena.

Inside the house, warmth greeted him first, followed by an uprising of voices as everyone was already there ahead of them. He smiled and shook hands, and when Lucas tugged on his belt loop, Trey bent down and picked the little boy right up. "Hi-ya, tiny cowboy." He touched the brim of Lucas's hat. "When did you get this?"

"For my birfday," he said. "I'm five now."

"I heard," Trey said, smiling at him. "You look like a real cowboy now."

"Yeah, like you," Lucas said, and Trey chuckled. He glanced around, realizing he was the only man there wearing a cowboy hat. Even Beth's father didn't have his on today. Her brother worked as a private consultant, and Sally's husband sold software all over the country. He traveled a ton, and Trey didn't think he took a cowboy hat with him.

Hugh joined him and Lucas, asking, "How's married life, Trey?"

Trey's pulse immediately moved to the back of his throat. He looked at Hugh, trying to decide what he was really asking. "Good," he said evasively.

"My sister can snore up a storm," he said, grinning across the room at Beth, who'd taken the pie into the kitchen and gotten stuck there talking to her sister and her sister-in-law. "Both of 'em can."

"He's not wrong," Mick said as he joined their little huddle. He looked at Sally, his wife, and back to Trey. "Are you and Beth going to have more children?"

Trey's eyes widened in less time than it took to breathe.

"Leave the man be," Hugh said with a laugh. "They've been married for a month."

"Sally was asking," Mick said, lifting his can of cola to his mouth. "She said Danny and Beth were trying for another child when he passed."

"Dude, you suck at conversations," Hugh said, his smile gone now. "How do you sell software like this?" He glanced at Trey. "Sorry, Trey. Come in. Get something to drink." He took his son from Trey and gestured for him to move further into the house.

My sister snores, Trey thought. *Are you going to have children?*

Something wasn't adding up right in his head. Why would they think he and Beth were even sleeping in the same room? They'd both told their families the marriage wasn't real. No one in his family had asked him anything about the marriage, the sleeping arrangements, or embarrassing things like when they'd have kids. Not even his mother, and that was saying something.

"Thank you all for coming," Clyde said, raising a glass of something amber and bubbly. Trey wouldn't be drinking any of that; his brain already felt too soft as it was.

Her father grinned around at everyone, and Hugh leaned toward Trey. "Ten bucks says he cries."

"Twenty," Mick whispered, but Trey kept silent.

"It's been a while since we've all been here together, and I'm grateful to host my children at Thanksgiving." His voice pitched up, and the older gentleman swiped quickly at his eyes.

"Winner, winner, chicken dinner," Hugh whispered with a light laugh made mostly of air.

"It's wonderful to see you all married so happily, with

the cutest grandkids ever." He reached out and tapped baby Tawny's nose. She blinked and laughed, and even Trey could chuckle fondly at that.

This family had a lot of love for each other, that was for sure. Trey could feel it beating through the very walls surrounding him.

"We welcome Trey and wish him luck with Beth."

"Hey," Beth said, though everyone else laughed.

"At first, I thought you guys were moving too fast, but looking at the two of you, I can see now that you're perfect for each other."

"Daddy," Beth said, her eyes nervous for some reason.

"What? It's my speech."

"Say something about Thanksgiving then," she said, tucking her hair behind her ear and deliberately not looking toward Trey.

"I always say what I'm grateful for on Thanksgiving," Clyde said. "It's you guys. My family. My posterity. I know Sally said she's not having any more kids, so I guess it's up to Hugh and Beth to get to work."

"Uh, Dad?" Hugh said. "We're done too." He met his wife's eyes, and Kait nodded.

"Let's just go around and say what we're thankful for," Beth said, a panicked note to her voice.

"You'll have more kids, right, Beth?" Clyde looked from Beth to Trey and back. He had no idea what to do or say, and he felt his defenses slipping into place.

A mask to cover how he felt. His jaw locked so he

couldn't speak. He folded his arms to make himself appear bigger and tougher.

Didn't her father get how awkward this was? Mick had basically brought up Beth and Trey's love life too. Did they want a play-by-play?

There wouldn't be one, Trey thought. What part of *fake marriage* did they not understand?

All at once, understanding flooded his mind.

She hadn't told them the marriage was fake.

He stared at her, silently screaming at her to look at him. The silence in the house pressed against his windpipe, and it just went on and on and on.

"Daddy," Sally said. "Let's go around."

"You didn't tell them," Trey said, and that brought every eye to his, including Beth's. "Tell me you told them."

Chapter 12

"Told us what?" Hugh asked, and Beth wanted to stuff socks down her brother's throat. Next to him, Trey fumed, and Beth needed to get him out of there before he exploded. Her legs felt like logs as she tried to get them to move, her joints and other bendy parts refusing to do their jobs.

"Can I talk to you outside?" she asked, pushing her good palm against his chest. Her left hand was almost all the way healed now, but she was technically only on week ten out of twelve. Her doctor said it was looking amazing though, and if she could stand it, to not keep it wrapped all the time.

Trey resisted for a couple of long moments that had Beth's mind wailing at her. Then he finally relinquished, spun, and stomped away from her and everyone else.

"Wow," Hugh said. "Your first lover's spat." He grinned at Beth like she and Trey were a cute teenage couple.

She was a widow, for crying out loud, and Trey had done

her a huge favor. He still did, every single day. She made sure he had food for when he went to the indoor track in the middle of the night.

A couple of times, she'd waited up for him on the couch in the office he'd started using when he'd moved in. He'd told her she didn't need to do that. That there was no sense in both of them being zombies the next day.

She sat with him while he worked on his schedules and invoices. She did all the laundry for him and TJ. She was doing everything she could to make his life easier and more comfortable, rationalizing all he did and all he paid for because it would end in just two and a half months. He didn't have to live like this forever; there was an end in sight.

An end to the busyness. Then, she'd been hoping and praying they'd have more time for each other. She wanted the marriage and relationship to be as real as her family thought it was.

Outside, she found Trey pacing at the mouth of the garage, his hands on his hips. When he heard her footsteps, he turned toward her. "They don't know," he said. "Do they?"

She hurried past her father's broken-down motorcycle, resisting the urge to shush him as if he were the five-year-old in her life. "No, okay? I didn't tell them it was fake." She was whispering by the end of the sentence, and she still cast a look over her shoulder to see if anyone had followed them outside.

"Why the devil not?" he demanded. "We agreed we'd tell our families, so we didn't have to have embarrassing conversations like that one." He gestured wildly to the house, not even bothering to keep his voice down.

Beth wanted to shrink before him. Instead, she raised herself to her full height and squared her shoulders, a fire igniting inside her that always glowed a little bit. "Don't you dare talk to me like that, Trey Chappell. Maybe I'm not perfect, and maybe I made a mistake, but you can still respect me."

He drew in a breath through his nose, his eyes almost wild. "This is *insane*," he said. "I called my brothers together for a meeting, fed them, and admitted everything. You think that was easy for me?"

"I never said it was easy for you."

"I told my parents about your little proposal before I even knew if I was going to do it. You should've *seen* my mother's face."

Beth could imagine. Or maybe she couldn't. Julie Chappell scared her half to death, despite the bit of sassy fire inside her. Beth felt it going out as pure helplessness washed over her.

She sucked in a breath as the panic descended, and she stepped away from Trey to balance herself against the nearby brick wall of the house. *Breathe*, she told herself, trying to find a rational thought and seize onto it.

She'd learned breathing exercises in her therapy sessions following Danny's death, and suddenly, she could both see and hear Dr. Shirley as he taught her some deep breathing exercises to help her find the right train of thought.

Trey's footsteps wandered away and came back, and finally he put his hand on her elbow. "Are you okay?"

She'd managed to ward off the impending panic attack, but she couldn't open her eyes just yet. The chill in the air actually helped her find a deeper part of her center, and she focused on the point of contact between her and Trey.

Warmth spiraled out from there, and Beth forced herself to breathe and think, both of them as slowly as she could.

"Beth," he said. "You're worrying me."

She finally opened her eyes, the world too bright beyond her. Trey filled her vision, and everything seemed right. "I didn't tell them," she admitted. "Because I knew they'd all try to talk me out of it."

"Would they now?"

"Absolutely," she said. "I didn't want to be talked out of it, Trey. I liked you—I *like* you. You'd asked me out before, and I—"

"And you weren't ready," he said, his dark eyes flashing with that dangerous fire she'd seen before when they'd argued. "I heard you, Beth, telling your dad you weren't ready. I made up some excuse and left."

Her eyes widened, as did the hole in her chest. Darkness filled it, and she felt certain that same blackness would consume her whole.

"Not one day later, you're asking me to marry you so you can enter this horse race, and I was so smitten with you, and I wanted to help you so badly." He pressed his teeth together, removed his hand from her arm, and paced away again.

Beth needed to sit down. She needed to find a way to make this right. She leaned against the back of her father's truck, almost sitting on the bumper.

He turned and came back toward her, his gaze narrowed and angry. "I didn't tell them, because I wanted to marry you," she said.

"For the horse race."

"Partially," she said. "I *do* like you, Trey, and everything we talked about before the wedding was one hundred percent true. I want it all, and I want you, and I want to see if we can make it into something real."

"It is already something real for me," he said.

"Me too," she shot back. "You think you're the only one with feelings here?"

"Of course not."

"Then stop acting like it," she said. "I *chose* you, Trey. I chose you, because you first chose me. You asked me out. You showed me kindness after kindness with TJ. I desperately need that money, and I chose *you* to help me get it." Tears filled her eyes, and she didn't bother trying to hold them back. "Isn't that what you wanted? To help me? You said it over and over, and I just…"

"Of course I want to help you." Trey paused in front of her, taking a moment before he reached out and wiped her tears away. "Baby, don't cry now." He gathered her into his chest, and with him as an anchor, she could stand tall and be brave.

"I have money, Beth. I could've just given it to you."

"Then it would always be between us," she said into his

brown, red, and black plaid shirt. "Trust me, I thought about it."

His anger seemed to have blown itself out, and Beth stepped slightly out of his embrace and wiped her face again. "I've had real feelings for you since the moment you knocked on my back door," she said. "The very first time you brought TJ home, I remember thanking God that he'd sent someone to take care of that maddening child, and that that someone was Trey Chappell specifically."

"I prayed about us too," Trey said very quietly. "I never do that, Beth. I don't, um, really have a relationship with the Lord. I haven't been to church in years, and honestly, I haven't missed it."

Beth looked up into his eyes, where that edge of darkness still rode. She searched his face for the rest of the story but didn't find it.

"I talked to my parents, and you know what they said? Pray about it, Trey." He shook his head. "I was angry. God doesn't hear me. He doesn't answer me."

Beth swallowed, because she'd felt the exact same way in the past. "I understand how that feels."

"I suppose you might," he said. "Anyway, I did what they said, and I...it's hard to describe. I just knew I was supposed to help you if I could. I felt peaceful about it, and I guess I still do. I just wasn't expecting to come here today and get asked when we're having kids and how I'm faring with how much you snore."

Beth blinked and then burst out laughing. A sob or two worked its way into the noise, and Beth flung her arms around Trey and held him very, very tight. "I'm sorry," she whispered. "Please don't be mad at me for very long."

"I'm not mad, baby," he whispered, his lips landing lightly on her neck.

Beth kept her eyes closed and her arms around her very sturdy husband. She started a prayer that she would know what to say and what to do in this situation.

Ask him, she thought, and while she wasn't sure if it was a thought inspired by her own mind or the Lord, she decided to follow it.

"What do you want to do now?" she asked, pulling away once more. Apprehension ran through her like swift-moving water, but with the truck behind her, she couldn't escape his gaze. "Do you want to tell them now?" She swallowed. She didn't want to do that, but she'd do whatever Trey said.

He gazed down at her. "This is not fake," he whispered. "I'm falling in love with you a little bit more every day, and I don't see why we need to tell them now."

A ray of sunshine entered her heart from the very first word he'd said. It curved her lips slightly, and Beth ran her hands along his shoulders to the long hair that curled beneath his hat. "I'm falling a little bit more in love with you every day too."

"Is that right now?" he asked, a smile touching his mouth too. "Why's that?"

"Because you take care of me and TJ," she said. "You're smart, and you're literally the hardest-working man I've ever met. You're kind to us even when you're exhausted, and I've literally never heard you complain about anything." She could go on and on, but she pressed against her emotions to steady them. "Why do you like me?"

"Because you have convictions," he said, and that surprised Beth. "You want that farm to be the best it can be, and you're not going to stop until it is. I love that about you. I watch you work around the house and the farm with your wounded hand, and it's like it doesn't even slow you down." He ran his hands through her hair, a look of adoration replacing the glinting, scary one. "You're brilliant with TJ, and I learn more about you and him and being a dad every time I watch the two of you interact. You've taught me how to peel apples and peaches, and you've taught me how to slow down when I want to speed up."

He cleared his throat. "Just to name a few things."

She smiled up at him, enjoying the feel of his hands along her back and waist. "I thought you were going to say it was because of the caramel pecan brownies."

He chuckled and leaned toward her, resting his forehead against hers. "Those too, actually."

"I'll make them tonight, if you want," she said, so many things shuddering through her chest.

"I'd like that, Beth." His breath wafted across her nose and cheeks, and he smelled like mint and lemons, as well as something richer in there—probably the black coffee he'd drunk for breakfast.

"Please kiss me," she whispered, and Trey didn't need to be told twice. He matched his mouth to hers, stroking and taking what he wanted from her. Beth gave it willingly, because he gave so much to her willingly.

As she kissed him in her father's garage, Beth fell a little bit more in love with him. Maybe all the way in love with him, because he'd forgiven her when she'd made a mistake, and there was no better feeling than that.

* * *

That evening, Beth dragged a knife through the pan of caramel pecan brownies that had been sitting on the counter cooling for the past hour. Trey had volunteered to put TJ to bed, and Beth had sent them both down the hall fifteen minutes ago.

She put a couple of brownies on a plate and went down the hall to her bedroom. With her tasty treat on the nightstand, she retraced her steps to the kitchen and put two more brownies on a plate for Trey.

This time, she paused in her son's doorway to find Trey half sitting up and half lying down in bed with TJ. The little boy was curled into the cowboy's chest, and Trey read in a soft, clear voice from the book he held for TJ to see.

He wasn't wearing his cowboy hat, and he looked softer, more approachable and less rigid. His dark hair curled around his ears and across his forehead, and Beth smiled at his handsomeness.

Her heart melted, and she wanted to take a picture of this moment so she could look back at it and remember, even when her memory had failed.

Danny had never read to TJ. Danny had never even

changed their son's diapers. Not even once. Trey would do that and more, and Beth knew it.

Trey closed the book, his eyes meeting Beth's. He smiled, the crinkles around his eyes so sexy and making him look so happy. "All right, bud," he said in the same calm, quiet voice. "Slide on under now." He got up so TJ would have room in the bed.

TJ snuggled into his pillows while Trey tucked the blanket around him. He bent down and pressed a kiss to TJ's head and whispered something. TJ reached up and put both arms around Trey's neck and said, "I love you, Trey."

"Oh, well. I love you, too, TJ." By the time her son had let go of Trey and he'd straightened, Beth's heartbeat had worked itself into a frenzy.

She held out the plate of brownies, almost as if they'd protect her from her own feelings. Those feelings surged and pushed against her defenses, the dam about to break. "Brownies," she said, and she barely recognized her own voice.

"Thank you," he said, crowding into her personal space to take them. She fell back and went into the hallway, her mind whispering crazy things about inviting him to her bedroom to share their treat together.

Crazy. Insane. Impossible.

"I'm assuming you have some of these in your bedroom already," he said, his voice filled with teasing.

"Your assumption would be correct," she said. "I'm all out of Ritz chips. A woman needs something in her nightstand to munch on."

"Mm." The sound got dragged out, and she turned to find him eating his brownie, his eyes closed in bliss.

He opened his eyes and finished the bite. "I don't think you can say one *munches* on brownies. These things are like cake." He stuck the rest of the brownie in his mouth, pure delight on his face.

She watched him chew, her pulse blitzing around her chest. What would he do if she stepped into his arms and kissed him? What would he say if she could somehow get him into her bedroom?

They *were* married, and Beth knew in that moment, standing in the hall after he'd read her son a bedtime story and put him to bed, that she was in love with him.

"What's goin' on in that head of yours?" he asked, and Beth didn't know how to tell him. Maybe she could just show him.

She took a small step toward him, swallowing against her nerves. "Trey," she said, her voice shaking on the one-syllable name. "I love you."

Her son had said it and gotten a favorable response. Maybe she would too.

Trey's shock showed plainly on his face. "Beth, you don't have to say—"

"I wouldn't," she said. "I'm saying it, because it's true." She took another step toward him, and he really had nowhere to go. Feeling strong now, with a touch of bravery somewhere deep inside her, she ran her fingers up his arm to where he held the plate with one remaining brownie on it.

She looked only at it, because if he said no to her next

question, she didn't want to be looking into his eyes. "Do you love me?"

He didn't answer immediately, which only lit her strength, confidence, and bravery on fire. As it burned and turned to ash, she closed her eyes against the stinging rejection.

Then he said, "Yes, I love you."

Beth's eyes flew open, and she met his gaze. They moved toward one another simultaneously, and the resulting kiss was nearly an explosion. She pulled in a breath as she ran her hands through his hair, lifting up onto her toes in an attempt to get closer to him.

She needed to be close to him; there was no way to get close enough.

She gasped as he broke the powerful kiss and moved his mouth to her neck. She clung to him and whispered, "Let's go into the bedroom, Trey."

"Yeah?" he asked, his voice rough and filled with desire. His hands seemed to be everywhere, and he dragged his lips toward her collarbone, sending a spray of sparks through her whole body.

"Yes," she said, lowering herself back to stand flat on her feet. She had no idea where the plate with that brownie was. It didn't matter. All that mattered was the two of them. She laced her fingers through his, looking at them in the harsh light from the hallway.

Then she led him into her bedroom, where she closed and locked the door behind them.

Chapter 13

"She's havin' a problem on that last turn," Trey said, consulting his clipboard.

"She wants to break there," Rob said. "It's extremely hard to hold her back."

Trey looked up to where Rob stood next to Somebody's Lady. "Maybe we should let her," he said. "Just let her break on that turn and see what happens."

Rob shook his head, though he wasn't necessarily disagreeing with Trey. "It's crazy. No one lets their horse loose on the curve."

"Let's just try it," Trey said. "Can we set her up again?"

"Sure." Rob stepped into Somebody's Lady and ducked his head to murmur something to her. They had a special bond, and Trey found it remarkable. A tingling feeling spread down his shoulders, and he knew the Lord had directly helped him find this trainer and jockey.

As Rob led Lady away, Trey put one foot on the bottom

rung of the fence and watched them. When they were out of earshot, he whispered, "Thank you, Lord, for Thy bounteous blessings."

Rob had made it about halfway back to the starting gate when the door to Trey's left opened. He stood straight and tall immediately, his heart pounding. He'd managed to keep his practice sessions under the radar, but when Lawrence entered the arena, it seemed that was about to come to an end.

Trey swallowed, his mouth semi-dry all of a sudden.

"What's goin' on in here?" Lawrence said, looking around like there might be a magic show he'd like to see.

"Nothing," Trey said, working very hard not to turn around and check on Rob's progress. He couldn't hide Somebody's Lady, though, and with Lawrence, he likely didn't need to.

Lawrence, who stood maybe an inch taller than Trey, looked past him to the track. "So this is how you've been training your horse for the Sweetheart Classic."

Trey's jaw jumped, but he said nothing.

Lawrence draped his arms over the top of the fence and looked down the track toward the black and white horse. He whistled appreciatively. "She's a pretty horse." He glanced a Trey. "How's she run?"

"Good," Trey said, relaxing slightly as he joined his favorite brother at the fence. Maybe Lawrence wasn't his favorite, but he was certainly up there, because he didn't normally ask a lot of questions. He was a lot like Trey;

content to be in the background while the louder brothers took the spotlight.

"You got Robert Merchant?" Lawrence asked, looking at Trey with wide eyes. "How'd you do that?"

"I texted him," Trey said. "He said he could do it."

"The Snape House has been trying to get him for months," Lawrence said.

"How do you know that?" Trey asked as Rob led Lady around the mobile starting gate they used for training. "He didn't tell me that."

"Conrad and Ian have been talking about it," Lawrence said. "I swear, sometimes they fixate on one thing for*ever*."

"Sometimes?" Trey quipped, and Lawrence chuckled with him. "She wants to make her break on the last turn," he said as Rob removed his hand from the gate, the indicator he was about to let Somebody's Lady run. "We're going to let her this time and see what happens."

The horse exploded from the gate, and Trey stood up on the bottom rung, his anticipation building in the back of his throat. The horse looked good, and Trey smiled as she thundered past him and Lawrence. He loved the scent of dirt and horseflesh, straw and sawdust and saddle leather.

The door opened again, and he muttered, "For the love," as he turned in that direction. Beth came inside, though, and Trey's whole being lit up.

"Is this how you find time to be alone?" Lawrence murmured, and Trey met his brother's eyes while his wife walked toward him.

"No," he said. "She's only come a couple of times. Looks

like she has food tonight." He patted his brother's chest. "Come see what she's got. She always over-packs." He walked away from his brother, a smile on his face for Beth.

"Hey," she said, glancing to Lawrence and then the track, where Somebody's Lady had disappeared around the curve to the far side of the track. Outside, they wouldn't have been able to see Lady unless they were up in the stands. Inside, though, without the trees and decorative hedges, the dark horse could be seen on the opposite side of the track.

He bent down and kissed her quickly. "You're a Godsend."

"It's peanut butter and peach jam," she said. "Don't get excited."

"I am excited." He took the paper bag of food from her and took out a sandwich. He handed it to Lawrence and added, "You remember my brother, Lawrence."

"Of course," Beth said, smiling at him. She looked drawn around the edges, and Trey wished he could clone himself so he could help out around Dixon Dreams more than he did.

Marc and his crew had been making steady progress, but Beth refused to be sidelined. Her hand was nearly healed now, and she had one final appointment next week to get the final check-off as to whether she could use it fully again.

She practically did now already, though he'd seen her taking painkillers and opening and closing her fingers slowing as if working out the kinks in her fingers and wrist.

"She's on the curve," Lawrence said, and Trey spun around. Though his stomach grumbled, he could wait another twenty seconds so he could see how Lady took the corner when Rob let her go as fast as she wanted.

"Holy cow," he said, his voice awed. Somebody's Lady had already been uncaged as she went past the top of the curve, and Rob leaned down into her as tightly as he could as she stayed right against the rail, practically leaning her rider into the fence as she literally flew out of the turn.

"My word," Lawrence said, plenty of shock in his tone.

"Look at her go," Beth said, joining Trey on the fence. "Trey, you didn't tell me she was so fast."

"She's your horse," Trey said as Somebody's Lady corrected back to the fence. She had come off of it slightly, and that would be a problem if there was another horse in front of her or one trying to take over on her outer flank. She'd have hit them with a cornering like that.

If she ran into another horse during the race, she'd be disqualified. Everything he and Beth had done would be for nothing.

Trey had grown up his whole life on the horse racing circuit, and he still marveled at how much hinged on a race that took less than two minutes.

Somebody's Lady flew past the group of them, and Lawrence whooped like she'd just won the Derby. He clapped, and Trey let himself smile too. He turned to check the time, and she'd shaved off two seconds from her last run just by cutting out sooner.

Rob slowed her and brought her back to the crowd. "She didn't seem to lose steam in the last eight strides," he called. "What did you think?"

"She was incredible," Beth breathed, climbing all the way to the top of the fence and swinging her legs over so they hung into the arena. Somebody's Lady went right to her, still heaving for breath. "You let her loose earlier?"

"About six strides earlier," he said. "I felt like she was going to lose me on that corner." He grinned. "I need to train in one of those astronaut apparatuses."

"Or do a bunch sit-ups," Lawrence said. "I don't even know how you held on."

"Sheer luck and a prayer," Rob said, looking down to the corner. "I don't know, Trey. What if I fall off? That really might have just been luck."

"She came off the rail too," Trey said. "We'll pull the feeds, and you'll see what I mean."

"She corrected brilliantly," Lawrence said. "Maybe with one stride, if that." He looked at Trey with wide eyes, almost begging him to let Lady do what she wanted.

Trey wished he could. He wanted everyone to be happy too, but if Beth wanted to win the Classic, it was his job to get the horse trained up the right way to do that.

"If there was any other horse on the track..." Trey shook his head. "We need her to practice with some training horses."

"Not for a few days," Rob said. "We ran her full-out tonight and last night. She needs a rest day tomorrow—not even any training from you. Not even a slow day. Then you can do slow, medium, and fast, and we'll race her in five days."

"Five days," Beth said. "I want to be here."

"Me too," Lawrence said.

Rob grinned at Trey, his eyes equally lit with an excited kind of fire that spoke of his enthusiasm for how far they'd come with Somebody's Lady. "Can you get two or three horses to race with her? Full racing?"

"I'll work on it," Trey said, wondering how he was going to do that. He knew all the trainers and boarders at Bluegrass, but the timing of their training would have to line up with theirs, and they'd have to actually be horses that could compete with Lady, not just leaders or one-ups.

He took a sandwich out of the bag. "Hungry, Rob?"

"Always." He took the sandwich and settled on the tiny saddle on Lady's back. "Good time tonight."

"I'll meet you in the stable," Trey said, and Rob got Lady moving. He'd make her walk the track a couple of times to calm her, and then the two of them would make sure she was clean and comfortable for the night.

"I can't believe this is what you've been doing," Beth said. "You made it sound so boring."

"It usually is," he said, taking out a sandwich for himself finally. "We don't race her full-out every night."

"You should be working with the horses here," Lawrence said.

Trey cut him a glance out of the corner of his eye and filled his mouth with peanut butter and Beth's homemade peach jam. He loved the combination of salty, creamy peanut butter, and tart-yet-sweet peaches. A moan started somewhere in his chest and he leaned over and pressed his cheek to Beth's.

She giggled and pushed against his chest without much effort to really keep him away from her.

"Tell him he should talk to Spur about training," Lawrence said, looking at Beth now. She looked at Trey, and with Lawrence switching his gaze to him too, Trey started to squirm.

"Leave it, Lawrence," he said once he'd swallowed. "I'm not talking to Spur about training."

"It's what you want to do." Lawrence frowned at Trey. "I don't know why you just won't talk to him about it."

"Conrad and Ian are the trainers," he said simply. "Who else is going to make the schedule?"

"Duke," Lawrence said. "He's got that incredible notebook where he keeps track of all the mares and studs. He's on the phone as much as you, and he could easily do what you do."

"He already works a full-time job," Trey said. "So do I. You think he can take on two full-time jobs because I'd rather train horses?" He shook his head. "I know my place on the ranch."

"Trey," Beth said, and he looked at her and took another bite of his sandwich. "Maybe you could talk to him."

Trey shook his head as he chewed.

"He's brilliant with them," Lawrence said. "He has a real affinity for animals."

"Children, too." Beth smiled at Trey, but he wasn't in the mood to stand around and listen to the two of them talk about how amazing he was.

"It's one-thirty in the morning," he said. "I'm going to bed."

"Conrad wouldn't even *consider* letting a horse loose on the corner," Lawrence called after him.

So what? Trey wanted to ask. He'd spoken true. He knew his place at Bluegrass Ranch, and it wasn't in the training facility—at least not for any longer than it took to make sure the people who'd signed up and paid got their scheduled slot.

Outside, he paused and looked up into the clear, dark night sky. He felt the weight of that sky settle on his shoulders, and he took a breath as he tried to hold it up. As he released the air in his lungs, all the troubles and cares of the world went with it, and he took a single step toward Thunder, who he'd saddled and ridden over from Dixon Dreams tonight.

Beth had driven her SUV, but Lawrence must've walked, because there wasn't another vehicle besides Rob's near the stables to his left.

"Trey," she said behind him, and he ducked his head and turned back toward her.

"I don't want to talk to Spur about training," he said. "I don't even know if I'm going to be at Bluegrass for much longer."

"What do you mean?" She looked up at him, and with the glow of the half-moon, he found the confusion on her face.

"Baby." He took her into his arms, where she pressed her cheek against his heartbeat. He didn't know how to say what he'd been thinking about in the past few weeks since Thanksgiving. He supposed if there was one person he could —and should—tell, it was Beth.

Hadn't that been his big mistake with Sarah? Hadn't she accused him of bottling everything up and not trusting her with the deepest parts of his heart?

After she'd broken their engagement, Trey had only retreated further inside himself. He put his head down, and he got the job done. He slept when he couldn't stay awake any longer, and he ate when his body demanded he did.

He'd improved in the past six months as he figured out how to be himself again. Since the day his mother and father had told him to pray about what he should do with Beth's proposal, he felt like his life had been put in a blender and set on high.

He was married now, for one. Not just on paper either, as he and Beth had been sharing a bedroom since Thanksgiving. He hadn't quite gotten up the courage to go to church with Beth and TJ, but he'd told her a few days ago he'd go to the Christmas service this weekend.

"Five days from now is Christmas Eve," he said, pulling away from Beth. "Who's going to want to race their horse on Christmas Eve?" He also needed to find a way to start training Somebody's Lady during daylight hours. The Sweetheart Classic wasn't run in the middle of the night, and she'd need to run in front of a crowd too.

The to-do list never seemed to end, and Trey pushed against the pure feelings of overwhelm as they threatened to suffocate him. He pressed his eyes closed, the burning there testifying to him that he really needed to get to bed.

"Wait," he said. "I scheduled daylight time on the outdoor track."

"You're doing that thing where you continue conversations out loud that you've only had with yourself," Beth teased. "Come on. I'll help you with Somebody's Lady, so we can both get to sleep sooner." She slid her arm around his waist, and the two of them started toward the stables.

Inside, they found Rob and Lawrence, and with everyone, the tack got cleaned and put away, Somebody's Lady got checked, brushed down, and bedded.

"I put the Sweetheart Classic on my calendar," Lawrence said, grinning at him and Beth as they left the stables. "I can't wait to see that horse really run." He clapped Trey on the shoulder, which made him laugh.

"Thanks, Lawrence. I'm sure you'll be the only one there." Trey didn't blame his family. They were all extraordinarily busy, and he could admit he hadn't even known Spur was dating Olli until the man was days away from proposing to her.

Spur did have a knack for knowing what he wanted and going after it once he'd identified it. Trey wished he was as courageous as his brother. As he got in the passenger seat while Beth started the car, he decided to just say what had been on his mind.

"Beth," he said. "I don't know what the future holds, obviously, but I've been thinking a lot about where I should be." He glanced at her, but it was too dark to truly see her face. "It might not be Bluegrass Ranch."

"I still don't know what you mean."

"I mean, we're married now, and maybe I should be working Dixon Dreams with you. Full-time. We could work it as a family and teach TJ everything he needs to know to inherit the place when he's older." He spoke very quietly, the inner workings of his mind coming out in somewhat coherent sentences.

Beth gripped the steering wheel, the tension between them real and palpable. She took a deep breath as she turned onto the highway and headed toward her farm. Only a minute down the road, she turned again, the white gravel in her driveway crunching under her tires.

"We should probably start thinking about a different name then," she said. "If that's what you really want."

Trey smiled into the darkness. He hadn't seen this curve in his life—he'd always envisioned himself living and working at Bluegrass Ranch. It sure seemed like the Lord was leading him down a different path, though, and Trey hoped He'd keep illuminating his footsteps so Trey would know if he was about to step off a cliff or not.

Chapter 14

Beth stepped out of the master closet and into her heels, looking up as Trey came into the bathroom. He hadn't even started getting ready for church yet. Beth didn't want to push him, but he had said he'd come with her this week.

She was an expert in making up excuses for why she couldn't attend family gatherings, church, anything she didn't want to attend. Trey matched her in that regard, but he'd said he'd come for the Christmas sermon.

"Morning," she said coolly.

"Yes, it is," he said grumpily. He'd be fine once he'd been awake for longer than five minutes. Beth knew, as she'd been dealing with this growly version of Trey for over two months now. He'd shower and brush his teeth, and she'd somehow feel like she'd held them up from leaving, the way she usually did.

"Is TJ awake?" she asked.

"He wasn't when I left," Trey said, continuing into the bathroom.

Beth left, annoyance singing through her, and went down the hall past her son's bedroom. He and Trey had begged her to make a blanket fort in the living room, where they'd slept last night.

"They obviously didn't sleep," she muttered to herself, her heels making sharp clicking noises once she'd left the carpeted hallway and arrived in the kitchen. When she'd gone to bed, the two of them had been giggling about something underneath their tented blankets.

Then, she'd found them both adorable. Now, she wished she'd told them they could have an hour in the fort and then put them both to bed where they could get a full night's sleep.

"TJ," she said, using her motherly authoritative voice. "Time to get up, son. We have church today."

If waking Trey before he was ready wasn't pretty, doing so for her five-year-old was akin to torture. She couldn't even see him, and she pushed back the blanket draped over the barstool to try to find him.

"TJ," she said again, her voice coming out like a bark. "I mean it. Time to get up."

He groaned, and she knew what that sound meant. It meant they were going to be late for church.

Beth suppressed her sigh and got down on her knees, thinking through what Trey would do to get TJ where he wanted him. She'd watched him deal with TJ, and the fact was, he got on TJ's level more than Beth did.

She was the taskmaster. The one who nagged TJ to get his shoes and backpack. The one who told him four times to eat his toast before school. The one who made him brush his teeth and wash his hands when he didn't want to.

Trey took TJ out to the ranch and let him work with horses and dogs. He picked him up and ran him out of the SUV when Beth left him behind because they were late. Trey grinned at TJ and listened to him talk and talk—and talk— about the things that had happened at school. Trey read to him at night when Beth was too tired. He held TJ on his lap while he let TJ watch his cartoons.

Beth never did any of those things, and therefore, her relationship with her son was a lot different than Trey's.

She found him curled into a ball amidst a pile of pillows, pressed back into the corner where the loveseat and the couch met. If she wanted to get back there, she'd have to crawl through all the blankets.

"Or I can rip them down." They were hosting a huge luncheon after church that day for all of the cowboys who'd been working at Dixon Dreams the past several weeks. Tomorrow was Christmas Eve, and then Christmas Day, and with all of their individual family parties and dinners, not to mention the training Somebody's Lady needed over the next couple of days, things were hectic.

"Come on," Beth said, straightening and then reaching to start taking down the blanket fort. "Get up, TJ. You have thirty minutes before we need to leave for church. I want you to go brush your teeth and wash up. I'll get your clothes out and come do your hair."

Her son didn't appear, and Beth finished folding the first blanket and reached for the second one. She pulled it down, then another and another. She could fold them later. She needed TJ to get up right now.

Her frustration grew with every passing second, until she finally realized she was one moment away from yelling. She paused and took a deep, cleansing breath.

"TJ," she said as calmly as she could. "Time to get up." She kicked off her heels and stepped over the blankets and pillows on the floor to her child. She stooped and scooped him into her arms. "Baby."

She sat on the couch, mostly because she couldn't stand on the uneven floor and hold TJ. He curled into her chest, and Beth took a moment to appreciate him for the little boy he was. She'd never have this moment again, and she breathed it into her memory and held it before she whispered, "It's the holiday sermon today, buddy. Remember how they pass out the candy canes at the end?"

He lifted his head, his eyes suddenly open and wide.

She smiled at him, proud of herself for pausing and trying a different tactic. "Teeth," she said. "Wash your hands and get your hair wet like Trey showed you. I'll get your clothes and come help you with them and your hair."

"Okay, Momma," he said.

She dropped a kiss on his forehead and set him on his feet to go do what she'd asked him to. She sighed as she looked at the mess in the living room.

It didn't matter. She, Trey, and TJ lived in this house, and it looked like a family lived here. Sudden emotion lodged in her throat, because she hadn't had this life in so long.

"Babe," Trey called from down the hall. "Have you seen my brown boots?"

"Which pair?" she muttered, pushing herself to her feet.

"No," she called louder. "You had that pair you left on the front porch."

He came striding down the hall, his hair damp and a cloud of cologne following him as he grinned at her. "That's right."

"You're wearing those to church?" she called after him as he continued through the kitchen and into the front room.

"They just need to be cleaned up," he said.

Beth went in the opposite direction and got TJ's pants and white shirt out of his top drawer. She helped him get everything where it should be, and by some miracle, the three of them ended up in Trey's truck right when it was time to leave.

Trey pulled up to the dark gray building fifteen minutes later, and Beth immediately reached for her bag and got out of the truck. TJ slid over on the seat, following her, and she slammed the door behind her.

She'd taken a few steps toward the entrance when she realized Trey wasn't coming too. She paused and looked over her shoulder. The weak winter sun glinted off the windshield in such a way that she couldn't see Trey sitting behind the wheel.

Just go.

The words ran through her mind, and she smiled in

Trey's direction, hoping that conveyed to him that he could take his time and come in when he was ready. "Come on, baby," she said, taking TJ's hand. "Let's go find Grandpa."

Beth took her son up the steps and into the church, the sun at such an angle that colored light danced through the foyer and chapel from the stained glass windows. TJ skipped ahead of her when he saw his grandfather, and Beth followed him.

"Daddy," she said in a low voice, setting her bag on the end of the pew. "Can you handle TJ for a minute?"

"Sure," he said, looking at her with surprise. "Why?"

"I just need to go grab something I left in the car." She indicated her bag. "There are snacks in here if you need them." She walked away before her father could ask more questions. She had left something in the car—her husband.

Something had told her to walk away in the beginning, but that same feeling was telling her to go back and find out if there was anything she could do to help him find the strength to come inside the chapel.

Her door wasn't unlocked, and when she opened it, Trey yelped. "Sorry," she said. "I thought you'd see me."

"I had my eyes closed."

She got back in the passenger seat and closed the door. Her heart pounded and she didn't know what to say. With a couple of breaths, her mind settled. "When I got home from Danny's funeral, I had no idea how to go on."

Beth hadn't anticipated telling this story, but it was there, right on the end of her tongue. "I'd been surrounded by people for so long. The house was entirely too quiet. Kait and Hugh had taken TJ, probably as a favor to me." She stared straight out the front windshield. "I'm not really sure. I don't remember conversations from that time."

"I'm sure you don't," he said quietly.

"I had no idea how to do anything," she said. "I couldn't make dinner, and I couldn't shower. I just laid on the couch until Hugh came the next morning. With him there, I was able to eat, and we went out on the farm together. I'm not sure what we did or said, but it was easier when I wasn't alone."

She turned toward him. "Eventually, I learned how to do things by myself. You don't have to go through this alone. I'll walk in with you. I'll sit right beside you. You can squeeze my hand as hard as you want. TJ will probably sit on your lap. My daddy will give you a hug." She stopped, because her emotion surged up her throat and choked her.

Swallowing against it, she reached her hand toward him. "Will you come in with me?"

Trey started nodding before she finished asking the question. He laced his fingers through hers and lifted her hand to his lips. "Yes," he whispered.

Beth tried to smile, but it fell away quickly. "Stay there." She slid from the truck and went around to his door. She didn't want him to have to take even one step alone. She took his hand before he got out of the truck, and she held it all the way across the parking lot to the church.

They went up the steps together, and Beth heard the choir singing. The sermon hadn't started yet, and by the sound of it, the choir had just started their welcome song.

Her heart filled with love and gratitude, and when she stepped down the row where her father sat with TJ, Trey was still right beside her.

He sat on the end after putting her bag on the floor near his feet. Beth stayed close to him, her leg pressing into his, and she looked up at him, questions moving through her. "Okay?" she asked.

"Yes," he whispered, his eyes scanning the front of the chapel. The choir stood up there in their poinsettia-red robes, their angelic voices filling the rafters with song. For a moment, she thought he might be looking for the nearest exit, and that he'd bolt at any moment.

When the choir started singing the first Christmas hymn, he visibly relaxed, and he released the vice-grip on her hand and lifted his arm around her shoulder. He bent his head toward hers, and she inched into his side a little more.

"Thank you, Beth," he whispered, and she once again took a moment to commit this scenario to memory.

***

"Come on, Momma," Beth said later that day, grunting with the effort it took her to pull on the calf's legs. All at once, the calf released, sliding out of his mother and onto the straw-covered cement in the birthing barn. Beth fell backward, crying out though she tried not to.

Walter moved in, a towel in each hand, and started rubbing the calf while he watched her. "You okay?"

"Yes," she said. The calf's mother lowed, and Beth got to

her feet quickly though her lower back pinched. She released the heifer from the restraints she'd put her in so they could assist with her calf's birth. The mother cow went to her baby, and the bond they had was exactly the same one Beth had experienced when the nurse had first laid TJ on her chest, only moments after his birth.

"That's sixty-seven," Walter said. "I think you're going to have a huge herd this year." He grinned at Beth, and she smiled back at him. It was nice to have help on the farm, she could admit that. Really, really nice.

A huge blessing, she thought, assigning the right term to what her life was. The preacher had talked about identifying and acknowledging the blessings in life, and Beth rarely did that. She'd spent so much of the last three years trying to fix what was wrong that she didn't even see what was right.

"I hope you're right," she said to Walter. "Come on. You're coming back to the house for lunch, aren't you?"

"If these cows will stop going into labor."

"Trey's ordered enough food to feed the whole county," Beth said with a smile. "You better come, and you should go get your family too."

"Jen's on her way with the kids." Walter smiled as he removed his gloves. "I'll go see where she is." He left the shed while Beth walked over to the sink in the birthing shed and washed her hands up to her elbows.

She pulled her sleeves down so she wouldn't freeze when she went outside, and she looked around the shed to make sure she didn't have anything else to do before she went up to the farmhouse.

The birthing shed sat on the far east end of the main part of the ranch, the farthest building from the farmhouse. Beth didn't mind the walk back, especially when she could take it by herself.

She couldn't help but notice how quiet her mind was these days. Her thoughts didn't run in fifteen different directions, and she wasn't five seconds away from a complete panic attack. The ranch still didn't have enough profit, but with Trey funding the salaries of the cowboys working with her and buying groceries and food—and anything else he thought the three of them needed or wanted—Beth didn't find herself worrying about money.

She hadn't asked her father for money since the wedding, and he hadn't brought it up either.

Happiness accompanied her every step, and she paused when she heard the joyful clucking of the chickens. "Thank you, Lord," she said, tipping her head back as she looked up into the sky. The sun had disappeared sometime during church, and a storm had covered the blue face of the sky.

It hadn't rained yet, but the growl of thunder rolled through the sky, and yet Beth stayed by the warbling of her chickens. She loved the silly birds and the sounds they made, and she wanted another perfect memory for today, and she wanted to acknowledge the blessings in her life.

Her chickens were a huge blessing, and she took a moment to enjoy them.

Too long of a moment, because the sky opened before she could reach the house, and the rains came pouring down. She shrieked and started running, though no one could outrun a winter rainstorm in Kentucky.

By the time she reached the back porch, where the roof protected her from the falling rain, her hair was drenched, as were her jeans and boots. "Great," she said, though laughter bubbled through her.

She stepped over to the patio table and bent to take off her boots and jacket. If she texted Trey, he'd bring her a towel, and she could at least dry off a little before tracking mud and who knows what else through the house.

Voices filtered out to her ears through the open window, and Beth paid them no mind—at least until she heard Trey's voice say, "That's exactly what I'm telling you, Clyde."

"It can't be fake," her father said. "It just can't be. How can a marriage be fake?"

"It just is," Trey said. "How else could she enter Somebody's Lady in the Sweetheart Classic?"

She shot straight up, her heart pounding.

It just is, he'd said.

It just is, rang through her head.

It just is?

Did he really think that? She'd been sharing her bed with him for almost a month—that was real. She'd walked him into church today—that was real. He'd become a father to TJ—that was most certainly real.

"I mean, it's going well," Trey said. "Really, it is. She's great, and—" His voice got covered by a child's scream, and Sally's voice entered the fray, as did Kait's. Her father said something; everyone was saying something.

Beth felt like she was being whipped around and around. Up and down. All of the talking just became noise, but it couldn't erase the sound of Trey's voice saying their marriage was fake.

She wasn't exactly sure when it had stopped being fake for her, because she hadn't pinpointed the moment she'd fallen in love with him. She thought their marriage was going well too. They talked about meaningful things.

He did things like let her sleep late on the weekends, though there were chores to do. She brought him food at the training track, and she always had lunch when he came in off the ranch. He picked up TJ from school. They served one another, and Beth had really liked how their foundation was shaping up.

What had she missed?

Why didn't he feel that way too?

"You sit right there," Kait said, her voice sharp. She plunked Lucas on the porch, and he wailed as he looked up at her. "You can't hit your cousins."

She looked up, clearly frustrated and angry. Her eyes went right to Beth's, and she visibly deflated. "TJ wasn't involved," she said, her frown only deepening. She turned back to the farmhouse. "You should probably come in and start explaining. Trey says the two of you got married so you could enter the Sweetheart Classic, and your father is upset."

She strode back inside too, and Beth knew Daddy wasn't the only one who was upset.

Chapter 15

Trey kept frowning at the back door, willing Beth to walk through it. Maybe another cow had gone into labor. Maybe he should be out there helping her instead of in here stirring cole slaw that didn't need to be stirred.

No one spoke now, except the parents to their little kids. Lucas cried just outside the back door, and Kait stood a few feet from him, but out of his sight.

He wanted to ask if she'd seen Beth out there. Walter had come in from the birthing shed several minutes ago, and the rain had started in earnest just after that.

"I'm going to go see where she is," he said into the relative silence. He wished he could go back in time twenty-four hours and fix all of the things he'd done wrong. First, he'd let TJ build a blanket fort, but he wouldn't be stupid enough to sleep on the hard floor when he had a king-size bed with a pillowtop just down the hall.

He was far too old for sleeping on anything but a bed for longer than an hour or two. He'd somehow box up his anxiety so his dear, sweet Beth wouldn't have to come back out to the truck and help him get inside the church.

He'd call the restaurant and request delivery of the food he'd ordered, no matter the cost. That way, he wouldn't be rushed, impatient, and cranky by the time he returned to the farmhouse with the food they were feeding her family and the cowboys who'd been working at Dixon Dreams.

Because he wouldn't be rushed, he wouldn't have dropped the quart of sticky barbecue sauce all over the living room floor, and he wouldn't have snapped at TJ to help him. He would've been personable when he'd answered the door to greet Beth's father and brother, and he wouldn't have nearly growled at them to come in.

He could live with almost all of that—he sincerely regretted letting his temper come out on TJ—but he'd been in such a terrible mood and place that when Kait had made an off-hand comment about how maybe Beth and Trey would be the next ones to have a baby, he'd snapped.

Is this all you guys ever talk about?

He'd said those words, and not in a kind voice either. They'd all gone silent, and Trey should've stopped talking then.

Beth walked through the back door, a sniffling Lucas in her arms before Trey could pull on his boots and jacket. He'd ruined his other pair of brown boots with all that blasted barbecue sauce, and his irritation with himself only increased.

Everyone looked at Beth, who scanned the living room and kitchen and dining area in under three seconds flat. "What's going on?" she asked.

All eyes volleyed back to Trey. He stood there, shame and regret moving through him. "I told them we got married so you could enter the Sweetheart Classic."

Kait stepped over to Beth and took her son from her, stepping back so there were no obstacles between Trey and Beth.

"Why?" Beth asked. "We talked about this, Trey."

How could he explain the perfect storm of things that had driven him to the breaking point of his patience?

"Momma," TJ said, running up to her. He wrapped her legs up in a hug and said, "Trey yelled at me, and then he yelled at Grandpa."

"I didn't—" Trey cut himself off, already feeling his frustration rise again.

"It's fine," Clyde said. "He didn't yell at anyone, TJ. He was just frustrated." He clapped his hands together. "Is everyone here, Bethy? Can we eat?"

Trey couldn't look away from Beth as she patted TJ's back. She looked like he'd betrayed her, and he probably had.

"Everyone's here," Beth said quietly. "We can eat." She crouched down in front of TJ and smoothed his hair back off his forehead. Sally said something to Hugh, and the two of them started bringing food over to the table from the counter.

Trey was going to leave it there and do a more buffet-style serving than having to pass the food around the table.

He honestly didn't care how things went, and he wished he'd gone out to the birthing shed to help the heifer deliver her calf.

He watched Beth hug TJ and straighten, and he wanted to take her out into the garage and have a private conversation. He wasn't sure how to just move past this as if it hadn't happened. At the same time, he didn't want to perpetuate the scene and continue to make everyone uncomfortable.

In the end, Trey faded into the background, taking up a spot with the men he'd worked with many times at Bluegrass Ranch. He knew them, and they knew him. He knew their wives and children, and Trey felt like he belonged on the sidelines in this house for the first time.

Marc exchanged a glance with him, and Walter said, "We've all been there, Trey."

"Is that right?" Trey asked, still a hint of bite in his tone. "You and Jen got married in less than three weeks to meet a racing deadline? Fascinating. I'd love to hear that story."

Marc started to chuckle, as did Dominic.

"Stop it," Jen hissed from the other side of Walter. She stepped in front of her husband, her blue eyes flashing. "We've all been there? What does that mean?" She rolled her eyes at him before turning her attention on Trey.

"And you," she said, plenty of displeasure in her eyes. "You're just going to let this dinner go on like this? You need to go talk to Beth right now."

"Mm, I don't think so," he said, watching her stick like glue to TJ as she went over to the table. Her siblings flanked her, a barrier between her and the rest of the world, which right now, was him.

"Hailey?" Jen looked at Marc's wife, who lifted a glass of water to her lips. "He should go talk to her right now, right?"

"He's about ten minutes too late already," Hailey said, her lips barely moving.

"You know what?" Trey asked. "I liked you guys a lot more when you were trying to set me up with someone, and that's saying something."

Both Jen and Hailey laughed, and Trey was glad they were there. Two women telling him to go interrupt Beth and talk to her? They couldn't both be wrong, could they?

"Do I need to explain to her family?" he asked, his voice softening.

"That's a tough one," Jen said, falling back to Walter's side. "She might want to explain, and she might want to do it when we're not all here."

"She knows you guys," Trey said.

"She's horribly embarrassed," Hailey said. "She'll likely want to explain via text."

Trey hated that, and he pressed his teeth together. "I just go ask her to...what? Step out on the back porch for a moment?"

"Yes," Jen said. "You're losing your window. TJ is almost settled at the table, and once Beth digs in there, you're not getting her out without a scene."

Beth picked up TJ's cup and turned back to the island.

"Now or never," Jen said, a warning tone in her voice.

Trey took a breath and left the group to join Beth at the island. She saw him coming, and she refused to look at him. "Can we talk for a minute, please?" he asked.

"I'm fine," she said.

"I'm not."

That got her eyes to meet his, and Trey found the betrayal and anguish he never wanted to see again.

"Please," he said.

"I'm hungry, Trey, and I've probably got three cows to babysit overnight."

"I'll do it," he said.

"Right." She shook her head. "You're riding Lady tonight. Hard, I think was on the schedule."

He wanted to say the horse didn't matter, but he couldn't bring himself to do it. Somebody's Lady was all that mattered right now. Beth had wanted this marriage so she could enter that horse in a race. He wasn't going to ruin that for her just because everything else he touched turned to ash.

"I'll pay Marc double time. He'll do it."

"No, thank you,'" Beth said, her eyes turning icy. "You've spent quite enough money on my farm." She finished filling TJ's cup and started toward the table.

"Beth," he said, his chest stinging and his thoughts screaming through his head. "I went out into the garage to talk to you. The least you can do is offer me the same favor." His voice was loud enough for everyone to hear, and Trey found he didn't care.

He faced the dining room table where her family had

mostly settled. The cowboys and their wives were just now filling in around them, and Trey could not see a spot for him at that table.

"Beth and I did get married so we could enter Somebody's Lady in the Sweetheart Classic," he said. "I've been working with the horse and a really great jockey, and I'm confident we're going to win."

"Trey," Beth said.

"She wanted to enter the Classic, because this farm is on the brink of financial collapse every month. Her previous husband had racked up quite a bit of debt and didn't tell her. She is strong, and capable, and one of the best women I know. She's worked tirelessly on this farm, because she loves it, and she can't lose one more thing."

He threw his hands up into the air. "So I said yes. Heck, I've liked Beth for months. I even asked her out before she suggested we get married. We were going to go to dinner one night, but she told her dad she wasn't ready. We were married less than a month later anyway."

He watched only her now, unsure if he was making things better or worse. She wore a shocked expression, and Trey honestly felt like he was digging his own grave. He couldn't stop, though, so he opened his mouth one more time.

"Even before the wedding, we agreed that what we were doing wasn't fake. That we'd work on making the relationship and our marriage real. Somewhere along the way, I fell in love with her." He chuckled, though he wasn't sure why, because he didn't feel an ounce of happiness in his soul.

He gazed around at everyone, adults, children, cowboys, family members. "I've just had a very bad day today, and I lost my temper a couple of times." His chest quaked, and he couldn't stop it no matter how deeply he breathed.

"I'm sorry, TJ. I did not mean to snap at you. I was just frustrated that I'd dropped all that sauce. You can understand that, right?"

"Trey," Beth said again.

He didn't look at her. "Honestly, I love all of you guys. I do. I think it's amazing how you rally around each other and how well you get along. It's nice to spend time with women and not just my brothers. I just...I couldn't hear one more thing about when Beth and I are going to have a baby. Frankly, I find it odd that that's the highest priority for a relationship."

He turned toward Beth. "I messed up. Everything turned against me today, and yes, I snapped at your son." He hung his head. "I ruined my boots, and I'd driven ten under the speed limit on the way back because some guy was out for a joyride on his motorcycle. So I was late getting here, and your family showed up right after I'd dropped the sauce. I wasn't nice when they arrived, because I was stressed. I know this is all just an excuse, and I'm sorry."

Trey's chest shook as he faced everyone again. "I'm sorry." He didn't know what else to say or do. He looked at Jen, who had one palm pressed against her heart. Maybe he hadn't messed up again, though it certainly felt like he had.

He stepped over to Beth and brushed his lips along her cheek. "I love you, Beth. Out of anyone, I can't stand the thought of you being angry with me. I'm sorry, and I hope you'll forgive me." He looked over to TJ. "Sorry, bud."

Touching his cowboy hat, he nodded at everyone at the table. "Excuse me, please." He started for the front door, aware of the silence behind him and that he wasn't currently wearing any shoes.

TJ went to Bluegrass all the time without shoes; Trey could too.

In all honesty, he expected Beth to catch him on the front porch. When she didn't, he told himself she'd call his name the moment he reached the bottom of the steps.

She didn't.

Trey made it to his truck and still no one had followed him or called his name. His heart pounded as he drove away from Beth's farm, thinking of it as hers and not theirs for the first time in a long time.

* * *

Trey kept his head down while he waited for his mother to answer the door.

When she did, she said, "Trey," her voice full of surprise. "You could've just come in."

"The door was locked, Momma." Trey's mask broke, and he swept his mother into a hug. "Mom, I messed up." He held her tightly, even when she tried to pull back.

"Honey," she said into his shoulder. "I've got lemon pound cake. Come tell me everything." His mother thought everything could be fixed with enough sugar, and honestly, Trey would take anything he could get at this point.

He finally released her and nodded. His father leaned in the doorway, his eyes concerned, but he didn't start firing questions at Trey. He never had. Daddy could say a lot without saying anything at all, and he could convey exactly how he felt with very few words.

Trey never wanted to disappoint his father, and he'd definitely done that in the past. Those were some of the worst words he'd ever heard. *I'm disappointed in you, Trey.*

He was plenty disappointed in himself.

"Hey, Daddy." He hugged him too while Mom continued into the kitchen to dish up the cake.

"We have banana cake too," she called, and for some reason, Trey found that funny. He half-laughed and half-scoffed as he stepped away from his dad.

"How do you not weigh five hundred pounds?" he asked. "She makes a new cake every single day."

Daddy chuckled and patted Trey on the shoulder as they moved into the kitchen together. "Maybe you can take some to Beth to fix whatever you messed up."

"I think it's going to take more than cake."

Mom put a plate carrying a huge chunk of lemon cake in front of him. "You can fix anything with cake," she said.

Trey picked up his fork, but he didn't want to relive the horrible parts of today. He'd rather focus on the good, the blessings he had, like the preacher had talked about today.

He took a bite of cake while his mother brought several pieces of banana cake to the table. She sat down beside him, her eyes wide. To her credit, she didn't ask him any questions, and he knew with every bite of cake and every moment that he said nothing was driving her a little closer to insane.

He finally put his fork down and said, "I went to church this morning."

Daddy's eyes widened, and Mom gasped. "You did? Why didn't we see you there?"

"I don't know," he said. "I was there. It was real nice."

"I'm glad," Daddy said. "Did you go with Beth and TJ?"

"We still want to have you guys over," Mom said, glancing at Daddy. "I know you said you were going to take things slow and see how they went, and I know you're coming to the big family party together." She cleared her throat. "I'd just love to get to know them better."

"I'll talk to Beth," Trey said, hoping that was really true. He hadn't exactly told her about his mother's invitation to dinner, but he should have. His parents would love TJ, and Trey wondered if he could bring the boy out to the house one day after school.

"How are things going?" Daddy asked.

"I fell in love with her," Trey said miserably.

"Don't sound so happy about it," Daddy said, chuckling.

Trey started to laugh too, and as he scooped a piece of banana cake onto his plate, they were all laughing. He sobered and looked at his cake. "I did mess up, but I've already apologized. She won't stay mad at me forever, right?"

He looked from his mom to his dad, hoping they'd both say that of course he was right.

"Right," Daddy said.

"Whenever I'm mad at your father," Mom said. "I do make him suffer for a little bit."

"Julie," Daddy said, shaking his head though he was smiling.

"He apologizes, and I start planning how I'm going to let him know I've forgiven him. There's always food, and if it takes a couple of days to plan...well." She shrugged, a smile lighting up her face. "By then, he's gotten me a gift, and when he comes in off the ranch, he presents me with that, and I have dinner ready, and everything is fine."

She got up and patted Trey's shoulder. "You'll see."

Trey sincerely hoped he'd see, and he thought his time that afternoon would actually be better spent at Beth's favorite clothing boutique than with his parents. If only he knew what Beth's favorite clothing boutique was...

Chapter 16

Beth couldn't stand the silence in the farmhouse. It reminded her of the night she'd been left alone after Danny's funeral. She'd told people she wanted to be alone; she'd cried grateful tears when Hugh had offered to take TJ, who'd only been two years old at the time.

Then, when it actually came time to be alone in the house? Beth had hated it.

She felt the exact same way right now.

The weight of her family's eyes made her feel like she was losing an inch from her height every few seconds. In addition to that, she'd invited all the cowboys and their families, and her humiliation knew no end.

TJ babbled happily with Lucas, and Beth wished she could be a child again, with childlike concerns, and no concept of awkwardness, money, hurt feelings, or mistakes.

She worked slowly on scooping macaroni salad onto her

plate and squeezing the wrong kind of barbecue sauce over her meat. Her mind buzzed with all Trey had said.

He'd been unafraid to stand in front of everyone and speak. She wanted to be like that. She wanted to clear the air so they could have a good afternoon, filled with laughter and chatter, a quick gift exchange, and the craft she'd picked up for the kids.

She'd spent time finding a couple of simple but meaningful gifts for her family members and the cowboys, and she wanted to hug them all, smile, and let them know how much she loved and appreciated them.

Trey had ruined that, but he'd tried to fix it. Her refusal to follow him out the front door and make things right had kept the tense feeling in the farmhouse.

She didn't know how to be brave like him. She didn't know how to open her mouth and say the right things.

Still holding her fork, she pressed her eyes closed and prayed. *Dear Lord...*

She couldn't even find the words for the prayer.

Just start, she thought, and again, she was sure it wasn't her thought.

Beth put down her fork and lifted her eyes. Her father watched her with a hooded expression, and Hugh kept himself busy with his infant, tearing up a roll into tiny pieces and putting it on Tawny's tray.

Kait and Sally both looked at her, both frowning like she'd handled everything wrong. She had; she already knew that.

"I'm sorry," she said. "This is supposed to be a fun afternoon together for the holidays."

"It's okay," Hugh said. A quick glance at his wife had him back-peddling. "I mean..."

"It is *not* okay," Kait said. "Sally?"

"I agree with Kait," Sally said quietly. "I don't know why you're even still sitting there."

Beth's irritation sparked. "Because I'm not you, Sally. I don't know exactly what to do and when." Her chest heaved, but her mind screamed at her that she'd just made things worse.

"I'm sorry, Sally." She shook her head. "I don't want to fight with you."

"Beth," her father said. "You don't have to shoulder everything alone."

"That's what she likes," Sally said, her dark eyes firing with plenty of danger now. "It's how she's always been, Daddy."

"Now's not the time," their father said.

Beth glared at Sally, who gave the gesture right back to her. They didn't always get along, but Beth had never realized her sister thought she was so...something.

"Tell me," she said, folding her arms and leaning away from the table. She glanced down the table to where Walter sat with his wife. They ate silently, and Beth wished she could just leave. But this was her house. "I'm sorry, guys. This has to be the worst company dinner ever." She tossed a smile down toward the men who'd been working around her farm. "But I'd really like everyone's input. Even yours, if you care to say anything." She looked back at Sally. "Sally's going to go first."

"Sally," Kait murmured. "Be kind."

Sally pushed her pulled pork around on her plate, her gaze dropping there too. When she opened her mouth, the cruelty had fled from her voice. "Beth, you've always played the martyr. When Mom died, it was always, 'poor Beth. What's Beth going to do?' It was never, 'poor Sally. What's Sally going to do?' It was 'Sally can give you a ride. Sally can get a job to help pay the bills.' It was 'Sally will take care of Beth.'"

Beth's chest pinched, and her tears started to gather in droves behind her eyes. She clenched her teeth and cinched her arms tighter against her chest.

"I didn't care," Sally said. "I *wanted* to take care of you, Hugh, and Daddy." She looked at the others at the table. "Then, when Danny died, it was 'poor Beth' all over again. It gets really old is all I'm saying. No one is ever asking me if I need help. Daddy doesn't offer to buy my children new clothes or pay for a birthday party they don't need."

"I haven't—"

"Let her talk," Hugh said over Daddy, and they both fell silent again.

"Mick lost his job six months ago," Sally continued. "You didn't even know. None of you knew until this very moment." She swiped angrily at her eyes, and Beth's whole chest collapsed.

She wiped her eyes too, her tears for her sister now and not herself. She wanted to say she hadn't known, but that was exactly the point. She hadn't known, and Sally was saying it was because Beth was selfishly wrapped up in her own trauma.

"I thought he's been working in Philadelphia," Hugh said.

"He's been up there doing some training," Sally said. "I've been supporting us with the lawn sign business and the address painting."

"For six months?" Kait asked, shock in her tone.

Sally nodded and barely glanced at her husband, who kept his eyes down. His embarrassment was obvious, and Beth hated that she'd caused this conversation. "No one asks me if I need help with my three children, my house, my yard, or either business while he's gone. I just get up every dang day, and I do whatever needs to be done."

Her eyes shone with angry tears now, making her twice as fearsome. "So, Beth, stop doing whatever you're doing. Just stop. I don't think any of us here cares *why* you married Trey. We have eyes, and we have ears, and I know I stood here and watched a man very much in love with you apologize several times. To you, to all of us. I heard him ask you to please go out into the garage to talk to him. I heard his anguish when he apologized to your son, who he obviously cares for very much." She looked at Kait. "Kait?"

"I agree with Sally," Kait said. "Sorry, Beth. I love you like a sister. I do. I don't know all the details with you and Trey, and I don't really care. It's as obvious that you love him, and he loves you, as the sky is blue. People make mistakes."

"Beth doesn't," Sally murmured.

"Sally," Kait said, glancing at her. "She does. She's making one right now by not going after him to make sure he's okay, and that he knows she's not going to abandon him every time he makes a mistake or has a bad day."

"We all have bad days," one of the cowboys said, and Beth turned toward Marc. She didn't know what to say. She felt two inches tall and insignificant, and she was desperately trying to find all the ways she hadn't done what Sally had just accused her of doing.

The problem was, she couldn't. She did like to play the martyr. She did get help from her father. She hadn't known about Mick's job, nor had she ever offered to help Sally with her kids, house, yard, or businesses while her husband was out of town.

She didn't know how to save someone else while she was drowning herself.

You don't have to, she thought. She drew in a deep breath and stood up. "Thank you," she said. "Anyone else?"

No one said anything, and Beth looked out at them. "I know this is my house, but I have to leave for a little bit." She looked at Sally. "I'm so sorry I haven't been able to help you. I am one breath away from drowning all the time, and I don't know how to throw you a line when I don't have one myself."

"I know that," Sally said. "It's why I've never said anything to you. But I'm telling you right now—stop thinking you're drowning. Maybe you were a couple of months ago, before Trey came on the scene and started pulling you to shore. But you're *not* drowning anymore, and it's annoying to watch you pretend like you still are."

Kait stood up and moved around her kids to hug Beth. "We love you, Beth. We'll forgive you when you leave to go get Trey and bring him back here so we can have our awesome holiday afternoon together."

Beth clung to her, trying to steal some of her strength. At least she didn't cry. "Okay," she said, taking another breath and stepping back. "Okay."

Daddy got up and hugged her, as did Hugh. When her brother stepped back, Sally stood there, waiting her turn. The two sisters looked at one another, and then Beth grabbed onto Sally and let her tears fall.

"I'm so sorry," she whispered. "Really, I am."

"Go get him," Sally said. "Find him, and tell him you forgive him, and tell him that none of us care about the fake marriage that I suspect isn't really fake anymore."

Beth nodded, pulling in another long, deep breath. She wiped her face and bent down to TJ. "Buddy, I have to go find Trey, okay? Will you stay here and listen to Grandpa, please?" She met her father's eye just past TJ, and he nodded.

TJ said, "Okay," and Beth pressed a kiss to the top of his head. "Where did Trey go?"

"I don't know, bud," Beth said. "Where does he go when he's upset?"

"Probably to see Thunder," TJ said. "He likes Thunder."

"Yes, he does," Beth said almost absentmindedly. She wasn't sure if Trey would go saddle his horse and disappear out into the wilds of the ranch or if he'd get in his truck and drive until he ran out of gas or the road, whichever happened first.

She collected her keys and her phone, left her dinner plate full of food in her spot at the table, and called Trey after she'd started her car so his voice would come through the speakers.

"Hello," he said after three rings, his voice cool and detached.

"Trey," she said turning toward Bluegrass Ranch. "Where are you?"

"The ranch."

Beth blinked, trying not to be irritated with him. "It's six hundred acres," she said. "Could you give me a better idea of where I can find you so we can talk?"

"We're talking right now."

"I'd like you to come back to the farmhouse," she said as the dirt lane that led back into the trees and to the ranch where Trey was came into view. "I love you, and I don't want to have this family party without all of my family."

Enough silence went by for her to drive down the road and make the turn onto the dirt lane. "I'm at my parents' house," he said. "I'll meet you by the little house at the first intersection on the ranch, okay?"

"Okay," Beth said. She wasn't entirely sure where that was, but she'd figure it out.

"Five minutes," Trey said.

Beth went around a corner and came to the first intersection. The road branched to her left and continued straight, and in the little pocket of land sat a little house. "I'm here right now, but take your time."

He said he'd see her in a minute, and the call ended. Beth pulled her SUV into the short driveway of the house, realizing it was more of a cabin than anything. It might even be a shed and not a house at all.

Her fingers gripped the wheel, all of her muscles tight. They kept her in place, and she tried to think through what she might say to Trey when he arrived. She couldn't come up with anything good.

When Trey's big, black truck finally came down the road, relief filled her and spilled out in the form of a long sigh. She got out of her car and started across the wild grass to the other road, so she was waiting there when he pulled up.

She yanked open his door and stepped up onto the running board. "I'm sorry," she said instantly. "I'm so sorry. I should've come after you immediately, and I should've just accepted your apology, and I should've done so many things differently."

She took his face in her hands and gazed at him through her tears. "I'm sorry. Of course I forgive you, and I hope you'll forgive me."

"I feel like a fool," he said instead, his eyes as soft as his voice. He let them drift closed, and while there wasn't really room for her on his lap with the steering wheel and all of that, he still pulled her into place, using one hand to slide his seat back as far as it would go. "What did your dad say after I left?"

"Nothing," Beth said, placing a kiss against his cheek. "None of them said anything."

"I don't believe that." Trey pressed into each touch of her lips against his skin, first his lower jaw, then right below his ear. He smelled like fresh air and barbecue sauce and musky leather, all things Beth wanted in her life for good.

"I love you," Beth said. "Everyone makes mistakes. Everyone has bad days. They don't care why we got married. Please, please come back and have lunch with us." She pulled away and opened her eyes, waiting until he did too. "With me."

"I ruined my boots," he said, and he sounded so wounded about it.

Beth smiled at him as she gently tugged on his cowboy hat to get it off his head. She loved this vulnerable side of him, and as she touched her mouth to his, a brand-new kind of fire ran through her veins.

She didn't kiss him for long before pulling away. "Trey, baby," she whispered. "You have enough money to get new boots."

"I liked those ones," he said, his voice rough around the edges and full of air. He kissed her again, threading his fingers through her hair and holding her in place this time. Beth felt cherished and loved under his care, but she didn't let the kiss go on too long.

"I'm starving," she said. "I had to tear down a blanket fort this morning and birth a calf today, and I still haven't eaten."

Trey licked his lips and opened his eyes. "Right. Let's get you back to the farmhouse for lunch."

"You're coming too, right?"

"Yes," he said. "I'll come." He glanced out the windshield. "Do you want to drive your car or come with me? We can come get it anytime."

"I'll come with you." She wasn't sure how she managed it, but she somehow slid off his lap and across the console to the passenger seat. "Let's go."

He started down the lane, one hand draped lazily over the steering wheel. "Thanks for not making me suffer for a few days," he said.

"What?" she asked.

He looked at her while they were stopped at the highway. "My mom said she always makes my dad suffer for a few days while she plans the food she's going to make to let him know she forgives him. That gives him enough time to get a gift, and they make-up that way."

Beth blinked at him before giggling. "I'll take a gift," she said. "I don't think I need to make you suffer, though."

"That's why I said thanks." He pulled onto the highway. "Your dad really didn't say anything?"

"Nope."

"Kait?"

"Not a word."

"What did Sally say?"

Beth sighed and looked out her window, the familiar annoyance only aimed at herself. "Do you think I'm selfish?" she asked.

"Not particularly," he said. "Did she say that?"

"And a whole lot more," Beth said. "The problem is, she's right." She folded her arms again as if that could keep the bad things out and the good things in. "I think she's right." Her brain seemed stuffed to capacity, and she didn't know how to sort through the thoughts and feelings fast enough.

He pulled into her gravel driveway, and Beth looked at him. "Trey, I apologize if I've ever done anything to make you feel like I don't care about you, or that I don't appreciate everything—and I mean every single little thing—you've done for me and TJ."

The Lord had been right; all she'd had to do was open her mouth, and there were plenty of words waiting to come out.

"For the farm," she said. "All of it." She watched him as he absorbed her appreciation and apology. "I didn't know you'd overheard me and my father."

His eyes came to hers then. "I did." He shifted in his seat and cleared his throat. "I've never wanted to push you somewhere you didn't want to go, Beth. You know that, right?"

"I do," she said. "I'm the one who asked you to marry me."

"I said yes," Trey said. "I don't regret anything I've done, Beth. Anything we've done. I *want* to be here with you."

Beth smiled at him. "I want all of that too."

He chuckled and shook his head. "All right. Might as well get this over with." He got out of the truck and took Beth's hand when they met in front of the house.

"Don't worry," Beth said, taking the first step with Trey at her side. "They like you more than me right now."

"I doubt that."

"Yes, well, I have a lot of work to do to be a better person," she said. "I knew I was failing; I just didn't know how spectacularly."

He paused when they got to the top of the steps. "I do not think you're failing at much, Beth."

"That's because you're blinded by my beauty," she quipped, unable to truly laugh. "Thank you, though. I really don't want to fail you or TJ." Her lungs quivered as she took a breath.

"You aren't," he said. "Come on now. Let's just go inside and have a good time."

She nodded, and this time, she let him lead the way through the front door and into the kitchen. Once again, everyone watched them, and then TJ jumped out of his chair. "They're back," he said, running toward Trey and Beth.

Trey laughed as he caught her son up into his arms and held him against his chest. Everyone else had gotten up in those few seconds, and they came over to hug Beth and welcome Trey back to the farmhouse.

Extreme gratitude and relief filled her, quickly morphing into love for her family and their ability to forgive each other.

Once things settled down, Trey sat beside her, his plate loaded with food. Conversations happened around them, and he reached for the barbecue sauce, his hand freezing in midair.

"Where did this come from?" he asked, glancing around. "I dropped all of this in the living room."

Beth looked at the bottle of barbecue sauce that had not been there when she'd left to go find Trey, then around the table at everyone.

"I ordered it on that food delivery app," Walter said. "They delivered it a few minutes ago." He forked another bite of mashed potatoes into his mouth and grinned at Trey. "Can't have barbecue sauce be the thing that ruins your whole day, right?"

Trey blinked, his eyes wide. He slid his fingers around the bottle and squeezed as if trying to throttle it. Then he started laughing, the sound loud and wonderful as it filled the empty space in the farmhouse until there was none left at all.

The others joined in, and Beth basked in the new brand of happiness that existed at her house, with all of these people she loved.

She met Sally's eyes, and her sister sobered and nodded, just once, before turning to her nine-year-old as she asked a question.

Beth still needed to do better; she knew that. She would, because her sister was right. She wasn't drowning anymore, and that all had to do with a man who'd said yes when she'd asked him to marry her.

"So," Hugh said. "When can we come watch your horse run?"

"Tomorrow," Trey said. "We've got a mock race tomorrow morning, actually. Could be a good Christmas Eve morning activity." He looked hopefully around the table, and Beth's nerves twittered though he clearly wanted her family to come to the track and watch Somebody's Lady run.

Beth knew that what Trey wanted, he usually got, and she wished she had even half of his confidence in the horse they'd entered in the Sweetheart Classic.

Chapter 17

Ginny Winters bent her head and lifted the diamond earring to her earlobe. The stem went through easily, and she secured the plastic rubber on the back before straightening her head. Behind her, on the bed, Sarge perked up, his eyes moving to the open doorway of her bedroom.

Her heartbeat tumbled through her chest, landing somewhere in her stomach while she pretended none of that had happened. If she didn't think too hard about that October night where all of the alarms except the one at her mother's mansion in the center of the property had filled the night with sirens and sound, she was fine.

In quiet moments, however, Ginny could really get lost inside the labyrinth of her thoughts. She'd always wanted to write a novel, as she enjoyed an active imagination. Sometimes, though, that imagination had her imagining dark, hooded figures entering her house while she wasn't there and waiting in closets for her return.

It also allowed her to fantasize about a certain cowboy who'd been escorting her to all of her holiday events these past several weeks.

Cayden Chappell.

He'd readily agreed to let her stay at the homestead for a few days, which Ginny had done. Her mother had not understood why she'd want to stay so far away from the distillery, but Ginny sure had enjoyed her limited freedom and the tiny break from everything Winters and Sweet Rose.

She'd told a little fib and said she was staying at Olli's. She had for one night, and she was almost forty-six years old, so she didn't feel too badly about the little white lie. No one had gotten hurt with it, and she relished the fact that she had something her mother didn't know.

Her imagination went wild right now, warring between the serial killer scenario and having Cayden for a real boyfriend.

He'd asked her some hard questions back in October, and she'd told him that she was interested in him. They'd never gone out, though, not unless it was a social engagement she was required to attend as the reigning queen of Sweet Rose Whiskey.

"Just like tonight's party," she murmured, noting that Sarge had laid his head back down and neither of the other two dogs had heard anything to alert them.

She stood from the vanity where she'd been painting on her perfect face and turned to look at herself in the full-length mirror mounted to the wall. Tonight, she wore a deep midnight blue dress with plenty of sequins across the bodice. The sparkle hid a lot of her extra weight across her very barrel-like middle, and Ginny lifted up onto one toe and looked at the line in her calf from the resulting use of her muscles.

She had great legs; she knew that. They seemed to be the only part of her body—along with her arms—that didn't store fat. When she worked out, she lost weight from her legs, arms, and neck first. It was much harder to slim down through her torso, and Ginny had honestly given up.

Most mornings, she shimmied into her workout pants to lift weights and do core training with a professional trainer. She sometimes walked a circuit around the property, which was a mile and a half loop. That way, she could tell her mother she worked out, though no one needed to know about the bags of mini candy bars she had stashed in various places around her house, in her office, and even in the glove box of her car.

Sometimes she just needed a Snickers to make it through one more meeting, or a Twix to endure a phone call later in the day.

Tonight, she hadn't eaten yet, because this Christmas Eve party was a formal dinner and dance for all employees at Sweet Rose. Mother had been planning it for months, and the only way anyone in the family would've been able to get away with not coming was if they'd died.

She inhaled slowly and put both feet back on the

ground. Tonight, she'd show up with Cayden, and he'd get to see all the Winters in action.

Dread filled her, and she said, "Come on, guys. Let's all go out so you're good for a while."

Each dog jumped down to follow her, Minnie, the littlest, running ahead of Ginny as if going out to the back yard to take care of business was akin to attending Disneyland. Ginny held onto the railing as she went downstairs, careful to not let her heels catch against the rug as she walked.

In the kitchen, she opened the sliding glass door the dogs used and left it open as she stepped over to her clutch to make sure she had what she needed that evening. A sigh filled her body. She didn't need anything but herself and her phone, and Ginny didn't own a single dress without a pocket.

The gowns she owned never had pockets, but she hired a woman named Louise to sew them in so Ginny could go to anything and have her hands free. Mother would expect her to have a clutch tonight, though, as that was what Southern socialites simply did.

Ginny was tired of all of it. She wanted to wear sweatpants and eat almond ice cream bars while she watched some trashy reality TV until she was so tired, she fell asleep. First, she'd have to buy some sweatpants, and second, she'd have to ask Olli for the best reality TV show to binge-watch.

The doorbell rang right when she clasped closed her empty clutch and remembered she hadn't spritzed on any of the perfume Olli had sent her home with last week.

Get Your Man was supposed to work amazingly well, Olli claimed. After Ginny had stood in Olli's perfumery, helping her label candles and bottles of perfume for the last shipment that would arrive before Christmas, complaining that Cayden had cooled considerably toward her, Olli had run up to the house and brought down her personal supply of *Get Your Man*.

In your hair, Olli had told her. *Along your collarbone. Make him lean it to smell that, and then, bam.* She'd snapped her fingers, a joyful smile on her face. *He's yours.*

Ginny wished.

She also ran her fingers through her perfume-less hair as she went to get the door. The dogs came inside, one of them barking while the others just slid on the hardwood as they met it. Their steps became more sure, and the clicking of claws accompanied her through the cavernous living room to the huge foyer, where she opened the door.

Cayden stood there in a deep, rich tuxedo, and all Ginny could think about was kissing him. Her smile felt like the most normal one she'd worn in months, and she had the crazy idea of making up a horrible illness, texting her mother that she simply couldn't make it, and asking Cayden to drive her to the nearest store that sold sweatpants.

She'd change, and he'd sit with her while she ate that ice cream and watched that reality TV. She'd eventually fall asleep, her legs across his lap, and everything in the world would be absolutely right.

His eyes slid down to her bright red heels and back to her face. "You're stunning," he said.

"Merry Christmas," she said, her smile instantly turning fake. She hated that, and she forced it from her face. She didn't want to be fake with Cayden, and in that moment, it was as if someone had thrown a lightning bolt at her.

It struck her straight through the chest, sending truth through her whole body.

She'd been fake with Cayden Chappell. Every date was a show. Every dinner for someone else, not the two of them. Every text and phone call an arrangement for the next lie she was going to tell through her body language, her plastic smiles, and her multiple body shapers that made people think she weighed ten pounds less than she really did.

"Come in," she said, her voice quivering slightly. "I'm not quite ready."

"All right," he drawled, easily stepping past her through the enormously wide doorway. Ginny closed the door as he picked up all three dogs, chuckling as they licked his face and neck. He'd come to pick her up at this monstrosity of a house before, and he seemed fairly comfortable here.

Comfortable enough to take the wiggly dogs into the living room and sit down on the couch with them, still talking to them in a low voice and letting them act like psychos as they all tried to get him to rub them first.

Ginny quietly slipped upstairs, her mind racing. In her bedroom, she pulled her phone from the pocket that had been sewed in the dress right above her heartbeat and quickly tapped to call Olli.

"Hey," Olli said, her voice bright. Noise in the background indicated she was at a party of her own. Of course she was. The Chappells were having their big family get-together tonight. Cayden hadn't invited her to it, but he'd said he'd had to work some serious magic to get out of attending.

He claimed to have a mother as intense as Ginny's, but she knew that wasn't true. Wendy Winters was a special breed of intense, even when she tried not to be.

"What's going on?" Olli asked. "Aren't you at your company party tonight?"

"In a few minutes," Ginny said. "I need your help for a second."

"No problem. They're just arguing about how often they used to go to some fishing hole."

Ginny could hear Olli rolling her eyes in her voice, and she smiled. "I've just realized that I've been pretending with Cayden. It's no wonder he hasn't kissed me yet." She stepped over to her vanity and picked up the bottle of perfume Olli had given her last week. She hadn't been out with Cayden since then, so she hadn't used it.

"You've got the perfume on, right?" Olli asked.

"I forgot," Ginny admitted. "I told him I wasn't quite ready, and I came upstairs. We're going to be late now, and I just don't care."

She turned away from the mirror, because she didn't want to see her unhappiness. The way it coursed through her whole body was debilitating enough.

"Ginny," Olli said quietly. "When are you going to tell your mother you need a break?"

"I'm going to get one," Ginny said. "The moment the

clock ticks to twelve-oh-one on January first." She honestly wondered if she'd make it that long, and she told herself it was only one more week.

Just one. She could do it.

"Just two sprays," Olli said, not calling Ginny on the fact that there was literally no break in sight for someone in her position. "Into the air, remember? Then you stand there and let it settle into your hair. One big spray in front of you, and you step through it."

Ginny did what her best friend said, envisioning the how-to videos Olli had been working on with Renlund United. She'd won a major grant with the massive home goods and distribution company, and she was going to single-handedly change how and when women wore perfume, one spritz at a time.

"Okay," Olli said. "Now, I want you to go downstairs and tell Cayden what you just told me."

"Which part?"

"The part where you've been pretending. Tell him you don't want to pretend, and you'd love to have him over for dinner, just the two of you."

"I can't," Ginny heard herself saying.

"Of course you can." Olli gave a loud laugh. "Ginny, you command a governing board of fifteen. How many of them are you afraid of?"

"None."

"Then why are you afraid of one cowboy?"

"I'm not afraid." Another lie. Another thing she hadn't known until that moment.

"I have to go, but I want you to text me on the way to the event and let me know if you did it or if you chickened out." Olli said something to someone else as she hung up, and Ginny looked at the bottle of perfume in her hand.

One more spray wouldn't hurt, and she committed what Olli called the cardinal sin and sprayed it directly onto the skin along her throat.

Downstairs, she found Cayden standing in front of the bulletin board where Ginny tacked all of her nieces' and nephews' artwork, cards, little gifts, and anything else they gave her that she could put on the wall.

She stepped next to him, the hint of his cologne touching her nose and setting her desire on fire. She focused on Clara's note and pointed to it. "This was her first attempt at writing cursive." She smiled fondly at the joined letters.

"It's great," Cayden said. "How many nieces and nephews do you have?"

"Nine," she said instantly. "Harvey has four kids. Elliot, three, and Drake has the twins."

He looked at her, but Ginny couldn't meet his gaze. Her blood felt too hot, but that could've been because he was the most handsome man she'd ever met, or because of what Olli had advised her to do.

"Should we go?" he asked. "We're already a little late."

"I don't care," Ginny said, immediately sighing. She studied the bright yellow star Grace had poured gold glitter onto. That thing had flaked glitter onto Ginny's floor for a week before it was all done, and she grasped onto that memory and held it tight.

"Are we not going then?" Cayden asked, his voice smooth and proper.

"No, we'll go," she said. "I just wanted to talk to you for a minute." She couldn't stare at the wall while she did, and she turned toward him. He wore a pure black cowboy hat with his tux, and with his perfectly trimmed beard, those dark eyes, and a look of interest in them, Ginny found her courage.

"I've been pretending with you," she said. "Just like I do everyone else in my life. I hate it."

His eyes widened, and Ginny couldn't blame him. Even when they texted, she didn't tell him much. He hadn't even known how many nieces and nephews she had, and he'd been taking her to events all over Kentucky for over two months.

"When we go out, it's not really *us* going out," she said. "I tell you about all the major players, and what's going on at Sweet Rose, and my word, you must be bored out of your mind." She watched him for a sign that she'd lied, but he didn't give one.

"I don't like this," she said, really on a roll now. "I want to go out with you, just the two of us. No gowns, and no tuxedos, and no expectations. I want to wear jeans—or pants with an elastic waist—and the ugliest Christmas sweater I can find, and the ugliest pair of shoes in my closet, simply because they're comfortable."

"Okay," he said. "That's fine, Ginny. We can do that."

Hope lifted her eyebrows, and she knew reality would

come crashing down sooner or later. It always did. "Can we?"

"Of course."

"You never ask me out."

"You've told me you don't have time," he said, his eyebrows folding in over his eyes. "What did you expect me to do?"

"I don't know." She sighed and stepped into his arms. "I realized while we stood in the foyer looking at one another that everything between us isn't real. I slip into this fake persona when I'm with you, because we only go to events where that's who I am." She looked up at him, the warmth and width of his hands on her waist setting her pulse to bumping again.

"This is not your fault," she said. "It's mine. One hundred percent."

He nodded, not arguing with her, which only made Ginny feel worse than she already did. She drew in a deep breath of him, getting leather and something fresh, along with a bit of fruitiness that had her mouth salivating to taste his mouth and see what kind of toothpaste he used.

"All right," she said. "We better go." She started to step away from him, but his arms tightened around her, and she paused.

"You smell amazing," he whispered, dropping his head and letting the brim of his cowboy hat trail along the side of her head as he got closer to her. "I want you to know my feelings for you haven't changed. I am ready whenever you are, and I'm willing to wait if you're not."

She nodded, enjoying this close, intimate moment with him. She didn't have many of them, with very many people. Ginny could not remember the last person she'd felt like this with who she wasn't related to or who wasn't Olli.

"All right, Ginny," he said, his voice still soft and whole and perfect. "You can tell me about your nieces and nephews on the drive to the restaurant."

She nodded, though she didn't want to talk about her nieces and nephews. She sure did love them, because she knew she wouldn't have children of her own and they brought her some form of maternal joy. If she spoke of them too much, though, her sadness over her own situation would manifest itself, and as Ginny had no defense against Cayden and his questions, she'd end up telling him everything.

Would that be so bad? she asked herself as he helped her into her white, fake-fur shawl, offered her his arm, and led her outside to his truck. By the time she got there, she'd answered herself.

No, it wouldn't be so bad, but he might not want you anymore if he knows you can't have his children.

Chapter 18

Cayden Chappell once again dressed himself in a fancy suit and a shiny pair of shoes. He combed his hair though it would stay under a cowboy hat, and he brushed his teeth until they sparkled like pearls.

Downstairs, he went into the kitchen, whistling. He didn't mind the dressing up and the polishing. He got to see and smell and talk to Ginny Winters every time he did, and he glanced back down the hall that led to the two bedrooms here on the main level of the homestead. She'd stayed in Spur's bedroom for four nights back in October, and Cayden reflected on them often.

He'd enjoyed seeing her in the morning and helping her get a cup of coffee before their day really started.

He didn't hate the events she'd dragged him to this holiday season either. The food was good, as she'd promised, and she was great company.

Last week, at the Christmas Eve party, she'd admitted

what he'd already known: she was pretending with him, just like she did with everyone in her life.

He suspected she had one person she was herself with, and that was Olli Hudson. Chappell. Spur's new wife. Cayden knew Olli and had for years. He wasn't going to ask her what he should do to crack through Virginia Winters's tough external shell, though.

He was figuring it out, one event, one phone call, and one text at a time. "Almost there," he said to himself as he poured a bowl of cereal and started eating it.

The door down the hall that led to the garage opened, and a couple of people entered. They were both talking right over the top of one another, and Cayden recognized their voices as Ian and Conrad.

"...can you believe it?" one of them said.

"That horse is amazing," the other said. "Coming off the rail like that? Incredible."

Before he'd finished, the other was talking, and Cayden knew about what.

Somebody's Lady. Trey had texted late the night before Christmas Eve and invited everyone in the family to come watch the horse he'd been training for the Sweetheart Classic.

Cayden had gone, and he'd been impressed. The horse could run, that was for sure.

Trey had explained that it was her first race with other horses, as well as a crowd larger than four. He wanted them to be loud, and he wanted them to cheer. He wanted to see how Somebody's Lady did when confronted with distractions and competition, and if he'd been worried, after the race, Cayden wouldn't understand why.

"There you are," Conrad said, actually interrupting himself in the middle of a sentence as he entered the kitchen. "You should've seen Lady tonight. She finished three lengths ahead of Lost Boy."

"Wow," Cayden said, glancing at Ian, who wore an equally excited look in his eyes. "You realize we don't own Somebody's Lady."

"Trey does," Ian said, his voice taking on an arrogant pitch that annoyed Cayden. "He and Beth own her together."

"You know the Sweetheart Classic isn't a race to brag about winning, right?" Cayden asked next. He loved goading Ian, because the man thought he was the best horse trainer in the south. He was good—very good—but Cayden knew there was always someone better. That was just the way of the world.

Even when he felt like he was doing well, there was someone doing better. On the flip side of that, there was someone doing worse, and he'd become content with his middle-of-the-road life.

At least until he'd met Ginny Winters. Now, he just wanted more. He wanted more dogs so he'd have something to talk with her about. More time with her. More opportunities to see her and what kind of incredible fashion she wore. More information about her. More insight into what made her tick. More knowledge of what she liked and didn't like, what she wanted and what she dreamt about. More, more, more.

"It has a purse of five hundred grand," Ian said, stepping past Cayden and opening the fridge. "Aren't you going out tonight? Why are you eating cereal?"

"I like cereal," Cayden said, not about to admit that the party tonight only had "light appetizers." He simply filled his mouth with the puffed rice cereal he loved and watched Ian look for something to eat.

"Mom has food at her place," he said casually, knowing that would earn him a scowl

Sure enough, Ian tossed him a growl and a scowl and said, "I'm ordering from HanaRamen. You want something, Conrad?" He pulled out his phone and started tapping to get to the delivery app.

Conrad didn't answer, his own phone completely dominating his attention. Cayden stayed out of it, because he wasn't going to order from the ramen noodle place in town that had everyone talking about how much they enjoyed Japanese food.

Cayden did not enjoy Japanese food, and he'd take a good medium-rare steak, a baked potato with all the toppings, and tall glass of lemonade for any meal, any time.

"Conrad," Ian barked, and Conrad looked up from his phone.

"What?" he barked back. "Can you leave me alone for five seconds? Hilde posted something." He strode into the living room, and Cayden and Ian exchanged a glance.

"What did she post?" Cayden asked, still watching Ian.

Conrad had dated Hilde for most of this year, but she'd broken up with him just after Thanksgiving, citing something about how she needed time to "find herself" and "decide what she wanted."

Conrad had been devastated, and he'd slept in Spur's room for a week just to be around the older, wiser brothers. His words. Cayden suspected he'd stayed here so he wouldn't have to answer any questions.

As Blaine and Cayden were the only two in the homestead now, and they both usually kept their questions to themselves, Conrad had found some measure of relief with them.

"She's going to India again," Conrad said. In the next moment, he sucked in a breath. "Look at this." He jogged back over to Cayden and shoved the phone in his face.

Cayden leaned away to be able to see it. "What am I looking at?"

Conrad shifted the phone to Ian, who actually took the device. "It's Jason."

"No," Cayden said, plenty of shock moving through him. "Do you think she's dating him?"

Conrad took the phone back from Ian, his face an angry, angry mask of himself. "Yes, I do. They're going to India together." He looked up and into Cayden's eyes, pure anguish in his. "I asked her to go to the East Coast with me, and she 'couldn't get away.'"

"I know." Cayden wished Blaine were here. He'd know what to say to help Conrad, and he'd likely pull him into a hug too while he whispered those things.

"You don't want her," Ian said.

"Yes, I do." Conrad glared at Ian and started for the door he'd come in a few minutes ago. "I'm going home. If you want a ride, you'll have to come now."

Ian looked at Cayden again, who could only shrug. "I'm coming," he said, and he quickly followed Conrad. Cayden put his bowl of leftover milk in the sink and leaned into the counter, palms down.

"Help him," he prayed. "I don't know what he needs, but if there's anything I can do to help, let me know, and I'll do it." He gazed out the window, the sky already dark. "Help me tonight, too," he added. "With Ginny."

He didn't know precisely what he needed help with, but he knew he needed it. With the prayer done, he grabbed his keys and made the long drive to Ginny's. Her house glowed with white lights Cayden felt sure would be able to be seen from space, and four valets waited in her massive circular driveway.

"Hello, Mister Chappell," one of them said as he opened his door. "Miss Winters has asked me to allow you entrance through the front door this evening."

"Thank you," Cayden said, feeling himself slip into his alternate persona too. He disliked it as much as Ginny had said she did, when they'd spoken last week. She'd talked to him on a more normal level on the way to the party, but the Real Ginny Winters had disappeared the moment she'd emerged from his truck and taken his arm.

He wasn't the first to arrive at the party she was hosting tonight, and she'd wanted it that way. He went left toward the front door while a few other guests went right to go around the house to the library entrance. Behind him, the valet said, "Eastwood is inbound."

Cayden's step stuttered, but he refused to turn around and ask him what that meant. He went up the steps to the door, unsure if he should knock or simply go in. There was a party inside, and he didn't need to ring the doorbell.

He twisted the knob and opened the big front door that probably weighed a hundred pounds. The foyer was dark, as was the living room. Light spilled out of the library, along with light music and laughter, and Cayden took a moment to just bask in the quiet out here.

His attraction to Ginny was inexplicable. He'd tried to make it iron flat and make sense, and it simply didn't. He barely knew her, even after all the events they'd been to, and he wanted so much more than she'd been able to give him.

Maybe you'll always want more than she can give, he thought, his worry and fear multiplying by the microsecond.

He wondered where Ginny put her dogs when she hosted big parties like this, because he loved her dogs, even though they were small. He'd always considered himself a big dog person, as they had a few dogs around the ranch and none of them weighed less than fifty pounds.

A moment later, someone came through the door leading into the library, and Cayden's soul lit up at the sight of Ginny.

"Happy New Year," she said as she came toward him. Tonight, she wore a more casual pair of black slacks, and Cayden smiled at her as she approached. She'd paired her slacks with an off-white sweater with a bright blue star on the front of it, and he'd never seen her dressed like this. The parties required more formal attire, and he suddenly felt overdressed.

He took off his jacket and held it at his side. "I don't think I need this. You look amazing in that sweater."

She brought the scent of vanilla, peaches, and something bright with her, and Cayden leaned down to breathe her in as they embraced. "Thank you," she said. "You look great too."

"No jacket, though, right?"

"No jacket," she said. "We're just chatting and eating and drinking."

Her chatting and eating and drinking happened in a much different way than his, though, and he couldn't even imagine his brothers here at all. They'd be wearing jeans and boots, laughing too loud, and double-fisting candied popcorn or M&Ms faster than anyone could refill them.

He and Ginny were so different on so many different levels, but Cayden didn't care. When he held her in his arms, he didn't care about the opposite ends of the world they came from.

They breathed together, and Cayden let a real smile drift across his face.

"Is everyone here?" he asked. "Your brothers and their families?"

"Just Drake and Joan," she said. "The others have their own parties tonight."

"Your mom?"

"Yes, she's here," Ginny said, stepping back.

Cayden quickly secured her hand in his and smiled at her again. "Great." He stepped forward, and Ginny went with him. He draped his jacket over the back of her couch and they went into the library together.

Cayden had never been in the library, but he'd seen such rooms on movies like *James Bond* and *Beauty and the Beast*. This library was all of those and more. It had two levels, with a domed ceiling that an enormous chandelier hung from.

Comfy-looking couches dotted the space from where he stood to the other side of the library, but many people stood around chest-high tables where flutes of snacks sat. Waiters moved through the crowd with drinks and trays of appetizers, and Cayden was reminded of the big fundraisers his mother sometimes made him attend for the ranch.

People who owned racehorses had plenty of money too, and everywhere Cayden looked, he saw money. More money. Pure money.

He edged closer to Ginny, because while he had a lot of money too, he felt completely out of his league next to her. "You know all of these people?" he asked.

"Yes," she said. "On some level."

"A business level?"

"Most of who I know comes through Sweet Rose, yes," she said, her smile painted perfectly in place. Ginny was flawless, and Cayden found himself wanting to peel her back layer by layer until he found the real her.

"Come meet a few people," she said.

He went with her, because he wanted to be at her side.

He'd gotten very good at meeting people he'd never see again in his life, and he too had a perfectly pleasant smile, a firm handshake, and several topics he could hit on for easy conversation.

She took him around the room, introducing him to people she knew. This man she'd met when they'd gone on a midnight hike in the same group. That woman she'd met when she'd bought half their whiskey supply as her husband's final wish before he'd passed away. This other person she knew because his grandfather had been working at Sugar Rose since he was sixteen years old.

Cayden actually enjoyed himself, and when Ginny threaded her fingers together behind his neck and said, "Dance with me, cowboy," he knew he'd go anywhere to be with her.

He grinned down at her, the bubble around them intimate and private. He saw through her façade for a moment, and he liked the woman underneath all the power, prestige, and perfume.

They swayed slowly, and Cayden kept her very close to him, right where he wanted her. His pulse had quickened in the beginning, but now it settled into a normal beat. "What's the first thing you're going to do on your vacation?" he asked.

"Find an off-the-wall place with great scones and honey butter," she said, her voice laced with a smile. "I hope they'll still be selling them when I roll out of bed about noon."

"What time do you get up now?"

"Oh, usually about six-thirty or seven," she said. "I don't

need any teasing about how late that is from the cowboy." She laughed lightly, and Cayden simply kept his smile on his face.

"It's winter," he said. "We sleep in during the winter too."

"Then I'm going to change into my swimming suit and find the least populated beach. I'm going to sit there and read and watch the water and daydream about moving to the Caymans permanently."

"Sounds nice," he said, spotting her mother as she came into view. He hadn't seen her yet tonight, and he immediately tensed.

Ginny felt it and pulled away slightly. "What?"

"How long will you be there?" he asked, keeping one eye on Wendy Winters as she moved over to a group of people Ginny hadn't introduced him to.

"A week," she said, glancing around.

"Mm," he said. "I miss you already."

That brought her eyes back to his, and he leaned down to press his cheek to hers. It had to be nearly midnight, if the tiredness in his bones and the way his face hurt from smiling so much was any indication.

Just then, someone called out, "Only five minutes."

Ginny pulled away suddenly. "Excuse me, Cayden. I need to get the ball on the screen." She bustled away from him, and he stood in the middle of the dance floor, alone, watching her weave through the crowd to the wall without the fireplace. She picked up a remote and pressed a button.

A screen started to lower, and the chatter in the room

increased. More buttons got pressed, and the next thing Cayden knew, the big ball in Times Square came up on the screen. A timer in the bottom of the frame said they only had one minute and twelve seconds until the New Year.

Ginny didn't have long to get back to his side. He didn't want to welcome a new year into his life without her. He wanted to kiss her as the very first thing he did in this next year, because if he did, he felt certain he'd be able to end the year with her too.

He started walking toward where she'd been to lower the screen, and with only twenty-three seconds to spare, they met up again. He took her hand and looked at her. She grinned up at him, and when the countdown reached ten, he joined his voice to those already chanting.

He kept his eyes on the timer on the screen, and when it reached zero, he cheered with everyone else, laughing though he wasn't sure why. He did know what he wanted to do next, and he tugged on Ginny's hand, pulling her closer to him.

Cayden had kissed other women before, and while it had been a while, he thought he could still do a decent job. He took Ginny into his arms, smiled down at her, noted the way she'd tilted her head up toward him, and bent his head so his mouth lingered near her ear.

"Happy New Year," he murmured. "Here's to it being a great year for both of us." He moved one hand up her arm and behind her head, holding her where he wanted her so he could kiss her.

He hesitated as Ginny whispered, "Happy New Year, Cayden," and then his mouth touched hers. Pure heat poured through him, along with plenty of joy. A hint of relief did too, because she hadn't pushed him away or dodged his advances.

She very much kissed him back, and Cayden fell into a familiar rhythm, his nerves quieting with his success. He wanted to accelerate the kiss, but he knew where he stood, and he knew who with.

He kissed her as long as he dared, and then he broke the connection he very much wanted to make again—and very soon. She giggled and pressed her forehead to his collarbone, and Cayden opened his eyes and glanced around to see how many people were staring at him and Ginny.

Hardly anyone, as they were all celebrating in their own way. Hugging, high-fiving, kissing, and laughing. They didn't care about him and Ginny.

Then his eyes met Wendy Winters', and Cayden actually flinched. She started toward him and Ginny, and Cayden bent his head again. "Your mother is headed this way."

Ginny stepped out of his arms, and he watched her shake all of the improprieties off as she prepared to receive her mother. "Mother," she said, dropping his hand as she stepped over to the older woman. She kissed her on both cheeks, her hands on her shoulders. "Happy New Year."

"To you too," Wendy said, her eyes cutting toward Cayden. "Hello, Mister Chappell."

"Evening, ma'am." He reached up and touched the brim of his cowboy hat. Then he extended his hand toward her to shake. She barely put her fingers in his, and he got a very cold feeling from her.

"Ginny, come meet Tristan Pike. He says he's been looking for you all night."

Ginny's shoulders squared, and Cayden drew in a breath and held it. Time seemed to stretch, and then she said, "No, thank you, Mother."

Wendy's eyes widened. "No, thank you?"

Ginny pressed in close to her mother and said something. She turned back to Cayden, a slightly wild look in her eye. "Will you please stand with me by the door as people start to leave?"

"Of course," he said quietly. He nodded at Wendy. "Ma'am."

Ginny slipped her hand through his arm, glared at her mother, and together, they turned and walked away.

"What was that about?"

"She's trying to set me up with Tristan Pike." She scoffed, the sound angry more than frustrated. "Like that's going to happen."

"She saw us kissing just now," Cayden said. "I don't think she approves."

"I told you she wouldn't."

"I still don't understand why." He could throw a party like this; he simply chose not to. As he stationed himself next to the door and next to Ginny, he realized that very simple fact.

He *chose* not to have parties like this. He chose not to hire waiters and invite over "friends" he barely knew. He'd rather spend the night with his rowdy brothers and bowls of candy they had to refill themselves.

It didn't make Ginny's choice worse than his; it just helped him realize that he wasn't beneath her or all that different from her. He just chose differently than she did.

After only a few minutes, Wendy stepped to his side and linked her arm through his. Surprise ran through him, and she kept her smile on her face as she started talking.

"I don't approve of your relationship with my daughter," she said. "She carries far too much responsibility to be tied to a man like you. I can see you like her, and it's obvious she is quite charmed by you."

Cayden didn't know what to say, and he had the distinct feeling he wasn't meant to say anything.

"She will do almost anything to spite me these days, so I'm going to appeal to you to end this before things get too out of hand." She laughed as an older couple hugged her, and she said a few things to them before they left.

Back at his side, she trilled out anther girlish giggle that didn't fit her age or sophistication. "I trust you're a smart man, Mister Chappell. I know you do many good things for the horse country and community. We are simply from opposite sides of Lexington, and if you respect her at all, you'll make sure tonight is the last night you two are seen together. Horses and whiskey simply do not mix."

She stepped away, gliding toward a man he'd seen her with earlier. She kissed him on both cheeks and continued on her way.

Cayden's chest vibrated in a strange way. Wendy Winters had just asked him to break-up with Ginny. He'd just kissed her for the first time, and he wanted to do it again.

How could he possibly break-up with her?

How can you not? he wondered. He didn't know everything about the Winters or Sweet Rose Whiskey, but he knew enough to know there would be serious consequences for him if he disobeyed Wendy Winters. They were old blood in the Lexington area, as was his family.

She was right that horses and whiskey didn't mix, because he'd never heard of anyone in his family dealing with anything whiskey or distillery related.

A break in the guests leaving gave him an opportunity to turn toward Ginny. "Do you need help cleaning up?"

"I've hired people to come in tomorrow," she said.

Cayden nodded, his emotions storming through his whole being. "I think I might head out then. I've got a long drive to get back to the ranch."

"Oh, sure," she said. "I'll walk you to the door."

"It's fine," he practically yelled at her. He needed to calm down, and he forced his voice into a lower volume. "I know the way, and you have guests still." He bent down and kissed her cheek, noting the way she pressed into his touch and put her hand on his arm. "Thank you for inviting me, Ginny. Have fun on your trip."

He straightened and adjusted his hat. "I can't wait to hear all about it." He grinned at her, his indecision raging through him. Then he turned and crossed the entire library and entered the living room. It was cooler and quieter out here, and he got a few moments of relief as he walked through the semi-darkness to the front door.

Outside, it was even colder, and he took a deep breath of

the winter air on the front porch. He went down the steps and waited for his truck, and it wasn't until he was halfway back to Bluegrass Ranch that he realized he'd left his suit coat on the back of her couch.

He had to go back for that, right?

"Dear Lord," he said aloud. "What am I supposed to do?" Tonight felt like the first time they'd both been real with each other, and Cayden didn't want to break-up with her.

He told himself he didn't have to figure it all out tonight. She was leaving for the Caymans in a couple of days, and she'd be gone a week. He had some time, but he knew all that time would get him was ten sleepless nights.

Chapter 19

Trey stood next to the passenger door of his truck, watching TJ skip toward him. "Look at me skippin'," he called to Trey.

"Looking good," Trey said with a smile. He took TJ's backpack and swung it over the side of the truck and into the back. "How was your art class today?"

"So good," TJ said, already standing on the running board though the door was still closed. He jumped down and Trey wished he had the energy TJ did.

"Yeah? Did you paint?"

"We got to use the stencils again." TJ hopped on both feet, and Trey couldn't help grinning at him.

"Remember we're goin' to the zoo today?"

TJ looked up at him, his eyes wide. "Yeah!"

He'd clearly forgotten, but it didn't matter. TJ didn't have to keep track of his schedule, and he had no plans for his afternoon anyway. Trey laughed and opened his door, saying, "Come on, bud. Get in. My mom and dad are waiting for us."

TJ ran over and started climbing into the truck. Trey helped him the last few inches the way he always did, and he told the boy to buckle his seatbelt before he closed the door. As he went around the front of the truck, he hoped he wasn't making a huge mistake by taking TJ to the zoo with his parents.

His mother and father were simply thrilled, of course, but Trey had his doubts about the "fun" this afternoon would hold. Beth had said TJ loved the zoo, and she was spending the afternoon with her sister as they put up a month's worth of freezer meals for next time Sally's husband was out of town.

His parents waited on the bench outside the zoo's entrance, just as they'd said they would. Trey held TJ's hand as they crossed the parking lot, his stomach clenching and unclenching with every step he took.

His mother stood the moment she saw them, her nerves apparent from paces away.

"Okay," Trey said. "There they are. Remember their names?"

"Julie," TJ said. "And Jeff."

"That's right."

"They have names that both start with J, like me and you have names that start with T." He beamed up at Trey, and Trey's heart filled with love for the little boy. Things between him and TJ had gone right back to normal, because children were the most forgiving humans on the planet.

He and Beth were in a good place, but it was a different place than where they'd been before Christmas. Somebody's Lady was doing amazingly well, and he felt like the race and the horse were all he and Beth ever spoke about now. They went over their schedule for the day, and they talked about the horse.

He couldn't wait until the Sweetheart Classic was over, and he hoped he could hold his patience for the next three weeks until the bell rang and the race began.

He'd been sleeping in the same room as Beth...sometimes. Half the time he fell asleep on the couch, and she left him there. Another part of the time, he read to TJ until they both fell asleep, and when he woke up, he went to the bedroom next door to his, and not across the hall to hers.

He wasn't sure why. They hadn't spoken about it. She'd come after him, and he'd forgiven her. There was just something about their relationship that was more...clinical now. *It's become about the race and nothing else*, he thought.

"Hey, baby," Mom said, and Trey pulled himself out of his thoughts. She bent down and put her hands on her knees. "You must be TJ. I've heard so much about you." She wore a grin two sizes too big, and Trey wanted to tell her not to try so hard.

She didn't have any grandchildren yet, as she'd been pointing out to Spur and Blaine and Trey and anyone else who would listen for the past few years. TJ wasn't technically hers either, but he could see she liked him a lot already.

TJ pressed into Trey's leg, and he nudged him away. "It's my momma, TJ. She's not gonna bite." He looked up at her, silently asking her to stand up. She did, and Trey passed TJ's hand to hers. "He loves strawberry lemonade."

"Oh, well, let's go find some of that," his mom said. "It's kind of cold for strawberry lemonade, though. Maybe you'd like some caramel hot chocolate?"

If she pumped him full of sugar, TJ would love her forever.

Trey followed them, hugging his father hello. "TJ," he said. "This is my daddy. Come say hello."

The little boy skipped back to him, all smiles now. He looked up at Trey's father, who smiled down at him. "Nice to meet you, TJ," he said. "I'm Jeff."

"Trey told me," TJ said. "My grandpa has white hair like yours."

"I bet he does." Daddy chuckled. "What do you want to see first? I saw a webcam of the polar bears, and they're always out now."

"I like the zebras," TJ said, looking back at Trey. "Can we see the zebras?"

"I'm sure we can, bud," TJ said, though he had no idea where the zebras were in this zoo. He hadn't been here in years, as he'd had no reason to come and walk around while looking at animals.

His life had changed so much in such a short time, and he didn't mind all the things that were different now. He actually liked them. He had a meeting with Spur after the Classic, in which he'd talk about his future at Bluegrass.

He did want to train horses, and he wanted to work Beth's ranch with her. He wanted to make it into *their* ranch, a place they both called home and both cared about.

They still hadn't talked about any of that either. She was still in the middle of birthing season, and she'd been paying more and more attention to her sister and sister-in-law. She made dinner every night, but the conversation rotated around TJ or Somebody's Lady, and Trey felt more distant from her than ever.

He let his parents handle TJ for the afternoon, and he simply trailed along in their wake, smiling when he needed to and speaking if he had to.

"Let's go to dinner," his mom said once they'd seen all they wanted to. That, and the zoo was closing. She clearly didn't want to allow the afternoon to end, and Trey liked that they wanted to spend time with TJ.

"Let me text Beth. She might have dinner at the farmhouse."

"Maybe we could go there." Mom's face lit up like a star, and Trey realized how far away he'd kept them.

"Let me call her," he said, tapping to dial her instead of text. He paced away from his parents and TJ while the line rang, his pulse bobbing somewhere behind his ribs.

He wasn't sure why he was nervous for her to spend more time with his mom and dad. His mother had done the catering for their wedding, and it had been fine. More than fine—great, even.

"Where the devil are you?" she asked instead of using the normal greeting of hello. "I've called you four times. We're all waiting at The Bluebell."

Trey's heart skipped a beat at the anger and annoyance in her voice. "What? Why?"

"It's my brother's birthday," she hissed. "How can you not remember this? I told you at least four times this week."

"I'm at the zoo with TJ and my parents," Trey said, frowning. "I told you at least four times we might go to dinner. You never said a word about it." Trey didn't normally forget things like this. The thing was, neither did Beth.

"I thought the zoo was next Wednesday," she said.

"No," he said. "It's been on the calendar forever on today."

She sighed like he was being difficult on purpose. "Well, can you come meet us?"

He looked over his shoulder, his mother's hope so bright. "Can my parents come?"

"I—why would they want to?"

"Because," Trey said, his voice taking on a sharp quality. Sometimes Beth could be infuriating, and he felt like she was arguing with him right now simply because she could. She'd done that way back over the summer when he'd first started bringing TJ back to Dixon Dreams on a more regular basis.

"They love your son," he said. "They want to be part of our lives." He ducked his head. "You know, Beth, we spend a lot of time with your family, and you haven't said two words to my mother since she planned and executed the dinner at our wedding."

She pulled in a breath, and Trey hated that he'd been the

cause of the sting he knew was now spiraling through her chest.

"I'm going to tell them they can come," Trey said when she remained silent. "It's dinner at a restaurant, Beth. They're perfectly capable of speaking to people like adults. It'll be fine."

"Fine," she clipped out. "How much longer should I tell everyone you'll be?"

"To The Bluebell? Probably thirty minutes. We're at the zoo."

"I heard you the first time," she said, another sigh accompanying her statement. "I wish you would've answered the first time."

"I didn't get any calls," he said. "There must be a dead zone in the zoo somewhere."

"Mm hm," she said as if she didn't believe him.

He needed to get off the phone before he said something he'd regret later. "I'll see you soon." He hung up before she could say anything else, and he turned back to his parents. "We need to get to The Bluebell. I apparently forgot about Beth's brother's birthday." He scooped TJ into his arms. "Come on, bud. We need to hurry."

"Oh, okay," his mother said. "I understand."

"You're invited," Trey said, smiling at her. "The Bluebell is good, right?"

"I love The Bluebell," Daddy said. "They have this open-faced brisket sandwich that they put all these caramelized onions over, with tons of gravy." He smacked his lips so loudly that Trey laughed.

"Great," he said. "We'll meet you there?"

His father didn't walk particularly fast, and Trey needed to get to the restaurant quickly.

"Sure," Mom said, and Trey leaned over and kissed her cheek.

"Great. See you there." He started walking much faster, swinging TJ up onto his shoulders. "Come on, bud. Your momma's not happy with us."

"Because we're late," TJ said, not asking. "She don't like it when we're late."

"Doesn't," Trey said automatically doing something Beth often did. "It's doesn't, Teej. She *doesn't* like it when we're late."

"She doesn't like it when we're late," he said correctly, and Trey thought the boy was speaking the honest truth.

* * *

"I'm just saying," Trey said much later that night. "We don't talk about stuff anymore."

"Yes, we do," Beth argued. "We just got the dates wrong this one time."

"It's more than that," Trey said, sighing. He sat in the recliner in her bedroom, and she was propped up in bed. He should've just laid down and taken an hour-long catnap before he had to head over to the ranch for Lady's training. He'd been able to schedule some practice time during the daylight hours, but the horse focused better at night, and Rob was willing to come at their usual time.

Trey saw no reason to rock that boat. Horses could be fickle and unpredictable, and with only a few more real races in Lady's future before the actual event, he needed to keep her as focused and stable as possible.

"What do you mean?"

"I mean we haven't talked about what I'll do after the race. We haven't renamed this place. We haven't talked about having more kids. Heck, I don't even sleep in here but a quarter of the time." Even when he did, there had *only* been sleeping happening in here.

Beth stared at him, her eyes searching for something on his face. "I didn't…"

She didn't what? Trey got up, ready to go across the hall and get at least thirty minutes of his power nap. "I need to get going," he said. She obviously didn't pay that close of attention to his schedule, so how would she know he was far too early to head to Bluegrass?

He felt the exact same way walking toward her bedroom door as he had leaving the farmhouse over Christmas. She wasn't going to call him back or follow him, he knew that already. He really needed to stop fantasizing that she would.

That's not fair, he thought. She had come to Bluegrass Ranch to find him and talk to him when they'd had their very public disagreement.

They had a very explosive relationship, and Trey really liked it. He liked the passion she'd poured into her kiss that day, and he liked that she'd come right up into the truck and onto his lap to tell him how sorry she was.

They'd always had this great chemistry between them,

and he suspected that the arguing fueled that chemistry.

"Trey," she said when his hand touched the doorknob.

He paused and ducked his head, almost looking back at her out of the corner of his eye but not quite. "What?"

"I've been trying so hard," she said. "Sally's just needed me a lot lately."

"I'm sure she has," Trey said, trying to decide how much to say. "I need you too, I suppose, and I guess it just feels like that doesn't matter to you."

"It does."

"I don't know if it does or not," he said. "I think what matters to you is winning the Classic, and this farm, and TJ. I don't think I've managed to get myself on the list at all." He hated saying that, but as he did, the truth of his words sank deep into his heart.

"I think you like having me around, because then you're not alone. I pay for the cowboys, and they've done an astronomical job cleaning this place up. You like that. You like that I go pick up TJ, and you like that I take him with me out on the ranch so he's not in your hair."

He opened the door, the paper-thin walls around his heart shattering. "But honestly, Beth? I think any man could show up here and do what I've been doing, and you'd be happy. It's not *me* that makes any of this special. I just happen to be the cowboy you knew best."

"That is not true," she said, but her voice carried no real weight.

"I'm late," he said, taking a step out into the hallway. "Don't wait up for me."

Chapter 20

Beth did wait up for Trey for as long as she could. He didn't come back to the white farmhouse down the road from Bluegrass Ranch, and she eventually fell asleep on the couch. She woke when she heard TJ singing somewhere else in the house, and she took a moment to open her eyes, because the light was so bright.

That meant one thing: They were late for school.

She heard TJ's bare feet skipping down the hall and into the kitchen, and he still sang as if it were a weekend and not Thursday.

The sucking sound of the fridge releasing as her son opened it met her ears, and she groaned as she got to her feet. "Hey, bud," she said, her eyes searching out the clock on the stove.

Eight-twenty. Kindergarten began in forty minutes, and TJ was still in pajamas, his hair sticking up. The drive to school took twenty-five minutes, and Beth warred with herself over rushing him through getting ready, not going at all, or simply taking him late.

"Momma," he said, his face brightening. "Can I have that sugar toast?"

"Sure," she said, though she already pitied his teacher. "We have to leave for school very soon. I'll make the toast while you go get dressed."

"Okay." TJ skipped back down the hall, and Beth took the bread out of the drawer and set it in the toaster. She could get dressed after she drove TJ to school, and she'd text Trey to find out if he was still okay getting him that afternoon.

She hated that she had to text; Trey had been getting TJ from school for a couple of months now. Every day, without being reminded or asked. It was just part of his day.

Her stomach vibrated, but she pressed her teeth together and took out the cinnamon-sugar mix Trey had put together. It was at least ninety percent sugar, which was why TJ called it sugar toast. She normally only let him have it on Saturdays, when he was going to go to Bluegrass with Trey.

Everywhere she looked, Trey existed.

In the fridge, his protein shakes took up half of the top shelf. On the counter, his phone charger waited, and he'd brought an air fryer into the house simply to reheat their leftovers.

"I have a microwave," Beth grumbled as she went down the hall to check on TJ. She'd likely find him playing with his Army figures, having forgotten all about his task of getting dressed.

Sure enough, Beth found TJ jumping on his bed, one fist curled around one of his commanders and the other slapping the wall with every leap upward. "Teej," she said, trying to be patient and kind. "We're going to be late. You'll have to eat your toast in the car as it is."

She opened the top dresser drawer as she kept talking. "Stop jumping on the bed and come put on some pants."

"Okay, Momma." He jumped down, the resulting crash making Beth think he'd broken right through the floor. He hadn't, of course, and in fact, he wasn't hurt at all.

It took a few minutes to get him dressed as he barely worked with her. Sometimes he had to suddenly go to the bathroom right in the middle of getting dressed, and sometimes she couldn't find both of his shoes. Today, thankfully, he stood there and let her pull his shirt over his head while he put his arms in.

He stepped into the jeans, and both of his shoes sat by the door. "All right," she said. "Let's get your backpack and your toast and go." She detoured into the master bedroom to grab a jacket and a pair of shoes, and she met TJ in the kitchen.

The toasted bread wasn't very warm, so she stuck it in the microwave for ten seconds, buttered it, and sprinkled a very little bit of the sugar mixture on it. "Here you go."

The backpack was almost as big as TJ, but he hardly carried anything in it. They got in her SUV, and if she could hit all the right lights, she'd get her son to school on time.

He reached for the volume button on the radio and said, "Momma, can you put on that Chicken Little singalong?"

"Yep," she said, tapping a couple of things on the screen to get the soundtrack to come up. It did, and TJ sang along merrily during the drive to school. She pulled into the circle drive out front and turned down the music. "Go on, baby. See you after school."

He opened the door and spilled down to the ground as she called, "Love you."

"Love you too!" He slammed the door and ran toward the building. Beth watched him go, her heart expanding with every moment that passed. She couldn't sit in front of the elementary school all day, though, so she sighed and got back on the road back to Dixon Dreams.

"Dixon Dreams," she said aloud. They needed to rename the place if Trey was going to think of it as his. He'd been right that they hadn't named it.

Alone in the car, Beth couldn't help that her mind lingered on all the things he'd said to her last night. "Of course he's on my list," she said, but even she wondered if that were true.

She'd been working for the farm and TJ for almost three years now. She'd been ignoring her family. Unintentionally, but the result was the same. Now that she'd started to focus on them, she'd started ignoring Trey.

Tears gathered in her eyes. "I don't know how to do it all," she said. Something had to give, didn't it? There were only so many hours in the day. Only so much energy she could expend. Only so much she could manage before the load was too heavy for her to carry.

"Lord," she whispered. "Have I been using Trey Chappell for his money and friendship?"

He did pay for the cowboys that now worked her ranch, and they did do absolutely amazing work. She turned into her driveway, the edges of the gravel crisp and perfect. The fences were straight and painted a bright white. The horses in the pasture seemed happy enough, and everywhere she looked, she found a well-functioning ranch.

She parked out front and got out, stalling in her sandals and pajamas right there in the driveway. Trey hadn't come back to the house last night, which meant he'd slept at Bluegrass Ranch.

He'd never done that before, and Beth wondered if things between them were really that bad. "Probably," she muttered. She'd just missed how bad it was, because she was trying so hard to be there for Sally, as Mick was in New Jersey this week, chasing down another new lead on a job. He'd interviewed for it over the phone, and they wanted him to come tour the facility and do another round of talking.

Beth enjoyed spending time with Sally and Kait, because then she didn't feel so alone. Trey had helped with that too, of course, and as she went up the steps to the front porch, the guilt filled her from top to bottom.

Her Christmas pillows still sat on the swing on the front porch, and she detoured toward them. She picked them up and took them inside. The storage closet in the corner held most of her seasonal decorations, and she took out her winter and Valentine's Day pillows and replaced them with the holiday ones she'd brought in.

She sealed the bag and went back outside. She fluffed everything and set out a blue and white pillow with a bright yellow scarf across the front of it. Above the scarf, in the same wavy, curved letters that indicated movement, it read *let it snow.*

It had snowed a few inches last week, and because the temperatures didn't get above freezing, most of it still lay on the ground. She tucked her hands into her jacket pockets and sighed as she sat on the swing.

She pushed herself with her toe to get herself to start to sway back and forth, deciding to take another few minutes to figure out what to do. Before she could come to a course of action, Marc came around the corner of the house with Walter.

"...we find her, we'll tell her. Simple as that."

"It's not going to be simple," Walter said.

"Beth deserves the facts," Marc said.

She stood up, the swing squeaking as she did. "Marc?" she called. How did she have the courage to face him and the potential problem he and Walter needed to tell her about?

"There you are," Marc said, swinging his attention toward her. "I thought you were going to be in the fields to decide what to rotate this morning." He went around the porch to get to her.

"I'm having a slow start this morning," she said.

Walter chuckled. "Boy, I feel that deeply in my soul." They all laughed as the two cowboys came up the steps, where Beth met them.

"Go on, now," she said, realizing how very much she

sounded like Trey when she tacked that "now" on the end of her sentence. "I heard you talking. Something not simple going wrong?" She looked between the two of them.

Marc cleared his throat, exchanged a glance with Walter, and said, "You've got a pipe leaking somewhere. There's a sheet of ice just past the chicken coop for the third morning in the row."

"That's not good."

"No, it's not," Marc said. "Because we don't know where it's coming from. Could be a sprinkler pipe going out to your units. Could be something in the coop—that would be the best option. Could be coming from the barn on the other side of the pasture, or the pump that feeds the pasture, or—"

"The stable," she and Marc said together. "I get it." She pulled in a breath and ran her hand through her hair. She needed to shower and get dressed. Pull her hair up and get to work. "I'll call Jake." She smiled at Marc and Walter. "Thanks, guys. For everything."

They nodded, and Beth turned to go into the house. She showered quickly, dressed in her usual ranch clothes—jeans, undershirt, sweater, thick socks—and dried her hair partially before pulling it into its customary ponytail. She'd probably still regret only drying her hair halfway, as the temperature wasn't supposed to get above forty today.

She'd cover her head with one of the beanies Kait had given her for Christmas, and she hurried down the hall to the kitchen. She knew better than to go out on the ranch and work without eating, so she grabbed a breakfast bar from the cupboard, pulled on her steel-toed boots, and shrugged into her jacket.

Outside, she dialed Jake Harguss, the best plumber in Dreamsville.

"Beth Dixon," he said with a smile in his voice.

She couldn't help smiling too. "You always sound so happy to hear from me," she said. "Because you know I'm going to pay your mortgage for the next six months with my plumbing problem."

He belted out a laugh, and Beth joined in with him. In the past, she'd be on the verge of tears with a plumbing problem, and while she felt slightly sick, it was nothing like the tension and terror she'd experienced in the past.

The last time she'd called Jake, it had cost her thousands of dollars to fix the problem, and she quieted as a bit of trepidation filled her.

"What's the problem?" Jake asked.

"I've got an ice skating rink behind my chicken coop," she said.

He exhaled, and Beth didn't like the sound of that. "I can come this afternoon and bring the cameras."

"Really?" Beth had expected him to say he was booked for the next two weeks. Jake was always busy, because he was fair and extremely good at his job.

"Yeah, I just had Penelope Sykes call and say her husband fixed their issue, and she was on my schedule for this afternoon. Let's see..."

Beth waited while he tapped and muttered, said something to his secretary, and then said, "How about one-thirty or so?"

"That would be great," Beth said.

"The sun's supposed to be out today," he said. "Take some pictures so I can see what I'm dealing with on the largest scale possible."

"Okay," Beth said, heading down the steps to the back sidewalk. "I'll go do that now. My cowboys told me of the problem. I haven't actually seen it yet."

"Text me," Jake said, and the call ended.

With a mission now, Beth kept her strides long and quick, arriving at the chicken coop only a few minutes later. Around the back, she found the ice skating rink she'd spoken of, and it was bigger than she'd like.

She tipped her head back and looked up into the bright blue sky. "Really?" There were only a couple more weeks until the Sweetheart Classic, and she already had enough problems. "Don't I have enough to deal with?"

She did, but that didn't matter. Life threw curveballs whether she was ready to receive them or not. She pulled out her phone and got snapping the pictures Jake wanted, then she got on the four-wheeler and made the rounds through the fields, taking notes on what she'd planted last year.

Then, right on the seat of the quad, underneath the winter sun, she made notes of what she'd plant in each field in another month or two, and which fields she'd leave for a year or two to rest and rejuvenate.

She still had sixteen cows that needed to have their babies, and with her notes taken, she buzzed over to the field closer to the house where they were. They were all standing, munching happily on the grass they could get to through the snow. Tad had fed them already this morning, and as Beth's stomach growled, she remembered the breakfast bar in her pocket.

She took it out and unwrapped it, finishing it as she returned to the shed and put the four-wheeler back in its place. She was on chicken duty, and that meant her birds hadn't been fed yet, nor had their eggs been collected.

Completing jobs she'd done hundreds of times in the past didn't take a lot of brain power, and Beth once again found herself thinking of Trey. She hadn't called him or texted him yet, and she got her phone out to do that.

Can you still get TJ from school today? she sent.

It didn't take long for him to respond. *Yes.*

One word, and Beth frowned at her phone. She didn't know what to say. *Thanks* seemed appropriate, and she sent that. She hadn't had time that morning to think about dinner, so she hadn't taken anything out of the freezer to thaw.

Will you be home for dinner? She stared at the words for a good ten seconds before she sent them, and this time, Trey's answer didn't come flying in instantly.

Beth got back to work, sweeping out the barn and moving onto the stables and the horses that needed fresh bedding and fresh water.

"Beth?" a man called, and she looked up, surprised.

"Here," she said, exiting the stall where she'd been working. Jake stood in the doorway down the aisle, and a smile sprang to her face. "I didn't realize what time it was."

"I'm a little early," he said. "Is now okay?"

Beth set the shovel against the wall. She'd moved Draconian next door to Harold's stall, and the two horses got along great. "Sure," she said, already moving toward him. "How are you? How's Sapphire?"

"She's great," he said. "I've been training her to roll over, and she does *not* like it." He chuckled. "I sure do miss Danny and his way with dogs."

"So do I," Beth said, but her emotions didn't surge to the surface. She reached Jake and embraced him. "It's so good to see you, though I wish we were meeting for one of those salty breakfast sandwiches and not that I'm about to show you a major plumbing problem."

He laughed too and stepped back. She looked into his eyes, searching his face for any sign of Danny. They'd been best friends growing up, and Jake had been a good friend to Beth once she'd married Danny.

He'd come to take TJ to a baseball class at the recreation center once after Danny's death, but Beth had never called on him again. At least not for personal help. If she had a plumbing issue, yes, she called Jake Harguss.

Looking at him now, she wasn't sure why she'd cut him out of her life. In the next moment, she realized she hadn't done that. Not intentionally, the exact same way she hadn't meant to ignore Trey or make him feel like he wasn't important to her. Of course he was, just like Jake was.

"I'm sorry," she said. "I should've kept in touch with you

better."

Jake ducked his head. "I'm fine," he said. "Things are going fine."

"Nobody special in your life yet?" she asked, linking her arm through his as they stepped out of the stable.

"I actually started seeing someone just before Christmas," Jake said. "Don't ask me her name," he added quickly. "I'm not going to tell you. It's still very new. I think we've gone out three or four times."

"In a whole month?" Beth asked. "Six weeks, Jake. Why so slow?" She must not be that special if he wasn't anxious to see her every night.

"She lives in Louisville," Jake said. "That's all I'm going to say. Come show me the ice skating rink." He grinned at her and they made the trek over to the coops. She just gestured toward the sheet of frozen water, which had shrunk in the past few hours.

He circled it, nudging it every few feet with the toe of his boots, as if that would tell him where the leak was located and how to fix it. When Jake returned to her side, he said, "We'll go through the drain in the coop first. Work out from there."

"Okay," she said, turning to lead the way into the little shed next to the henhouse. It was pretty cramped in there for even one person, as Danny had built it as an attachment to the henhouse simply as a mudroom to clean up in before he continued into the farmhouse from the muddy outer fields.

Jake lifted his case to the sink, balancing it on two edges to open it. "Oh, Henri said to say hello."

"That's nice," Beth said. "How is she handling Georgie being in school?"

"I think her exact words were 'I've died and gone to heaven.'" He laughed, and Beth joined in.

"I think I felt the same way," she said. "Though the drive definitely adds time to my day."

"Yeah." Jake bent over his case to get out the equipment. "I heard you have help now." He lifted his eyes to hers for a moment, pure curiosity there. He quickly looked away, back to the long cable he began to feed down the drain.

He tapped the screen in the top of the case, and something gray and garbled came up.

"Uh, yes," Beth said. "Trey Chappell and I got married."

"I heard," he said.

"We didn't invite anyone but family," she said. "He has a lot of brothers, and the deck was full."

"That's what Cheyenne said."

"Cheyenne Wool?" Beth asked, surprised. "How would she know?"

"I don't know. That's just what she told Henri, who told me."

Great, Beth thought. Everyone in town had been talking about her. She didn't know what to say, so she said nothing.

"You know," he said, still feeding cable down the drain. "I thought about asking you out, but I wasn't sure if it would be weird."

Beth blinked, because she had not given Danny's best friend a second thought. Her heart started to pound, and she certainly didn't know how to respond. She tried to back up simply to put a little bit more space between them, but there was nowhere for her to go.

"I don't know if it would be either," she said quietly.

"Guess we'll never know." He flashed her a smile and reached the end of his cable. The case teetered and started to slip. They both lunged for it, because it was a very expensive piece of equipment, and she didn't want it to get broken on her ranch.

His boots had plenty of mud on them from his trek around the edges of the frozen water, and he slipped. He grunted as his hip hit the floor, and Beth tripped over his now-splayed legs.

She landed right on top of him, a cry coming from her mouth. He steadied the case with one hand and said, "Don't move. It's right against your back."

Beth froze, though she wanted to scramble around until she could find solid ground and get to her feet.

He strained to balance the case, and when he did, he relaxed onto the ground. He started to chuckle and said, "Ow. I'm old."

She laughed too, relaxing into her position though her kneecap was resting uncomfortably against the cement and one hand pressed on Jake's chest.

Their eyes met, and Beth knew she needed to get out of that shed right now. "Okay," she said. "Let me—"

"What's going on?" someone asked, and she whipped her attention over her shoulder to see Trey standing there, his tall frame and wide shoulders filling the doorway and blocking her only escape.

Chapter 21

Trey couldn't believe what he was seeing. His heartbeat had been accelerating minute by minute since he'd picked up TJ forty-five minutes ago. He'd been looking for Beth for the past twenty minutes, and now he had to find her laying on top of another man.

"There you go," that other man said, and Beth managed to press one hand against the wall and get to her feet. She faced him, taking the single step toward him to close the distance between them.

Behind her, the man got up, and Trey finally saw who it was. "Jake Harguss?" he asked, his eyes flying back to Beth. "You and…wasn't he Danny's best friend?"

"Can you back up?" she asked, her voice pitching up.

Trey did what she said, because he wasn't sure what else to do. He'd stayed at the homestead last night, unable to face coming back to this farmhouse. He'd never intended to stay away forever, though.

He'd always planned on picking up TJ and bringing him home for lunch. He, Beth, and Trey usually ate lunch together, but today, the house had been empty and there had been no lunch. He'd told TJ he'd be right back, and knowing the child, he was probably scrambling eggs and burning down the house by now.

He actually glanced toward the farmhouse to check for smoke. None rose into the sky, and he turned his attention back to his wife. Beth had left the shed, though, and she'd walked away from it. She stood several paces away, staring out over her ranch.

Jake came out of the shed too, a black case that looked like a bulky briefcase made of hard plastic. "Nothing here," he said. "Where should we look next, Beth?" He glanced at Trey. "The stables?"

Beth didn't move, and Trey stuck out his hand. "I'm Trey Chappell. I'm not sure we've ever met formally. My brother probably handles all our issues. Spur?"

"Sure," Jake said, smiling. "I'm Jake Harguss." The two shook hands, and Trey gritted his teeth so he wouldn't squeeze the other man's hand too hard. "You've got a leak somewhere here. I'm just trying to find it."

"It's not my ranch," Trey said automatically.

"What?" Beth demanded, and Trey hadn't realized how closed she'd come. "This is too your ranch. *We're* working the ranch together."

He looked at her, trying to decide if he was going to get into this with her right now. He didn't decide fast enough, and Beth threw her hands up and scoffed. "Let's try the stables, Jake," she said. "Are you going to take TJ to Bluegrass, or should I go check on him? Jake doesn't need my help to find a leak."

"I..." Trey didn't know what to say. He did take TJ to Bluegrass with him every afternoon, and they returned to Dixon Dreams about four to finish a few things before dinner. He was a good friend to Trey, and he did whatever Trey said.

Pathetic that one of his best friends was a five-year-old.

"I am not doing anything with Jake Harguss," Beth said, plenty of anger in her tone. "*We* have a giant sheet of ice behind the chicken coop, and I need him to find the leak and fix it. *We* need to sit down and talk about what we want to call this ranch, and *we* need to talk about what we both want."

"Do you want to do that?" Trey asked.

"Yes," she said, raising her chin slightly. "I am not perfect, Trey, but I am trying so hard. For so long, my focus was on TJ and the ranch. I didn't have room for anything else. I do now, and I'm really struggling with where my time and energy should go. I know you don't get the attention you deserve. I know my sister doesn't." She wiped quickly at her face. "I'm trying, and I've been praying all day for the right solution, and I just don't know what it is."

"Okay," he said.

"I know how to feed chickens. I know how to clean out stalls, so I've been doing that. The fact is, I might just not be good at being married." Her chest heaved, and she didn't brush away the tears this time.

Trey frowned, unsure of where this particular item had come from. "Beth," he said. "What does that mean?"

"I'd been married to Danny for only three years before he died. He was already cheating on me. I obviously wasn't a good wife—at least not good enough for him. Maybe I'm just not good enough for anyone, as we've only been married for three months, and I'm already disappointing you."

Trey felt the fight go out of him. "You don't disappoint me."

"You're a liar," she said. "You can't take it back now, Trey. I know now. I know I'm not good at being married, and maybe...well, maybe I should just get used to that fact and learn how to be happy alone."

Trey didn't know what to say. Beth wiped her face and let her hands fall back to her sides. "I'll go make sure TJ has lunch."

"I can do it," Trey said. "Then we'll go to Bluegrass."

She shook her head. "No, it's okay."

"Beth, I don't mind."

"*I* mind," she said. "*I* mind, Trey. If we aren't going to be a family, then you don't just get to take my son to your ranch as if he's yours. He's *not* yours. He's mine."

Trey felt his whole world slipping away from him, and no matter how hard he tried to grasp it, he couldn't. Something lodged in his throat, making it difficult to breathe. "I want us to be a family."

"No," she said, backing up a step. "You love *TJ*. You've always loved TJ more than me, and I've been fine with it, because I never thought there'd be anyone who would love him like I do, or who would want him along with me." She sniffled, and Trey wanted to wrap her up and tell her he'd been wrong.

"I guess I didn't realize that someone would want him *more* than me."

"I don't want him more than you," Trey managed to say, but the words were weak and soft coming out of his mouth. "I just—I got a little frustrated, that's all. I'm allowed to be frustrated."

"So am I." She folded her arms, and Trey watched her wall herself off.

"Okay," he said. "You don't want me to take TJ for the afternoon, then?"

"No," she said. "I'll take care of my son. If he tries to come over there, you send him straight back here, do you hear me, Trey Chappell?"

"Yes, ma'am," he said, ducking his head. She'd said once that if she didn't text him, TJ didn't have permission to be at Bluegrass Ranch. She hadn't had to do that, because TJ had been taking the boy with him with her full knowledge and blessing.

"Thank you," she said quietly.

"Beth," Jake called from around the corner of the barn, and they both turned that way. "Found it."

"Praise the Lord," Beth said, moving toward Jake quickly. Trey watched her walk away and disappear around the corner of the barn. He suddenly had no idea what to do now. He had plenty of work to do at Bluegrass, and then he was to come back here and help Beth transfer hay from her hay barn to the loft in the stables so she could feed the horses for the rest of the winter.

She didn't want his help with TJ. She likely wouldn't want his help with the hay tonight. She didn't want him anymore, and Trey wondered if she ever really had. As long as he even had that tiny inkling infecting him, he wouldn't be able to stay here.

They'd agreed to pretend going into the marriage. He didn't want to be pretending coming out.

He quickly went back to the house, finding TJ sitting on the couch with his game machine. The boy didn't even look up at him, and Trey went past him to the mouth of the hallway. He turned back and looked at the dark-haired child, his heart positively tearing right in half.

He did love that little boy. He loved him with his whole heart. He loved Beth too, and he hated that he'd pressed her into a corner where she felt like she wasn't good at being married, and that she'd disappointed him.

Maybe he had been disappointed. Maybe he had been upset. Maybe he'd stayed at Bluegrass Ranch last night to get some distance. "Only for clarity of thought," he said to himself.

"What?" TJ asked, and Trey shook his head.

"Nothing, bud." He walked down the hall and into the bedroom where he'd first stayed when he'd moved in here. He didn't have much in this room, but he had kept his suitcase in the closet here. He pulled it out and picked up the few things he'd left in this room.

Then he took the suitcase across the hall and started

filling it with his clothes and toiletries. He was sure he'd forget something—he had food here that he'd bought for himself. Things Beth didn't even like. He wasn't going to go through every cupboard and closet. Whatever he left behind, she could throw away.

He hesitated, because he didn't want to make more work for her. He simply didn't know what else to do. Breaking off an engagement was easier than this, and that had been the most horrific situation of his life. This would be worse, and to tell his parents...

Trey's chest hitched, and he zipped the suitcase closed, desperate to get out of the farmhouse before Beth returned.

He did so quickly, leaving his suitcase by the front door and jogging back to TJ. He picked the boy up off the couch in one swift move and held him so tight that TJ grunted. "Hey," he said, his voice a squeak.

"Sorry," Trey whispered, his throat so narrow. "I love you, buddy. Okay? No matter what happens, or what tomorrow is like, I love you."

"Okay," TJ said. "I love you, too, Trey." He hugged him tight too, and then Trey set him back on the couch. He picked up his game machine and went right back to it.

Trey watched him for another moment and then said, "Be good for your mother," before leaving.

He drove away from Dixon Dreams, so many things up in the air while his heart was down in the bottom of his boots.

* * *

"No, we're still doing the Classic," Trey said a week later. "It's only nine days away." He looked at Rob, glad when the man nodded instead of asking another question.

"I just wasn't sure," he said. "When I talked to Beth, she said the two of you weren't really talking right now."

"Mm." Trey wasn't going to go into all the details. He'd been sleeping and living at the homestead on Bluegrass Ranch since their discussion last week, but he'd texted her several times.

They were respectful exchanges. He'd asked her to please let him finish with Somebody's Lady and run the Classic.

She'd agreed.

She'd said he had a case of protein shakes at the house and that she'd put them on the front porch for him to pick up at his convenience.

He had.

He'd told her he was willing to keep picking up TJ from school.

She'd said her sister was taking him, and it was a great time for both of them to visit in the evenings when Beth went to get TJ from Sally.

Trey tried not to think about the life he'd enjoyed at Dixon Dreams. If he dwelled on it for too long, he lost hours of his day, and he simply didn't have that luxury.

"I'm going to take her around the other way," Rob said, drawing Trey back to the training track. It had been dry for a few days now, which meant their outdoor track was prime running ground.

"Okay," Trey said, looking down at his clipboard. "We

need to press her to do two laps at almost race speeds, and then we'll be done." He had note after note of Lady's training over the last few months, and he didn't know what he was going to do once the Classic ended.

He wanted another horse to train, but he hadn't spoken to anyone at Bluegrass about it.

Rob rode off on the black and white horse, and Trey climbed into the stands to watch them. They had fifteen minutes of their time left, and then Trey would have to get next week's reminders out to everyone. He had March's schedule to review and finalize, and he needed to call no less than six trainers about the stable spots that had opened up in their row houses.

How he'd managed to keep up with his work here, keep TJ at his side, and go home to Beth in the evenings, he'd never know. "It was a miracle," he said aloud, feeling the truth in those words the same way he'd felt the Lord telling him to help Beth by marrying her.

He sat down in the stands and hung his head as he put his elbows on his knees. "What do I do now?" He wasn't happy, and surely everyone on Earth knew it. The Lord had to as well.

God didn't answer him, something Trey was used to, but this time, he didn't let the bitterness and disappointment touch his heart. He simply looked up and found Somebody's Lady out on the track.

Rob ran her fast, and she did whatever he asked her to. They were an incredible pair, and Trey saw with earthly eyes the answer to his prayers—and to Beth's.

A few minutes later, Lawrence sat next to him. "Spur's on his way up."

"Yeah? Why?" Trey didn't take his eyes off Rob. He let Lady slow and start to cool, leaning over and saying something to her. He'd get her to the starting gate, and they'd get their race in.

"He said he wants to see how Lady's doing."

"Mm." Trey suspected Spur would ask all kinds of questions about him and Beth. Blaine had only asked a few, and Cayden had simply listened. Trey had told them that it just wasn't going to work out, and that once the Classic was over, he and Beth would likely end up divorced.

There was no *likely* about it. It was going to happen. He was just trying to decide how much time he should let go by before he filed. He didn't want anyone at the Sweetheart Classic to know or even suspect that the marriage wasn't real, as he'd heard about the founders of the race stripping winners of their titles in the past.

Word had gotten around about him moving back to Bluegrass, but only Lawrence had spoken to him about it.

"How are you doing?" he asked.

"I'm hanging in there," Trey said, smiling at his brother. For that single moment, it felt like heaven opened and the sun's rays shone down.

"Good," Lawrence said. "I suppose that's all we can ever do."

"Yeah." Trey sighed. "What about you? Gonna survive working with Cayden?"

"Doubtful," Lawrence said dryly. "He's been so sour since breaking up with Ginny."

"Did he actually break up with her?" Trey asked. "I never did hear that story."

"According to him, he just didn't call her once she got back from her trip to the Caymans. But." He really hit the T. "She didn't call him either, so he's just Grumpy Gus all the time. It's exhausting."

"I wonder why she didn't call," Trey said. "She seemed to like him a lot."

"He's smitten with her still," Lawrence said. "I told Blaine we need to stage an intervention, and Blaine just laughed. Said he liked having all ten of his fingers, thank you very much."

Trey laughed, because Cayden was always saying stuff like he'd do some physical damage to someone if they didn't leave him alone.

"I'm not sure why Wendy Winters doesn't like him," Trey said.

"Yeah, well, he's organizing this huge event just to impress her, though he won't admit it." Lawrence pointed to his right. "There's Spur. And now I have to deal with some marketing firm we've never worked with before, and it'll be up to me to be Cayden or I'll get chewed out." He sighed, but he wasn't wrong.

Spur came down the aisle and sat down next to Trey. "Heya, boys."

"Spur," they said together.

"How's she look?"

"Great," Trey said. "I think we're going to win."

"I can't wait to see it," Spur said.

"Rob's setting her up now," Trey said, nodding to the track. The three of them sat side-by-side and watched as Rob took his time with Lady. Finally, he nodded, and whoever was up in the booth sounded the bell.

Lady took off like it was a real race, and Trey pulled in a breath at her magnificence.

"She really is amazing," Spur said. "You've done a phenomenal job with her."

"I think it's mostly been Rob," Trey murmured. The hole in his chest widened when he realized that he'd lose Somebody's Lady as soon as the Classic ended. He'd have to take her back to Dixon Dreams, and he'd likely never see her again.

"Beth should keep training her," Spur said. "She's not a Derby horse, but she could win the smaller purses at a dozen races."

"I'll tell her," Trey said, a blip of hope entering his heart. If Lady kept racing, maybe he could keep training her.

They fell silent after that, and Trey didn't dare look down at his phone, which he'd started as close to the sounding of the bell as he could. She ran like the wind on the far straightaway, and Trey tensed as the corner approached.

He'd seen Rob let her loose many times before, but he always felt the need to hold his breath.

Lady entered the turn, ready to break, but Rob held her back. He could see the concentration on the jockey's face, and the desire to run on Lady's.

"There she goes," Lawrence said the moment Rob let her go.

"Holy cow," Spur said as horse and rider flew off the corner. She'd tightened her turn, and Rob was sure he could get her into a position where she wouldn't touch another horse.

Lawrence stood up and started cheering, and that made Trey smile. He wanted to do the same, but he was too nervous. Lady looked like a winner as she streaked toward the finish line, which would be more pronounced at the actual Classic.

She crossed it, and Rob put up his fist. By then, Trey couldn't see his face, but he felt the joy in the fist pump that would surely show on the jockey's face.

"I can't believe it," Spur said. "Makes me wonder if we have some sleeper racers in our row houses."

"Why don't you let Trey find out?" Lawrence asked as he sat back down.

Trey looked at him, his eyes widening. "Lawrence."

"Come on," Lawrence said. "You want to train horses, and you're good at it." He leaned forward to see Spur on Trey's other side. "He should be training horses. He can obviously do it and keep up with his track scheduling. He can go through our horses and train the ones you think aren't Derby-worthy, but that could still bring home good money."

"Half a million dollars is nothing to sneeze at." Spur kept his eyes out on the track, and that raised a red flag in Trey's mind.

"Nothing at all," Lawrence said, and the conversation suddenly felt rehearsed.

"You guys," Trey said. "Come on. You've talked about this before."

"So what?" Spur said, some of his favorite words. "You are good at this, and maybe you should be training our lower-level horses."

"Just what I want," Trey said dryly. "The seconds and thirds. Tell me Conrad or Ian could've taken this horse from where she was to what we just watched."

"Of course they can't," Spur said. "They're divas, just like the horses they work with. You wouldn't like working with the divas, Trey. That's not you."

"He's right," Lawrence said.

"Oh, stop it," Trey said, growing surlier by the sentence.

"They're not seconds, besides," Spur said. "They're great horses, and they'll love you, and you'll love them. And if you can get Rob to sign on with us full-time, you can keep twenty percent of any winnings you guys get. He can keep ten."

Trey sucked in another breath and finally turned to look at Spur. "That's triple what you pay Ian and Conrad."

"You'll not say a word to them about it," Spur said. "Rob will have to sign an NDA too." He wore a dark look. "The last thing I need is to deal with diva racehorses and diva trainers in the family."

Trey blinked a couple of times, trying to find a downside to what Spur had just proposed. He couldn't find one right now. "I'll think about it," he said, because he knew better than to just accept something without at least a little bit of time to examine things from all sides. He'd also like to pray about it, strange as that still was to him.

"What are you guys wearing for that photo?" Lawrence asked.

Spur practically growled next to Trey, which almost got him to laugh. "There's a wardrobe specification," Trey said. "Didn't you get your shirt?"

Trey had received his blue, black, and white plaid shirt in the mail, and it had fit great. He'd been told to wear clean, "as new as possible" blue jeans, clean cowboy boots, and a dark cowboy hat.

"I got it," Lawrence said. "I meant, are you going to put on your fancy belt buckle?"

"I am," Trey said. The city was taking a picture of the eight Chappell brothers and putting a giant billboard up on the highway leading into Lexington. That required a big, shiny belt buckle.

"I think I will too," Lawrence said.

"Just don't be late," Trey said. "Cayden said that about fifty times, and while I know he's a little overbearing about some stuff, this feels important."

"No one will be late," Spur said.

"You'll likely have to stand in the middle," Trey said. "Just start gathering your patience right now."

"Great," Spur said, standing up. "Can't wait for the Classic."

Trey looked at Lawrence, and Lawrence looked at Trey.

"What he means is he can't wait until this picture is over," Lawrence said, grinning.

They both laughed, but Trey had to agree. Once the photo had been captured, Trey could stop getting a million reminders from Cayden.

* * *

The photo for the billboard got taken without much fanfare, and the Sweetheart Classic arrived in record time. Trey met Rob and Somebody's Lady in the row house where she'd been living for a few months. "How'd she do last night?"

"Great," Rob said. "She's ready." He stroked the horse's neck, a fond smile on his face. "I'm going to miss this horse. She's got a special spirit."

Trey looked at Somebody's Lady, his own fondness moving through him. "She sure does." He reached into his pocket and pulled out a butterscotch candy. Her ears perked right up, and her lips drew back.

"You're going to spoil her," Rob said.

"It's one candy," Spur said. "The race isn't for hours." He gave the treat to Somebody's Lady and stepped back. "Let's get going."

The Classic wasn't for hours, but they had to get to the track and check in, find their stall, and get used to the grounds. Lady would have track time, where she could practice and run, and Trey had almost paid the overnight fee to be on the grounds last night.

He'd decided he didn't need to spend the money on

that. He'd called Jake Harguss's office to ask about the plumbing bill at Dixon Dreams, and he'd paid the seventeen hundred dollars for the pipe repair.

If Beth knew about it, she hadn't texted to say.

Trey didn't want to think she knew and hadn't said anything. He also didn't want to think about watching this race without her at his side.

It was a couples' race and the whole reason they'd gotten married in the first place. They should be together today. As he helped Rob get the horse in the trailer, along with all the gear they needed, he mentally composed several texts.

Once behind the wheel of his truck, with Rob in the passenger seat, he quickly sent a message to Beth.

You'll be there today, right? We should at least be seen together.

It wasn't the message he wanted to send, but Beth had been very clear in her feelings for him and what she thought of their relationship.

I'll be there, Beth said.

That was all. Trey would have to take it, because he couldn't force Beth to do anything she didn't want to do.

Chapter 22

Beth sat with her father and TJ for about a half an hour before everyone else showed up. Sally arrived with her children; Kait and Hugh each carried a child in their arms when they joined them only a few minutes after that.

Three rows ahead of her, Trey's parents sat. TJ had been down to talk to them at least three times, and even now, Julie turned and looked over her shoulder. Thankfully, her family started arriving too, and Beth had a hard time focusing on the early races as Chappell after Chappell arrived.

All seven of Trey's brothers had come, a few of them with women at their sides. She and TJ knew them—they'd all been at the wedding, of course. Julie had also hosted a family Christmas party that she, Trey, and TJ had attended.

None of them turned around to look at her, but TJ yelled down to Blaine, who turned with a smile. "C'mon down, bud."

"Can I, Momma?" TJ asked, and Beth couldn't tell him no. Her nerves were already frayed and tight, and she didn't need to deal with a cranky five-year-old. To make matters worse, TJ had asked again that very morning if they could invite Trey over for his birthday.

TJ would be turning six in just three weeks, and Beth wasn't even sure Trey knew. She hadn't told him, but she wouldn't be surprised if TJ had. To her knowledge, her son had not gone over to Bluegrass Ranch, and he'd started asking why Trey didn't pick him up from school anymore.

He'd asked every day this week to go over to Bluegrass, and each time, Beth had been able divert his attention to something else to keep him home.

TJ held the railing as he went down the steps, and Blaine pulled him right onto his lap. Blaine's fiancée, Tamara Lennox, handed TJ something, and everything seemed light and easy between them.

For a while there, Beth had enjoyed the same kind of relationship with Trey. She wanted it again. She missed him more than anything, and the only reason she hadn't been over to Bluegrass Ranch to get him back was because she hadn't told anyone in her family that she and Trey were separated.

If she had, Sally and Kait would've sat her down and told her what to do.

She didn't want to be told what to do. She wanted to follow her heart. She'd been thinking and praying for weeks, and she felt like an answer lay just on the horizon.

"Aren't you supposed to be down there with Trey?" her father asked, and Beth turned toward him.

"Yes. Do you see him?" Though she wore sunglasses, she shaded her eyes to look toward the ground.

"He just came out."

"That's my cue," she said, standing up. She actually had no cues; she and Trey had not worked out any system. He'd texted to say they should be seen together, and she'd agreed. She knew enough about how the Classic worked that she'd made a plan in her own mind about meeting him in the owner's space at track-level during the race.

She made her way down the steps, sweating though the weather was still fairly cool. A man stood at the gate leading into the owner's area, and she gave him her name. He checked something on his phone, and then smiled her through the gate.

She could barely return the gesture, and her mind felt fuzzy as she stepped past the guard. Trey heard the gate and twisted to look over his shoulder.

Beth's feet froze. Everything that had been wrong in her life was suddenly right. The answer she'd been searching for was right in front of her.

He turned all the way around, the smile on his face wide and wonderful. It was also very fake, and Beth remembered where she was, who was watching, and what was at stake.

Not only her ranch, but her reputation. Worst of all, her heart.

She took a step forward when Trey did, and he swept her into his arms. They breathed together, and Beth whispered,

"I miss you, Trey. I love you. You have to come back to the ranch. I'll do better. I'll figure out how to be the wife you need. Please."

He pulled away from her, his gaze coming to hers. He searched her face, and Beth did everything in her power not to cry. She wouldn't cry just seeing her husband who'd merely left earlier than she had that morning.

"You don't have to answer right now," she said, drawing together all of her courage. "Think about it. I want you, though. I miss you. I love you. I hope we win today, but I don't care if we do or not. I just want you to come home." She stopped when the announcer started talking about the main event.

Trey took her hand and they went up to the highest row in the owner's box. Other people were already there, and Trey shook a few hands and nodded to people. They all seemed to know him, and with her hand in his, they accepted her too.

He sat down with a sigh and said, "Here we go now."

It wasn't exactly what she wanted to hear, but just the sound of his voice made her smile.

It seemed to take forever for all the horses to come out, and she stood when Somebody's Lady was finally announced. She wore the number four on her flank, and she and Rob had been dressed in pink. She loved the sight of them, and a new kind of excitement built in her chest.

She suddenly had too much energy, and she couldn't sit back down. Trey stayed in his seat until only moments before the bell sounded, and they both watched as Lady exploded out of the gates, along with eight other horses.

"Go!" Beth yelled, unable to stop herself. Cheering sounded above her, and Trey chuckled at her side.

"My brothers are loud," he said, but Beth could barely hear him over everyone else yelling at their horse too.

Most of the owners didn't, though, and Beth told herself not to blink as the horses sprinted in front of her. There one moment, and gone the next, she followed them as they approached the first turn.

"She's in sixth," she said, her voice awed. She'd seen Lady run before, and she didn't like the back of the crowd.

"Rob will bring her out," Trey said calmly. He did take her hand though, and when he squeezed, Beth finally felt his nerves.

Sure enough, though, Rob brought Somebody's Lady off the rail and around two horses in just a couple of strides.

"She likes to chase on the second straightaway." Trey lifted up on his toes to see, but Beth had already switched her attention to the huge screen in front of her. Lady was in fourth now and gaining ground on horse number three.

"He's got to get her around two more before the turn," Trey said.

Beth didn't think they'd catch the lead horse, who was two lengths ahead of the horse in the second position. Lady was easily six or seven lengths behind the leader, and Rob got her around one more horse before the turn, not two.

"Here she goes," Trey said, his voice excited.

It was like Rob flipped a switch, and Lady finally got to

run. She leaned like nothing Beth had ever seen as she exploded around the corner, overtaking another horse within a stride. She was on the outside, so she didn't have to worry about running into another horse, and within three more strides, she was ahead of another horse.

Beth started screaming as the horses thundered toward the finish line. Somebody's Lady looked like she'd just started while the first-place horse had already started to fade.

"Come on!" Trey yelled, and Beth found herself screaming the same thing.

Lady drew up to the brown and black horse who'd been in the lead for the entire race. Her head reached the saddle, then his neck.

"Go! Go!" Beth screamed. The finish line was so close and yet still strides away. Lady just needed a few more.

The announcer was yelling; everyone added their screams to the fray.

Lady drew even with the leader, Rob spurring her on as he rode her to perfection.

The horses crossed the finish line, and Beth had no idea who'd won. The yelling and chaos quieted enough for Beth to hear, "It's a photo finish, ladies and gentlemen. What a race. Those horses can run, folks!"

Trey stood still at her side, his pulse in his neck throbbing.

"This is torture," Beth said just as the screen came to life. The footage was terribly slow, and both horses were clearly giving it their all. The announcer explained that it's any part of the horse that crosses the line first.

The finish line came into view, and they'd put a solid yellow line over it for the spectators. In the next moment, Beth knew.

Trey started to laugh, because he'd seen it too.

Lady was on the right track to be fully stretched out in her stride when she crossed the line. The horse beside her wasn't.

"She won," Beth said, actually dumbfounded. "I can't believe it." She turned to Trey and grabbed onto him, both of them laughing now. "She won!"

"There it is, folks. By about three inches, with an incredible stride and stretch, your Sweetheart Classic winner is Somebody's Lady!"

The crowd went wild, and Beth enjoyed the feel of Trey's arms around her as she looked up at the screen and saw Somebody's Lady frozen, her nose touching the yellow line while the other horse's wasn't.

Trey whipped off his cowboy hat and waved it, whooping along with the others in the crowd. "Let's go," he said, quickly smashing his hat back onto his head. He took her hand, and they left the owner's box. Someone led them down a sidewalk no one else was on, and she opened a gate Trey went through like he owned the place.

They'd been in the small alcove for only a few seconds before Rob rode Somebody's Lady into the space. She got dressed in flowers and a sash, and Rob lifted both hands above his head.

Trey grinned as he stepped over to Lady and stroked her neck. He reached up and shook Rob's hand, and he opened his other arm for Beth to step into. She did, and he held the reins while she held him, both of them smiling for all they were worth.

Pictures got taken, and the festivities started to wind down. Beth felt like she was on a roller coaster, with incredible highs and devastating lows.

There were no more races that day, and the crowd had started to thin. Not her family or his, though, and they waved up to them. Beth took a good look at everyone up there. She loved her siblings and her nieces and nephews. She loved her father. She loved her son.

She loved and wanted Trey. She couldn't imagine not being at his side for this—or for anything else life had to offer, good or bad.

He started to pull away from her, and Beth turned to see Rob swinging Lady around to leave the alcove.

"Trey," she said, suddenly desperate to go with him.

"I'll call you in a bit," he said. He took another step and then turned back to her. He swept his arms around her and kissed her, the movement hard and a little wild. The kiss only lasted two seconds, and he pulled away.

Their eyes met, but again, he only looked at her briefly. She didn't have enough time to decipher everything in his eyes before he turned and left with Rob and Somebody's Lady.

She sighed and went back through the gate. As she passed the Chappell family, they all cheered and congratulated her. Blaine stepped out into the aisle and hugged her, and Beth almost started crying. She wanted to belong to this good family, and she wanted it to be real.

Lawrence met her on the next step, and he hugged her too. "Trey's wondering if you and your family would like to come to Bluegrass for the celebration dinner."

Though surprise ran through Beth because she didn't know he'd planned a celebration dinner, she immediately answered, "Yes." She stepped back and met his eyes. "I can't speak for everyone, but TJ and I will be there."

Lawrence smiled and nodded, and Beth continued up the steps to her family. Hugh and Daddy engulfed her, and it was then that Beth realized what had just happened.

Her horse had won the Sweetheart Classic. Five hundred thousand dollars for her ranch.

No, she thought as she buried her face in her father's chest. *Our ranch. Mine and Trey's.*

She'd thought of the perfect name. She just needed to talk to him. Maybe if she told him again that she loved him, he'd forgive her and come home.

* * *

A couple of hours later, Beth pulled up to a pavilion on Bluegrass Ranch. "Wow," she said at the same time Hugh said, "Who has a pavilion on their property?"

"The Chappells," Beth said. Julie flitted around, moving bowls and utensils, giving directions to her sons, who did what she said, and stepping over to her husband and pressing a kiss to his forehead.

She got out of the SUV and reached to open the back door so TJ could get out too. He went running toward the pavilion, where a couple of the brothers greeted him. She felt strange walking up the sidewalk with Hugh and Lucas but without anything in her hands. She'd offered to bring something, but Julie had insisted they had everything covered.

"Hello, sweetheart," Julie said, receiving Beth. She kissed both of her cheeks and looked at Hugh.

"This is my brother," Beth said. "Hugh."

"Nice to meet you, ma'am." Hugh could play the proper Southern gentleman, and he shook her hand dutifully.

"Is your father coming?" Julie asked.

"He wasn't feeling well," Beth said. "My sister took him home." She glanced at Hugh, who nodded. "It's just us. Hugh's wife just found out she's pregnant again, and she's not well right now either."

Kait wasn't especially happy about the pregnancy, and while Beth knew she'd come around, she also knew Kait and Hugh had wanted to be finished with two children.

"Oh, I'm sorry," Julie said. "Who are you?" She crouched down in front of Lucas, who clung to Hugh's leg like there were monsters at this luncheon. Julie reached up and took a cookie from the tray, offering it to Lucas.

He took it, and then took her hand when she promised to get him some chocolate milk to go with it. Just like that, she'd charmed him, and Beth marveled at the softer side of the woman.

She stood next to Hugh, feeling very out of place. She couldn't explain anything to him, so she just got out of the way as another truck pulled up to the lot in front of the pavilion.

Spur got out of the driver's seat, and he walked around to the passenger side. He whistled between his teeth, and everyone turned toward him. "Here he is," he called in a loud voice. "The newest championship horse trainer at Bluegrass Ranch…Trey Chappell!"

He grinned and started to clap as the door opened. Trey got out, his smile huge as his family cheered for him. Beth joined in, those pesky tears filling her eyes as she clapped. She couldn't get her voice to work, so the applause would have to be enough.

After only a few seconds, Trey lifted his hand in a sign to tell people to quiet down. They did, and he and Spur walked up the sidewalk. He hugged his family, his eyes never leaving hers for long.

When he finally reached her and Hugh, Trey shook her brother's hand first, and then lifted her right off her feet.

She squealed and held onto his shoulders to keep her balance.

"We did it, baby," he said, setting her down. He gazed down at her, and underneath the brim of that big, black cowboy hat, they got some inkling of privacy.

"*You* did it," she said. "She was incredible, Trey."

"I'll do it, Beth," he whispered, pressing his cheek to hers. She closed her eyes and drank in the words. "I'll come home."

"You will?"

"Let's sit down and talk after this," he said, pulling away from her.

She could only nod, because a promise to talk was more than she could've even hoped for. It wasn't more than she'd prayed for, but she didn't dare to hope for the happily-ever-after her fantasies had started to conjure up.

"Trey!"

He stepped around Beth and caught TJ as he raced up to him. They both laughed, and Beth's heart warmed all over again.

She knew she'd made the right choices for the three things she had on her priority list.

TJ.

Trey.

The ranch.

Trey stood right by her as his father said a prayer over the food. He stayed at her side while they ate, the family talking and laughing over one another.

"I'll take TJ," Hugh said when it was clear Beth wanted to linger with Trey.

"Okay," she said, staying next to Trey as Hugh gathered up the two little boys and took her SUV.

Finally, Trey slipped his fingers between hers and said, "Walk with me, Beth."

She did, and the moment she felt sure no one left at the party would overhear her, she said, "I have room in my life for three main things. The most important things. Lots of other things can get done, but they're not the priority."

"Hm." He kept his head down, his eyes trained on the ground.

"I know what they are for me," she said. "I'm not perfect, and I'm not going to be perfect all the time. But they're TJ, you, and the ranch. I need those three things in my life, Trey. You're not just some cowboy I know."

She'd hated hearing him say that, and she hated that she'd ever said it out loud to him.

"I want to name the ranch The Triple-T Ranch," she said. "One T for TJ. One for Trey. And one for Turner."

He looked up at her, his expression storming with emotion. "That's actually perfect," he said. "I don't need the ranch named after me, though. Maybe just The Double-T?"

"No." She shook her head. "I want you there. I don't want the ranch to be more important than you. I'll work on balancing my family life with our life, I will. But I want Triple-T. The Turner is for me, Trey. It's okay for me to leave the Dixon behind now."

She swallowed, but it was true. She couldn't live with Danny's betrayal and sting in her heart forever. She also hadn't been able to let go of him for a long time. She could now.

"The three of us is what makes that ranch what it is. It should be Triple-T."

"Okay," Trey said, pausing. "The grass gets wild here, and there's still some snow. We should go back." He turned back to the pavilion but didn't move in that direction. "I've missed you."

"I miss you too," she said. "TJ misses you like crazy. He asks about you every day. I don't know what to tell him."

"I don't love him more than you," Trey said, dropping his head again. "It's just different."

"I know," Beth said. She reached up and cupped his face in her hand. "Will you kiss me, please? Soft and slow, baby."

Fire danced in his eyes, and he took her face in both of his hands and kissed her, just the way she wanted him to.

Chapter 23

"It's got to go up," Trey called, realizing Cayden was about to lose his end of the pole. Trey lunged toward him, catching it just as Cayden's fingers slipped. "Spur."

His oldest brother jogged through the white gravel to help too, and once Spur and Cayden both had a grip on the pole, Trey went back to standing near the highway entrance to the ranch.

The new Triple-T Ranch, where a new sign was going in today.

Warm sunshine shone down over them, though it was only the beginning of March. Trey felt the light of it on his skin and throughout his soul. "Conrad," he said. "Up. It has to go up."

"I can't lift it any higher," his brother complained, and Blaine stepped over to help him, though he was needed to secure the new face to the existing sign.

"There," Trey said. "Right there. Hold it steady. Let's get it attached now." He flew forward and got into the basket with Lawrence. Ian lifted them up, and when the basket was level with where they needed to be, Trey used the cordless drill to get the new sign attached to the arch that had been installed a week or two ago.

He'd rented this truck to trim the trees that had been growing wild near the stables here at the ranch, and it was perfect to finish this major project too. Everyone had come out to help, and Beth had the scent of maple and bacon floating in the air.

"Trey," TJ called from the ground, and Trey looked down at him. The little boy simply waved up at him, his smile wide and full of happiness.

Trey chuckled, waved back, and finished attaching the sign in his section. "Move us right," he called to Ian, and then grabbed onto the side of the basket as it lurched. "Dude, slowly," he muttered so only Lawrence could hear.

"He's just mad, because Spur said he could learn a thing or two from you."

Trey looked at Lawrence. "What?"

"You didn't know?"

"No." Trey had moved back into the white farmhouse the very evening of the Sweetheart Classic. He and Beth had taken some great strides in their relationship, which was real as real could get. They talked every day about real things—kids and chores and allowances. Schedules and wants and dreams.

He'd learned that she didn't own the land to the south

of the ranch, and he'd figured out who did. He wanted it, because he wanted his own practice track. Bluegrass was *busy*, and he didn't want to compete for the time his horses needed on the track. Once he'd learned who owned the land, he'd gone to Beth and confessed his desires to buy it.

He'd told her what he wanted his day to look like. Breakfast with her and TJ. Work at Bluegrass to keep up with the scheduling of their tracks. Pick up TJ from school. Work at The Triple-T, whatever that entailed, and training horses for the tier two and three races around the south.

She'd listened to him, her smile growing warmer and warmer with every word. She'd said, "You should have everything you want, Trey."

"But are you fine with it if that's what I do?" he asked. "It's a lot of money. He seems to know exactly how much I want that land—and that I have the money to pay for it." He wasn't happy about that, but he wouldn't miss the money, and he did want the land.

"Let's think about it for a day or two," she'd said.

He had. He'd prayed about it, but he hadn't felt strongly one way or the other. He'd come to realize that that wasn't the Lord ignoring him. It was the Lord letting him make his own choice, and that it honestly didn't matter if he did or didn't do it. He wouldn't be harmed if he did.

Trey had put in an offer on the land two days ago. Burt Barnes only had eighteen more hours to accept it or counter.

He pushed away the frustration and focused on getting the left side of the sign attached, then the right.

Back on the ground, he stood back with everyone and looked up at the sign.

"It's great," Blaine said, clapping him on the shoulder. "Look at you, a new ranch owner."

"I don't own the ranch," Trey said, unable to take his eyes from the sign. "I just belong here." He wasn't aware he'd spoken out loud until he started to feel the weight of so many pairs of eyes.

He looked away from the sign, where one of the T's was for him. Blaine stood right next to him, with Lawrence only an inch behind him. He looked around at all of his brothers. Ian was still pretty sore at Trey for a variety of things, he supposed, but nothing was said as they huddled together, all of them lifting their arms and settling them on the closest brother to them.

"You do belong here," Spur said. "You belong at Bluegrass too. All of you do."

"We belong to each other," Cayden said, his voice gruff. "No matter where life takes us, or how far away we go."

"You're turning into Blaine," Duke said, and everyone laughed—except Blaine, who said, "Hey," in a wounded voice.

Trey kept laughing and grabbed onto Blaine individually. "Don't let them make you feel bad for your heart," he said quietly.

"Okay, *Mom*," Blaine said, but he hugged Trey back with equal tenacity.

"How's it looking?" Beth asked, and Trey immediately stepped over to her. He slung his arm around her shoulders as she turned to look up at the sign. "Trey." Her voice sounded like mostly air. "It's beautiful."

"Lawrence made it."

Beth sniffled and stepped over to Lawrence to hug him. Surprise shone in his eyes, and then he melted into Beth's embrace, his smile growing.

"Thank you all," she said. "It's amazing. I love it so much." She returned to Trey's side and gazed up at the sign again. After taking a deep breath, she said, "Okay, breakfast is ready, and TJ is so excited you're all here for his birthday breakfast."

She grinned around at everyone before leading the way down the driveway and into the house. Trey simply moved along with everyone else, listening to them talk to each other and laugh, the crunching of gravel under their boots. It was comforting to be with them, and while he'd felt like he belonged at Bluegrass Ranch, when he stepped into the farmhouse, he felt like he was coming home.

He wasn't the first to arrive in the kitchen, and someone had stopped and clogged up the doorway. "What's going on?" he asked, trying to see past Cayden and Lawrence, but they had shoulders as wide as his, and he couldn't see anything but jackets and cowboy hats.

"You can't just stop here," Ian called from the back. "Some of us are starving."

"You're always starving," Duke called back.

"Where's Trey?" Blaine asked.

"Here," he said. "I can't get past anyone."

"Let him up here."

People shifted and moved, and Trey made his way through them to the front. Beth and TJ had been busy while he'd been outside with his brothers, because two long tables had been set up in the dining room and living room. They'd been covered with TJ's favorite color—blue—and a table setting had been placed in front of each chair.

A scrumptious-looking cake sat at each setting, every dessert with a six-shaped candle in it. They hadn't been lit yet, and Trey finally got to the part that had caused Spur and Conrad to stop.

Beth and TJ stood directly in front of the doorway leading into the back of the house from the front. She held a cake in her hands, as did her son.

The tops of the cakes hadn't been decorated, but the front. Beth's said, *Marry me?* And TJ's said, *Be my dad?*

Trey's emotions surged, and he couldn't speak or move.

He'd already married Beth, besides. He'd thought of himself as TJ's father before, and he and Beth had already been talking and making arrangements for the three of them to be a permanent, legal family.

"These are yes or no questions," Spur murmured. "What's it gonna be, Trey?"

"Yes," he said, striding forward with the strength of his family behind him. He took both cakes and turned to set them on the counter. Then he swept Beth and TJ into his arms, the three of them laughing together. "Yes," he whispered into her ear. "Always yes."

She stepped away and he lifted TJ up with a big roar. "I

love you, bud," he said while his brothers cheered and clapped.

"I love you too, Trey," TJ said, smiling at him. "Can we have cake for breakfast?"

"I think you already have it out, bud," Trey said, grinning at the child.

"Hello," Kait called from the front of the house. She brought more noise with her, and everyone started to file into the kitchen. Within minutes, his parents had arrived. Clyde came with Sally and her kids.

TJ's other grandparents arrived, and his mother moved right over to Trish and Taylor Dixon and hugged them hello. TJ ran over and showed them the cowboy hat Trey had bought him for his birthday, and they smiled and hugged him tightly.

Trey hadn't thought about how much they'd be involved in TJ's life, but watching them, he wasn't worried. Their son had been TJ's father; they belonged there as much as he did.

"We're ready, baby," Beth said quietly, looking at him.

He pulled himself together and cleared his throat. "Yeah? You're ready?"

"Yes," she said, taking his hand in hers. "If I start to cry, you'll finish for me, right?"

"Yep."

She nodded, her jaw set with determination. She looked at Lawrence, who she'd clearly worked something out with, because he put his fingers in his mouth and whistled. "Quiet down now," he said. "Beth has an announcement."

"Oh, brother," Trey said. "That's how you decided to

start this?" He looked at Beth and Lawrence, but both of them just smiled back at him. "You know they're going to think you're pregnant."

Beth turned to face the crowd gathered in the farmhouse for TJ's birthday. "Thank you so much for coming. It's amazing to see how many people love TJ." She reached down and ran her fingers through her son's hair. "He's very blessed to have all of you."

She cleared her throat. "Welcome to the new Triple-T Ranch. Trey and I just wanted to announce that we'll be getting new rings and renewing our vows this summer in a real ceremony." She looked up at him, tears in her eyes but so much joy shining through them. "He's also—" Her voice shut off, and her face folded as she tried to hold back her tears. It was a losing battle, but Trey gave her another few seconds.

He squeezed her hand and looked up at everyone. "We talked to TJ about it, and I've filed to adopt him. That way, he can be mine, and I can be his." He smiled, because he thought he might start to cry too.

"Will you change his name?" Trish Dixon asked, anxiety all over her face.

"Yes," Beth said. "Once the adoption goes through, we'll file for a new birth certificate. It will still list Danny as his father." Her voice shook on the last word. "Danny *is* his father. He just gets to have two in this life." Her hand tightened in Trey's again, and he knew it was his turn to continue the explanation.

"He's going to be Taylor John Dixon Chappell." It

wasn't that much of a change. They'd basically moved his current last name into his middle name position. Trey knew he didn't understand everything though. Trish and Taylor Dixon had lost their son, and in a lot of ways, they probably felt like they'd lost Beth and TJ too.

Trey didn't want to take any more from them. "Dixon will be his middle name now," he said. "He wants it. We want him to have it." He powered through the emotion in his throat, making his eyes burn. "It's a good name, with a long legacy, and we want him to know who he is and where he came from."

Trish's tears flowed down her face, and it was Daddy who put his hand on her shoulder and turned her toward him for comfort.

"Okay, I can't take it," Kait said, her own tears fresh on her face. "These cakes look so good, and I'm starving."

The tension broke, and a collective sigh filled the farmhouse.

"We have to sing *Happy Birthday* first," Beth said. "Help me light the candles."

Movement and chaos happened for the next few minutes as people found seats and candles got lit. Trey stepped over to Trish and Taylor and hugged them both, his head right between theirs. He couldn't think of anything to say, and they remained silent too. Sometimes, though, the tightness of a grip could convey more than words ever could.

Once he sat next to TJ, his candle flickering, Beth called, "Okay, one, two, three. Happy birthday to you…"

Trey joined his voice to the song, the rendition getting

louder and rowdier with every word sung. By the end, he laughed and shook his head, and he held up his phone and took a ton of pictures as TJ leaned over and blew out his candle.

He blew out his own and picked up his fork. "Cake for breakfast," he said. "This is amazing."

He took his first bite of the mini chocolate cake and looked around the room. The really amazing thing was this huge group of people he belonged to. He narrowed it down to his family, then Beth's family.

Then to just him, Beth, and TJ, and he leaned over and kissed the top of TJ's head and said, "Happy birthday, bud." Then he turned to his wife and kissed her right on the lips. "I love you," he murmured.

"I love you too," she said back, kissing him again.

* * *

She'll do anything to spite her mother and find her own happiness...even keep her cowboy billionaire boyfriend a secret. Keep reading for more about Cayden and Ginny - the first 2 chapters of **PARADING THE COWBOY BILLIONAIRE** are included.

Sneak peek! Parading the Cowboy Billionaire Chapter One:

Cayden Chappell pulled up to the farmhouse where his brother lived now. The new sign had weathered its first rainstorm, and the whole state of Kentucky had come through the weekend's downpour just fine.

Cayden felt like he'd had that storm cloud raining on him for almost three months now. The invisible weight he carried on his shoulders made him sigh as he got out of his truck. He knew where it came from, but he didn't know how to shrug off Virginia Winters.

She'd captured him completely, and while their relationship hadn't been traditional before, it was better than none at all.

He pushed her out of his mind, though he knew she'd just come back. She always did, and Cayden had lost way too much sleep to thoughts of the woman he'd only kissed once.

Once.

She shouldn't have such sway over him, and yet, she did.

He obviously hadn't made that big of an impression on her, because she'd never called him after she'd returned from her Caribbean vacation two months ago.

He went up the steps and rang the doorbell at the farmhouse, listening to it ring on the other side of the door. It sang through the country stillness too, and Cayden gazed out over the pasture that sat in the front left corner of the ranch. The grass was starting to green now that it was almost April, and Beth had two horses there, their heads down as they grazed.

There was something peaceful and serene about it that called to Cayden's soul. As the public relations manager, he didn't spend nearly enough time with the horses at Bluegrass Ranch. He could spend whole days in his office, in the administration building where few people normally came.

The only time the administration building was busy was during one of their events—the yearlings sale or their auctions. Then, the whole ranch bustled with activity, and Cayden was the one responsible for all of that.

He needed to get outside more, and he wandered away from the door and toward the railing on the far side of the porch. He'd just leaned against the railing when Beth said, "Cayden?"

"Mm." He continued to gaze at the pasture for another moment before he turned to his sister-in-law. Beth wore a denim skirt that narrowed at her knees and a black blouse with brightly colored flowers on it. She was exactly the kind of woman Trey should be with, and Cayden smiled at her.

"Sorry. I got lost looking at your horses. I need to get outside more." He'd finally finished wrapping up the horses-of-all-ages sale that had taken place at the ranch last month, and he was ready for a tropical vacation now too. It would be hot in Kentucky soon enough, and then he'd be wishing for cooler mornings like this one, with plenty of breezy afternoons.

"Those are actually Trey's," she said. "He brought them over last night."

Cayden crossed the distance between them. "You told him I don't want to go to this, right?"

"Repeatedly," she murmured without looking at him. "He has it in his head that if you two will just get yourself into the same room together, you'll remember why you liked each other so much."

"I don't need a reminder," Cayden said darkly. He'd never thought of himself as a growling, moody man, but since Ginny's disappearance from his life, he'd certainly become exactly that.

"Maybe she does," Beth said. "There's nothing wrong with reminding her of certain things."

Cayden pressed his teeth together and kept the words he wanted to bark at her contained. He'd told two people what Wendy Winters had said to him. Exactly two—Lawrence and Trey. Neither had bothered him much about calling Ginny or trying to breathe new life into a relationship that had gone quiet.

Until now. Now, Trey seemed to think it was his job to make sure Cayden embarrassed himself at every turn.

"If I'm so forgettable," Cayden said. "Will the reminder really matter?"

"You're not forgettable," Beth said. "Come on in now. TJ wants to ask you somethin' before we go." She turned and went into the house, and Cayden had no choice but to follow her. He wouldn't disappoint TJ if he could avoid doing so. The child had some sort of magic about him that made everyone bend to his will.

"He's here," she called as she went past the comfortable couches in the living room. The farmhouse had huge windows flanking both sides of the front door, letting in plenty of light. Cayden had never given much thought to where he lived, but as he'd gotten to know Ginny and seen her house, he'd been stewing on it more and more.

He wasn't even sure why.

She hadn't called him. He'd been very busy with the horses-of-all-ages sale, sure. He hadn't asked her to stay away, though. He hadn't given her any indication that he didn't have time for her.

Not only that, but another month had passed since that event, and she still hadn't called. He hadn't called her, because she'd been prepping for the Sweet Rose Gems & Gin event.

His mind seized on that thought, but he couldn't examine it before TJ yelled, "Cayden!" from the kitchen.

The little boy came running through the doorway Beth had just gone through, and Cayden braced himself to receive the kid. He had a battery that never seemed to run out, and Cayden had seen him trailing behind Trey several times.

He'd think TJ had gotten tired, but it was never true. He'd pick up the pace a moment later or see a dog and go chasing after it. Or Trey would say something to him, and he'd perk right up, running to catch Trey and get swung up onto a horse, where his face would glow like a lantern.

The little boy had a bright personality and a shock of dark hair that made him look like Trey's son, even though he wasn't.

"Heya, boy," Cayden said, his soul warming with the hug of the smaller human. "Your momma said you had something to ask me."

"Yeah." TJ released the tight grip around Cayden's neck and pulled back. "My teacher asked if anyone had a mom or daddy who knew how to make banners, and I was talkin' to Trey and he says you do."

"Said," Beth said from a few feet away. "Trey *said* you do."

Cayden grinned at TJ and then Beth. "I do know how to make banners," he said. "I know lots of people who make banners, actually."

"She wants to talk to you, then," TJ said. "I guess she needs some help with it."

"Okay," Cayden said, not sure what he should do here. He looked at Beth, who rolled her eyes.

"Trey can give her your phone number," Beth said. "If that's okay."

"Is it okay?" TJ asked, his eyes bright. He started playing with Cayden's collar, a hint of nerves in his movement.

"Sure," Cayden said. "Why not? What's her name?"

"Miss Robertson," TJ said. He wiggled, and Cayden put him on the ground just as Trey came in the back door.

"You're late," Beth said, and Trey just smiled at her, grabbed her around the waist, and kissed her. She giggled and made a lame attempt to push him away. Cayden couldn't help staring, and he felt bad for doing so once his brother looked at him.

Cayden was three years older than Trey, and three years younger than Spur. They were both cut from similar cloth—a rough, scratchy cloth. They didn't speak as often as the younger brothers. They held their emotions tight.

Blaine had the biggest heart and showed the most emotion. Duke, Ian, and Conrad were the loudest, always jockeying for a position of attention in the family. Lawrence was a mix of Cayden, Trey, and the younger boys, and Cayden got along really well with him.

Cayden felt like a black sheep in the Chappell family. He wasn't overly emotional, but he did feel things deeply. He didn't have to be the center of attention, but he didn't mind speaking his opinions either. He wasn't a natural-born leader, but he did possess a level of charisma that made him the natural choice for the public face of the ranch, something he'd been doing for twenty years now.

Trey had told him that he was the brother TJ talked about the most. He asked when Cayden could come over, and whenever Beth and Trey were going out, TJ asked if Cayden could watch him.

Cayden wasn't sure if that made him likable or pathetic.

"Do you have the invite?" Trey asked, stepping around Beth to the fridge.

"You need to go change," she said. "We're eating there."

"I have the invitation," Cayden said, reaching into his inside jacket pocket. "You guys can just take it."

"It says right on it that the person it was sent to has to be there. Guests are encouraged, *with* that person."

Cayden had read it a hundred times. He knew what the postcard said. When he'd gotten it at the homestead, he'd been two seconds away from tossing it in the trash. Trey had seen it, and since it had a glinting diamond taking up the entire front, he'd grabbed it.

He and Beth were in the market for new wedding rings. Rather, he and Beth were going to buy their *first* wedding rings. Since they'd gotten married last fall in an unconventional way, they didn't have a lot of the same things a more traditional couple would.

Cayden could see how much they loved each other, though. He wanted that same kind of giggling, doe-eyed woman in his life. He'd used to not care if he had a girlfriend or not. He was focused on his career, and as one of the only brothers with a college education, he was determined to prove to everyone that it mattered. *He* wanted to matter.

"Maybe once this is over, you two will be able to get your schedule to line up," Beth said, and Cayden's mind returned to that thought he'd stalled on before TJ had distracted him.

"I don't know," he said. "Is texting hard?"

"Have you texted her?" Trey challenged.

"Go change your clothes," Beth said, her irritation plain

on her face. Trey nodded and headed down the hall, leaving Cayden alone with Beth and TJ.

He didn't want to hear more about what could maybe happen with Ginny at the event. He met Beth's eye and said, "I'll go wait outside," he said. They'd asked him to drive and everything, and somehow Cayden had said yes.

He went back the way he'd come while Beth said something to TJ. Several minutes later, everyone was in the truck and Cayden was following his map to her father's house. She ran TJ inside and returned to the truck less than a minute later.

"Ready," she said, exhaling heavily.

"Let's do it," Trey said.

Cayden could make the drive to Sweet Rose Whiskey in his sleep, and he let Trey and Beth talk amongst themselves as he navigated them across town. The parking lot was fairly full already, as the event had started about ten minutes ago. It was an open house, so it wasn't like they'd needed to be there exactly on time.

He turned right and went toward the huge field adjacent to the lot, as he drove a big truck and could handle the rougher road. He parked and handed the postcard to Trey, who promptly pushed it right back at him.

"You're coming in," he said. "Just get us through the door."

"No," Beth said. "He's coming in, and he's staying. He's our ride."

Cayden wanted to argue with her, but he said nothing. He got out of the truck and took a deep breath. The evening had started to darken and cool, and Cayden loved the slower, quieter evenings in the country.

He knew what the event inside would be like, and he inhaled the calm before the storm. Before he knew it, he was stepping up to a gentleman at the door and handing him his postcard.

"Evening, Mister Chappell," the man said. He looked up and met Cayden's eyes, and Cayden's breath stuck in his throat. He knew this man. He'd parked his truck at Ginny's New Year's Eve party.

"Evening," he managed to say.

"Two guests?" he asked, glancing at Trey and Beth.

"Yes, please," Cayden said, slipping into his more formal personality. He hated that, and he pulled himself right back to his cowboy roots. If Wendy Winters was going to think him unworthy of her daughter, he might as well act like the heathen she thought he was.

Cayden had never been much of a rule-breaker, though, and his natural instinct was to please people. His mother. His teachers. Spur. Ginny.

Wendy.

He wondered if Ginny's mother had said anything to her, and he almost laughed. Of course she had. Wendy wasn't the type of woman who would hold back.

"We have drinks straight ahead," the man said, and Cayden blinked to focus back on the conversation. "Once in the first room, you'll find the food. Beyond that are the gems. Have a great evening."

"Thank you," Cayden murmured, and he went first into

the building. He hadn't been inside this one, and the hallway in front of him was long and dark. It opened up into a cozy room with a western theme. Dark brown leather couches dotted the room, with black and white cow-patterned rugs in front of them. A longhorn skull sat above the fireplace, and all of the tables looked handmade from hewn logs. A pair cowboy boots acted as a lamp base on the light fixture closest to him, and Cayden reached out to touch it.

Cowboy boots. He wore a pair right now, and he was actually surprised Ginny's mother would allow such décor anywhere on her property.

"Sir," someone said, and he turned toward a man who held a long tray with several glasses on it. "Would you like to try one of our gins?"

"I would," Beth said, stepping to Cayden's side. "Tell me what you've got."

He smiled at her like he was the happiest man on earth. "Down here is our classic gin," he said. "It's got that juniper taste you associate with gin. Next to it is our orange blossom gin. It's got the strongest citrus flavor out of any of our fruit-flavored gins." He continued to outline the alcohol on the tray, and as Cayden wasn't a fan of whiskey or gin or any alcohol really, he declined them all.

Beth selected the orange blossom, and Trey picked up the one with more anise in it. He took one sip and made a face. "This is why I don't drink."

The waiter had already moved away, thankfully, and Trey simply put his glass on the table next to those cowboy boots. Beth nursed hers as they looked around the room and then went through the doorway and into the next one.

This room was twice as big as the one with the cocktails, and there were far less people. Apparently, the drinks were more alluring than the food. Not to Cayden, and he took whatever the first man had on his tray and popped the whole thing into his mouth. Something salty and vinegary mixed with the beef, and then a bright pop of cilantro exploded in his mouth.

"Tartar," he said. "That was *good*."

"The chef made it with farm-raised cattle right here in Kentucky," the man said, beaming as if he personally owned the farm.

Cayden wanted to pull him aside and ask him if he really was that happy to be working here tonight. He suspected the Winters paid very well, and that they insisted their people wear smiles for miles.

Instead, he picked up another wafer with the beef tartar on it and threw it back as if he was eating oysters.

He hadn't seen Ginny yet, and some of the tension he'd been harboring in his chest and shoulders dissipated. She'd likely be in the gem room, where all the goods were. Sweet Rose had partnered with Down Home Jewelry for the event, as both were local Dreamsville corporations that had expanded to worldwide giants while maintaining their Kentucky roots.

Cayden drifted away from Beth and Trey and toward another tray of food. Then another. If he ate enough, coming here tonight would be worth the risk to his heart. As if on cue, it skipped a beat, and he reached for another Southwest eggroll.

Ginny had pulled out all the stops for tonight's event. Low music played in this room, and there were multiple places to sit and relax. Talk and get food and order additional drinks. Nothing ever ran out and while Cayden had seen behind the curtain at an event like this, he suspected most of the people here had not.

Trey appeared in front of him. "We're going in. You'll be okay here?"

"Yes," Cayden said, biting back on the sarcastic remark that popped into his head. He watched Trey and Beth duck through the door at the back of the room, and he took another crabcake when the tray came around again.

He'd just finished it when Ginny exited the room where Trey had gone.

Cayden got to his feet without even knowing that he had. He soaked in the sight of Virginia Winters, sparks flying through his whole body.

Beth had been wrong; the reminder wasn't for Ginny. It was for him.

Go talk to her, he commanded himself. He had to talk to her tonight. He had to explain that he'd gone silent because of her mother.

He couldn't believe he'd cared what Wendy Winters thought of him. He couldn't believe he'd given up the curvy, gorgeous woman currently smiling at a couple of men. Ginny wore an elegant off-white dress with plenty of lace everywhere. Her dark hair had been piled up on top of her head and secured with glinting gems that probably cost more than most people made in their entire lifetimes.

Her heels made her legs tight and slender, and Cayden's mouth turned dry.

It was her eyes that always captured him, and as she laughed and looked his way, he caught sight of those navy blue pools that pulled him in every time.

He knew the moment she saw and recognized him. The smile slipped from her face, and her eyes widened.

One hand flew to her mouth, which had dropped open, and then lowered to press against her chest. Her dress had wide straps that went over her shoulders and left a lot of skin to be observed.

Cayden couldn't move, though he wanted to. He could at least wave or something to indicate to her that he'd seen her. If he could just get his blood to stop burning him up from the inside out, he'd go talk to her.

Ginny had frozen too, and then she seemed to shake herself. Her masks flew into place, and she took a step toward him—and collided with a waiter carrying a full tray of sea bass and tomato canapés.

Sneak Peek! Parading the Cowboy Billionaire Chapter Two:

Virginia Winters had ruined many dresses in her lifetime. None as spectacularly and as publicly as the Victoria James gown she currently wore. She never wore a formal dress more than once, but that didn't mean she wanted tomatoes, balsamic, and fish juice embedded in the lace.

She certainly didn't want it to happen in front of anyone, least of all Cayden Chappell, who now loomed above her as if he'd sprinted across the drawing room to be there for her when she first opened her eyes and realized what had happened.

What had happened was that she'd been so entranced by his presence that she hadn't looked at anyone or anything but him. She'd run into a waiter carrying a full tray of canapés, causing both of them to tumble to the floor. She'd shown too much leg to everyone within the near vicinity, and she'd ruined her twenty-thousand-dollar dress.

Her hair brushed her face, and she realized she'd ruined that too. Embarrassment heated her whole body, and she watched Cayden's mouth move but no sound come out. Around her, everyone seemed to be looking at her with equally alarmed expressions, and Ginny wanted to tell them to back up and let her breathe.

Cayden reached out and touched her face, brushing that errant hair back. "...can you hear me?" Cayden's voice finally broke through the haze in her mind.

"Yes," she said, and sound rushed at her from every side. She couldn't grasp onto any one thought, and her mind raced through what she should do now. Change her clothes and come back to the party? Call it a night?

Just get out of here, she thought, and when Cayden asked, "Can I help you up, Ginny?" she put her hand in his, sparks flying up her arm and into her shoulder.

She looked at him, and so much was said between them. Her chest pinched, though, because he hadn't called.

She managed to get to her feet, pull down her dress, and wipe back her hair.

"Which door?" Cayden asked her, his voice low and meant only for her. She could still hear her name coming from his mouth, and he'd spoken it with a great deal of care.

"Straight ahead," she said, nodding to the door dozens of paces away. If she could just make it there, she could figure out what to do. "I'm sorry," she tossed over her shoulder to the waiter still trying to clean up the things she'd spilled.

Cayden kept the pace brisk, and Ginny pushed to keep up with him. "I feel so stupid," she muttered, the feeling intensifying when he didn't answer. Maybe he hadn't heard her.

Yeah, she thought dryly. *Like all those times you thought that maybe he'd forgotten your phone number.*

Or that he'd gotten a new phone.

Then had a complete memory lapse and couldn't remember where she lived and worked.

In her most desperate moments, she'd even started to think he'd been in a terrible accident and was in a coma in a nearby hospital.

Anything to not have to face the fact that he'd kissed her, wished her well on vacation, and then dropped her without another word.

He twisted the doorknob and let her go through first. Ginny immediately kicked off her heels, because one of her ankles was throbbing from her fall. Her palms stung, and everything felt out of place.

She made it to a small settee from the 1600s that had been reupholstered in the ugliest fabric on the planet. Her mother loved it, but Ginny did not, so it got stuck in here. If Mother wanted it, she should take it to the mansion where she lived alone.

Ginny was so tired of being alone.

Her emotions stormed, and before she could contain it, a sob wrenched itself from her throat. She lifted her foot to her knee and started massaging her ankle, though it wasn't hurt that badly.

"Ginny," Cayden said. "Can I get you anything? A drink. Some medication." He actually looked around like this storage room would have anything like that. It didn't look like a storage room, so she could understand his desire, she supposed.

"No," she said, looking down at her stained dress. The scent of fish hit her squarely in the nose, and a fresh wave of tears got triggered.

"Sweetheart," he said softly, coming closer to her.

"Don't you dare call me that," she said, lifting her eyes to his. She was so tired of being so proper all the time. She wanted to rage and scream. She wanted to tell him what she really thought of his behavior. Then, she wanted to eat ice cream and tell her dogs all about it, probably while she cried.

She stood, raising herself to her full height, though she was nowhere near as tall as him. "You have a lot of nerve, Mister Chappell, coming here."

"I got an invitation for this event."

"You never called." She folded her arms and fixed him with a hard stare.

He glared right back at her. "Last time I checked, phones make outbound calls too." He took a step toward her.

"I wasn't going to call someone who wasn't interested," she said.

"Neither was I."

They stared at one another, and Ginny's anger started to ebb away. "What happened?" she asked.

Cayden opened his mouth to say something, then promptly bit it closed again. She'd never known him to keep his mouth shut when he had something to say. He'd told her multiple times that he was interested in her, and that he wanted their relationship to be more than him escorting her to fancy parties.

He looked away, the indecision plain on his face despite the low lighting in the room. Watching him, she could feel his tender heart and his sexy vulnerability. She tasted him on her lips again, something that had been haunting her since their New Year's kiss.

"Let me tell you how it looks from my end," she said, her voice powerful but not loud. "You came to my New Year's Eve party. We danced and laughed. We kissed, and it was amazing. Then you left, and I went on vacation. When I got back, you didn't call. The one time we spoke, you said you were worried about Trey, the Sweetheart Classic, and the horses-of-all-ages sale at the ranch."

She stopped and took a long breath, blowing it out slowly as if she were doing one of her yoga exercises. "I figured you were quite busy, so I left you alone, thinking you'd call when things wrapped up. You didn't."

Familiar nerves ran through her. Ginny had grown up with a cruel father and a proper mother, and she knew what inadequacy felt like. She'd been inadequate since the moment of her birth, and it was something she had not overcome yet.

With Cayden, though...he'd always made her feel like royalty, like her life was a gift to him personally. She hadn't realized how much she'd needed that—needed *him*—until he was suddenly gone.

"I apologize," he said stiffly, still not looking at her.

"You apologize?" She took several quick steps toward him and touched his chest. "Look at me."

He swung his head toward her, but ducked it, not truly meeting her gaze.

"You don't say, 'I apologize.' That's something *I* say."

"I don't know what you want from me," he said.

"I want the truth." She pressed her palm against his chest again, not really pushing him, but needing to get his attention somehow. "Tell me what happened."

He lifted his eyes to hers, anger and danger there. "I don't want to tell you."

"If you met someone else, just say so."

"I didn't."

"You broke your phone, then."

"No."

Ginny's desperation spiraled out of control, and she couldn't stop herself from looking at his mouth. Oh, that mouth. It had claimed her so completely, and she couldn't comprehend what could've happened to drive him away.

He'd kissed her like no man ever had, and Ginny wanted him to do it again right now.

Without thinking or second-guessing herself, Ginny put her hands on his shoulders and tipped up onto her toes. She pressed her mouth to his and kissed him, a sob working its way through her stomach.

He stood very still for a moment, then two, then his hands ran up her arms and into her hair. A growl started somewhere in his throat, and his mouth softened, receiving hers and kissing her back.

The rough version of Cayden disappeared after a few seconds, and he turned the kiss sweet and sensual, dragging it on and on until he finally pulled away, his chest heaving as he breathed hard.

Her heartbeat sprinted in her chest, and she couldn't open her eyes and look at him. If this was all she got of Cayden Chappell, she wanted it to end with a kiss like this. One filled with passion and yet respect, with love and desire, and with all the tenderness of a man who cared about her.

She dropped her hands from his face and opened her eyes, and he cleared his throat and stepped back. She wasn't going to apologize, because she wasn't sorry for what had just happened.

"The only other thing I could come up with was that you'd been in a terrible accident and had been in a coma the last few months." Her voice hardly sounded like hers, especially at the end when her emotions got the best of her.

"Ginny," he whispered, stepping into her personal space again and gathering her right against his chest.

"Here you are," she said. "Obviously not in a coma." She wanted to push him again, but instead, she sank into him. He smelled like leather and horses, sunshine and freshly laundered cotton. Blast Olli for her perfect male scents.

"If I tell you, you have to promise not to do anything."

"Do anything?" She pulled back enough to look up at him. "What does that mean?"

"You're going to be very angry."

Ginny's pulse pounded, and she needed a clear head to hear what he was going to say.

"Because you obviously don't know." He pressed the tips of his fingers together and turned around. "Dear Lord, is this a mistake?" he prayed right out loud.

Ginny watched him with wide eyes, fear running through her now. "Just tell me," she said. "Because no, I don't know."

He took his sweet time turning back to her, and it should be illegal for a man to look as good as he did. Long legs clad in black slacks. Bright blue dress shirt, open at the throat. Dark leather jacket, black cowboy hat, with a little scruff on his face since he hadn't shaved since that morning.

He wasn't wearing a tuxedo, but this look was so much better.

He ground his voice in his throat as he removed his hat and put it back on. "Your mother asked me to stay away from you." He nodded once, like that was that.

Instant fury roared to life within Ginny. "She did *what*? When?"

"At the New Year's Eve party," he said. "After we kissed. She said horses and whiskey don't mix, and that if I respected you at all, I'd break things off between us."

"I am going to kill her." Ginny had never felt such rage.

"That's not quite right," he said, frowning. "She said if I respected you at all, I'd make sure that that night was the last time we were seen together."

Ginny didn't care what wording her mother had used. She'd overstepped her bounds—again. Ginny stepped around Cayden, her destination the mansion in the middle of the family land.

"Whoa, whoa," he said, darting in front of her and blocking the door. "You're not going back out there."

"Yes, I am," she said calmly. "Get out of my way."

"I said you couldn't do anything if I told you."

"I didn't promise," she said, stepping right into him but not for a good reason this time. "You don't get to tell me what to do."

"I—don't," he said, his eyes wide and alarmed. "Of course I don't."

Ginny took a step back, refocusing her anger on the right person. Mother. "*No one* is going to tell me what to do," she said, her teeth gritting. "I'm forty-six years old, and if I want to go out with Cayden Chappell, I'm going to."

She needed to find her core again, because she didn't like this wild feeling coursing through her.

"Ginny," he said, his fingertips landing lightly against her forearm.

That grounded her, and she looked at his hand and then up into his eyes. "Yes?"

"What are you going to do?"

"I'm going to go find my mother," she said. "I'm going to tell her she was right—I should always pack a second outfit for formal events. I don't do it, because well, because she said I should. Then I'm going to tell her she had no right to speak to you about our relationship. Once that's ironed out, I'm going to call you and ask you to dinner."

A small smile touched his mouth. "You're scary when you're mad," he whispered. He bent his head and trailed a line of fire up the side of her face with his lips. "You don't need to ask me, sweetheart. Just tell me when and where, and I'll be there."

"You're still interested?" she asked, her voice breathy now.

"Was that not obvious from that kiss?"

"Maybe I need you to show me again."

"Mm...I can do that." Cayden took her fully into his arms and kissed her again, every stroke a reminder of how much she liked him and how much he liked her. Every touch became fuel for the courage she needed to talk to her mother. Every pulse of her heart beat only for him, and while she'd have to deal with that and what it meant later, right now, it sure felt nice to be in his arms again.

* * *

Ginny didn't ring the doorbell or knock. She didn't even use the front door. Her mother lived in ten percent of the house, the bulk of that at the back, away from the public face of Sweet Rose Whiskey.

She'd parked five feet from the servant entrance, and she'd used her key to get through the door. To her right sat the kitchen, and to her left a set of stairs that went up. Harvey and Elliot had tried to get Mother to live on the first floor, but there was only one bedroom on the main level, and it was in the front corner of the house.

Mother wouldn't even go in that room, as Daddy had lived there. There had been little love left between them, and by the time he'd left Sweet Rose in an advanced stage of heart failure, they hadn't been speaking.

Ginny knew exactly how her father felt as she turned and marched up the steps. She went right at the top and down a hallway that had been torn out and rebuilt to accommodate Mother's flowing ball gowns. She owned more than anyone else on Earth, it seemed, and she always had a back-up plan for her back-up plan.

"Mother," Ginny called as the sound of the television met her ears. Her step almost faltered, but she kept going. Things had been building and frothing between her and her mother for months now. This was just icing on a poisoned cake that needed to be thrown away.

"Mother," she said again, pushing into the room where her mother spent her evenings at home. She sat in the recliner, gently toeing herself back and forth, a crochet needle working on the outer edge of a baby blanket.

"Ginny, dear." Mother looked up from her work, a smile soft and easy on her face.

Secrets, Ginny thought, her gaze stuck to that blanket. They both had plenty of those.

"I thought it was the Gin and Gems event tonight?" Mother phrased it like a question when it wasn't. She knew exactly what happened on the two-thousand-acre farm that was a distillery.

"It is," Ginny said, tearing her eyes from that blanket. Why couldn't Mother be wearing a black dress and stirring something nefarious over a fire? To find her crocheting a border on a handmade baby blanket while a cooking show droned on made her so...normal.

"Did you tell Cayden Chappell that horses and whiskey don't mix?" Ginny asked, making her voice as strong as she could.

Mother's fingers stumbled, and that was all the answer Ginny needed.

"Mother, you do not get to dictate to me who I will see and who I won't."

"He is all wrong for you."

"*You* are wrong about that," Ginny said. If there was one thing Mother hated, it was being told she was wrong. "I'm not sixteen anymore, Mother. I'm not even twenty-six. I'm almost fifty years old, and I've been doing everything you've told me to for my entire life."

Her frustration and annoyance blossomed and bloomed, expanding rapidly as her breathing increased. "I'm done, Mother. I like him, and you have *no right* to boss him around."

"Ginny, do think rationally," Mother said in a disdainful voice. She set her crocheting aside and sighed as if Ginny had interrupted the most wonderful moment of her life. "You're always over-reacting."

"I am *not* over-reacting," Ginny said. "I've lost almost three months of my life, wondering what I did to drive him away, only to find out it was *you!*" She advanced on her mother as she pushed herself up out of the chair.

She took a moment to steady herself on her feet, but when she looked at Ginny, the fire in her eyes was just as prevalent as it always had been. "He does not fit at Sweet Rose."

"He doesn't need to," Ginny said. "He owns and operates a hugely successful horse farm."

"Spur does that," Mother said, shaking her head. "I don't know what the Chappells are worth, dear, but there are eight of them. I doubt he could keep you in your current state of comfort." She turned away from Ginny and started for the small kitchen in the back corner.

"I don't need any of that comfort," Ginny spat back. "I hate that house. It's fifty times too big, and I hate coming home to it all by myself."

Mother paused and twisted back to Ginny, her eyes wide. "Your ingratitude is unbecoming."

"I am not ungrateful," Ginny said. "I'm *lonely*. I'm tired, Mother." She laughed, but it wasn't a happy sound.

Mother turned fully toward her, a malicious glint in her dark eyes now. "Of course I can't forbid you from seeing him. Go see him. Go to dinner with him. Fall in love with him. See if he has anywhere for you to live on that cattle ranch he shares with seven brothers."

"It's a racehorse operation, Mother."

"Whatever," Mother said, her appraising eyes sliding down to Ginny's feet. She'd left her heels in the car, and suddenly, all the smells and stains leapt out from where they'd been hiding. "Good Lord," Mother said, pressing her hand to her pulse. "Did anyone see you like this?" She reached out as if she'd touch the gown, but she yanked her fingers back before she did.

"Yes," Ginny said. "Everyone at the Gin and Gems event."

Mother's eyes flashed again, probably because of Ginny's blunt tone. She lifted her chin, not a tremble or tremor in sight. "If you choose him, you'll be choosing to walk away from Sweet Rose."

Ginny's eyes widened and she pulled in a breath. "I can have a husband and run the distillery."

"Not *him* as a husband."

"Why not?" Ginny asked, desperate to see Cayden through her mother's eyes. A horrible thought entered her mind. "Did Daddy... He's not a Winters, is he?"

"No," Mother said quickly. "But not for lack of trying."

Ginny watched the agony and betrayal roll across her mother's face, though Daddy had died years ago. "Him and Julie Chappell?"

"They even dated in high school," Mother said, her voice pitching up a little. "I won him, of course. Julie is a beautiful woman, but she failed to understand your father on a level I always did."

Ginny had no idea what that meant. "Mother?"

"You knew your father, dear. You'll put it together." She continued into the kitchen and began filling a teapot with water. Ginny didn't want to think about her father and his many affairs. No other illegitimate children had come forth, but Ginny and Mother had already agreed not to tell the boys if they did.

Harvey had taken Theo Lange's existence particularly

hard, which Ginny could understand, as they were only one month apart in age.

She watched her mother in the kitchen, unable to move. She was so used to siding with her. Mother and Ginny. Ginny and Mother. They'd been two peas in a pod as Ginny learned the whiskey business from her mother.

Daddy had always handled the business side of the distillery, while Mother tended to the fields, the flavors, the people, and the events. She was the public face of Sweet Rose, and she'd built it from a small regional operation to a global powerhouse in the world of whiskey.

"Money," Ginny said.

"Bingo," Mother said, not bothering to turn or look at Ginny. "Your father valued money above almost anything. Julie had nothing to offer him." She turned around then and leaned into the counter behind her. "I, of course, had all of this." She swept her hand toward the ceiling as if the room she'd converted into a living room and kitchenette was a grand ballroom. The smile she wore almost felt predatory, and Ginny wanted to run back to her house and lock herself in her bedroom until things made sense.

"Cayden is not related to me," she said slowly. "Daddy didn't cheat with Julie. Your objection to my relationship to him is because of…because his mother dated Daddy in high school?"

"She kissed him the day before we got married," Mother said, lifting her teacup to her lips as if she'd just said it would rain tomorrow. She lowered it a moment later, her eyes hard, dark marbles.

Mother did not like Julie Chappell, plain and simple. Mother could hold a grudge for a lifetime, something Ginny had always known and joked about with her brothers. To see it manifest itself as reality, though, was a much harder pill to swallow.

"I do not want that woman anywhere near my life," Mother said. "She will get nothing from me, certainly not my only daughter. She will not ever be welcome on my property." She set down her cup with hardly a clink, despite the venom and power in her voice.

"So, Ginny, dear. If you want to be with Cayden Chappell, you will need to walk away from Sweet Rose. From your family. From me." She folded her arms, a knowing glint in her eyes, as if she knew such a thing was impossible.

It *was* impossible.

Ginny's fury roared again, and her fingers curled into fists. "I'll think about it." She spun and stalked toward the exit.

"You'll think about it?" Mother called after her.

Ginny didn't answer. She had to get out of there before she started sobbing. She made it back to her SUV, everything clenched tight. She peeled out, spitting gravel behind her as she tore away from the mansion she hated.

"I hate this," she said aloud, pounding her palm against the steering wheel. "I hate whiskey. I hate Sweet Rose. I hate this dress, and this car, and I hate my mother."

Tears rained down her face and she put her car on the highway leading south from Sweet Rose, and she just drove as the storm inside her swirled and brewed, blew and raged.

When she'd calmed, she only had one thought left: Her mother owned her. She'd been wrapping Ginny in thin bands of barely-there control for almost five decades. She couldn't break free, even if she wanted to.

She was stuck. Trapped. Subject to her mother's whims and wishes—at least if she wanted to be part of her family and take over the whiskey business.

Her car started to slow down, and Ginny looked down at the speedometer. "No," she said, pressing harder on the accelerator.

It was no use—she was out of gas.

With the late hour, there wasn't anyone on the stretch of Kentucky road, and Ginny was able to easily maneuver to the shoulder and ease onto it as her car continued to decelerate. When she finally came to a stop, it was as if everything in her life now existed on a hinge.

Her next decision would decide the rest of her life.

She didn't have shoes she could walk very far in.

She wore a stained and stinky designer gown.

She had no food or water in her car.

She closed her eyes, everything burning inside her. "Time to be reborn from the ashes," she whispered, and she reached for her phone.

After dialing, she held the device to her ear and exhaled one long stream of apprehension and nerves.

"Ginny?"

"Cayden," she said. "I know it's late, but I'm stranded on the side of the road, and I'm wondering if you could come get me."

He started chuckling, of all things. "Is this going to be a pattern with you?"

"Probably," she said, trying to tame her crying into laughter and failing. "You should know that upfront, I suppose."

"You sound upset," he said.

"Yes." She could admit it. "I also have no idea where I am. I'm going to have to look at my map and send you a pin."

"How long have you been driving?" he asked quietly, the slight jangle of keys in the background.

She pressed her eyes closed, because he was going to be her knight in shining armor again. "What time is it?" she asked.

"Almost eleven."

"A while," she admitted.

He didn't sigh or huff. He didn't press for more information. All he said was, "Send me the pin, sweetheart."

* * *

Can Ginny and Cayden's love truly survive in the shadows? Or will they both end up broken-hearted if the truth comes out? **Read PARADING THE COWBOY BILLIONAIRE in paperback and find out today.**

Bluegrass Ranch Romance

Book 1: Winning the Cowboy Billionaire: She'll do anything to secure the funding she needs to take her perfumery to the next level...even date the boy next door.

Book 2: Roping the Cowboy Billionaire: She'll do anything to show her ex she's not still hung up on him...even date her best friend.

Book 3: Training the Cowboy Billionaire: She'll do anything to save her ranch...even marry a cowboy just so they can enter a race together.

Book 4: Parading the Cowboy Billionaire: She'll do anything to spite her mother and find her own happiness...even keep her cowboy billionaire boyfriend a secret.

Book 5: Promoting the Cowboy Billionaire: She'll do anything to keep her job...even date a client to stay on her boss's good side.

Book 6: Acquiring the Cowboy Billionaire: She'll do anything to keep her father's stud farm in the family...even marry the maddening cowboy billionaire she's never gotten along with.

Book 7: Saving the Cowboy Billionaire: She'll do anything to prove to her friends that she's over her ex...even date the cowboy she once went with in high school.

Book 8: Convincing the Cowboy Billionaire: She'll do anything to keep her dignity...even convincing the saltiest cowboy billionaire at the ranch to be her boyfriend.

Chestnut Ranch Romance

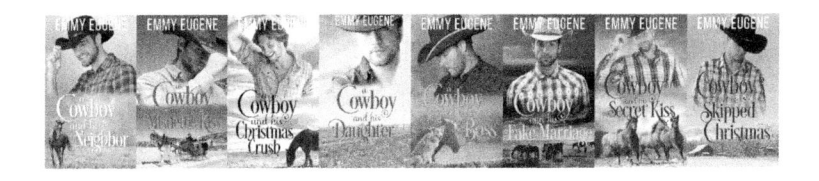

Book 1: A Cowboy and his Neighbor: Best friends and neighbors shouldn't share a kiss...

Book 2: A Cowboy and his Mistletoe Kiss: He wasn't supposed to kiss her. Can Travis and Millie find a way to turn their mistletoe kiss into true love?

Book 3: A Cowboy and his Christmas Crush: Can a Christmas crush and their mutual love of rescuing dogs bring them back together?

Book 4: A Cowboy and his Daughter: They were married for a few months. She lost their baby...or so he thought.

Book 5: A Cowboy and his Boss: She's his boss. He's had a crush on her for a couple of summers now. Can Toni and Griffin mix business and pleasure while making sure the teens they're in charge of stay in line?

Book 6: A Cowboy and his Fake Marriage: She needs a husband to keep her ranch...can she convince the cowboy next-door to marry her?

Book 7: A Cowboy and his Secret Kiss: He likes the pretty adventure guide next door, but she wants to keep their relationship off the grid. Can he kiss her in secret and keep his heart intact?

Book 8: A Cowboy and his Skipped Christmas: He's been in love with her forever. She's told him no more times than either of them can count. Can Theo and Sorrell find their way through past pain to a happy future together?

Texas Longhorn Ranch Romance

Book 1: Loving Her Cowboy Best Friend: She's a city girl returning to her hometown. He's a country boy through and through. When these two former best friends (and ex-lovers) start working together, romantic sparks fly that could ignite a wildfire… Will Regina and Blake get burned or can they tame the flames into true love?

Book 2: Kissing Her Cowboy Boss: She's a veterinarian with a secret past. He's her new boss. When Todd hires Laura, it's because she's willing to live on-site and work full-time for the ranch. But when their feelings turn personal, will Laura put up walls between them to keep them apart?

About Emmy

Emmy is a Midwest mom who loves dogs, cowboys, and Texas. She's been writing for years and loves weaving stories of love, hope, and second chances. Learn more about her and her books at www.emmyeugene.com.

Printed in Great Britain
by Amazon